DARKNESS BETRAYED

He stepped toward her, allowing his cool power to wash over her. Brigette shivered in pleasure.

"Until we've discovered who is ultimately behind the attacks, someone must keep an eye on Maryam." His dark gaze swept down her body before returning to rest on her upturned face. "Besides..."

"Besides what?"

His smiled revealed a hint of fang. "Besides, I intend to keep an eye on you."

More shivers raced through Brigette. Along with a white-hot anticipation that clenched her stomach. She tried to hide her fierce reaction behind a pretense of indifference.

"I've told you guys I don't need a babysitter."

His smile widened. "Babysitting is the last thing on my mind."

For a breathless moment, Brigette's gaze was mesmerized by the sight of those razor-sharp fangs. She'd always been isolated. First, by her overprotective pack, and then by the curse of the Beast. But she'd heard stories about what a vampire could do with his bite. The pleasure was supposedly so intense a creature could become instantly addicted.

Did she want to find out for herself?

Books by Alexandra Ivy

Some Like It Brazen

Romantic Suspense

Pretend You're Safe
What Are You Afraid Of?
You Will Suffer
The Intended Victim
Don't Look
Faceless

And don't miss these Guardians of Eternity novellas

Taken by Darkness, in Yours for Eternity
Darkness Eternal, in Supernatural
Where Darkness Lives, in The Real Werewives of Vampire County
Levet (Ebook Only)
A Very Levet Christmas (Ebook Only)

And don't miss these Sentinel novellas

Out of Control
On the Hunt

Published by Kensington Publishing Corp.

Darkness Betrayed

Alexandra Ivy

LYRICAL PRESS
Kensington Publishing Corp.
www.kensingtonbooks.com

LYRICAL PRESS BOOKS are published by

Kensington Publishing Corp.
119 West 40th Street
New York, NY 10018

All Kensington titles, imprints, and distributed lines are available at special quantity discounts for bulk purchases for sales promotion, premiums, fund-raising, educational, or institutional use.

Special book excerpts or customized printings can also be created to fit specific needs. For details, write or phone the office of the Kensington Sales Manager: Kensington Publishing Corp., 119 West 40th Street, New York, NY 10018. Attn. Sales Department. Phone: 1-800-221-2647.

Lyrical Press and Lyrical Press logo Reg. U.S. Pat. & TM Off.

First Electronic Edition: May 2021
ISBN-13: 978-1-5161-1095-7 (ebook)
ISBN-10: 1-5161-1095-1 (ebook)

First Print Edition: May 2021
ISBN-13: 978-1-5161-1098-8
ISBN-10: 1-5161-1098-6

Printed in the United States of America

To David, who is always there. Thanks for all you do.

Chapter 1

The lair of the Anasso, King of the Vampires, should have been a dank, musty place filled with bats and a few shabby coffins to emphasize the whole creepy vibe. Or at least dug deep underground to avoid the dastardly sunlight.

Instead, Styx had chosen a sprawling mansion on the outskirts of Chicago with lots of marble and gilt that was supposed to give it a classic sophistication. Okay, it had been Styx's mate who'd chosen it. Styx personally thought it looked like something an aging rocker with too many burnt brain cells would choose, but it pleased Darcy. And since she was a pureblood Were with claws that could literally rip out a male's throat, he tried to keep her happy.

Styx was currently in his office, which had been stripped of most of the gilt, although there was nothing he could do about the marble. Or the fluted columns that grew like a forest throughout the mansion. He'd intended to spend a few hours enjoying an ancient manuscript that had been loaned to him by Jagr. Darcy had recently gone to Kansas City to visit her twin sister, who was mated to the King of Weres, Salvatore, and their litter of pups. It'd been his suggestion that she take the trip, but she'd been eager to agree. She claimed that late fall was the perfect time to travel to see the leaves changing colors.

Styx had declined her invitation to go with her. He wasn't interested in foliage, no matter what color it might be. More importantly, the Were pups had reached an age when they spent an enormous amount of energy racing through the house, shrieking and yipping at the top of their lungs. It didn't matter if they were in their human form or their wolf form. The noise was enough to raise the dead.

And not in a good way.

Unfortunately, his decision to remain behind hadn't gone as he'd planned. He'd barely settled into his large leather chair when a male shoved open the door to the office.

Xi was one of his Ravens, the personal guards who'd sworn to protect him. Unlike Jagr, who was the leader of the Ravens, Xi wasn't bulky or as strong as an ox. He wasn't even the most powerful warrior, although anyone stupid enough to challenge him would quickly find himself with a dagger shoved into his chest and his heart cut out.

But he possessed a unique talent for stealth that made him the perfect choice for Styx's latest assignment.

Setting aside the manuscript, Styx regarded his Raven with a lift of his brows. The male was just under six foot, with short black hair that was shaved on the sides to reveal, on his scalp, the tattoos of two coiled snakes. His eyes were dark and his finely carved features so perfect he didn't look real. He was standing in the open doorway wearing black jeans and a black T-shirt. Keeping with the theme, his heavy boots were also black. The clothing was more about blending into the background than any particular fashion choice.

Styx, on the other hand, was wearing black leather pants and a white silk shirt because that's all he had in his closet. Darcy had finally accepted that he was never going to dress like a king.

"Are you looking for me?" Styx demanded when the male continued to stand there, eying him with an inscrutable expression.

"Yes."

"Then what are you waiting on? An engraved invitation?"

Xi's dark gaze drifted around the room before returning to Styx. "I'm attempting to decide whether or not I have the courage to enter."

Styx scowled. He'd witnessed this male battle a horde of orcs with nothing more than his fangs and a dagger.

"The one thing you've never lacked is courage, amigo."

"Normally, I would agree with you, but you have been..."

Styx lifted his six-foot-five body out of the chair. "I've been what?"

"Volatile over the past weeks," Xi told him.

The Raven was right. The past month had stretched Styx's limited patience to the breaking point. It was nothing he could put his finger on. Unexplained fires. Sudden riots. Vandalism. Brutal attacks on lesser demons.

Every night, he woke to discover a line of demons waiting to make a complaint or plead for his assistance. It was enough to stress out the most Zen vampire. And there was nothing Zen about Styx.

Which was why he'd requested Xi to investigate the various incidents. With an effort, Styx leashed his burst of annoyance at the interruption. He even managed to force a wry smile to his lips.

"According to my mate, I'm always volatile."

Xi didn't argue. "More volatile than usual," he clarified.

"Mount Etna volatile or Mount Vesuvius?"

Xi answered without hesitation. "Definitely Mount Vesuvius."

Styx tapped a finger on the edge of his desk. He was often short-tempered. It was part of his charm. But the past month had rubbed his nerves raw.

"I've had stressful times, terrifying times, and the world-is-about-to-end times. But this..." He shook his head. "I feel like I'm being tormented by a thousand unseen ants. Each biting when I least expect it."

"The city is seething."

"Seething. Yes. That's exactly what's happening," Styx agreed. It was like they were sitting on a simmering pot that might boil over at any moment. "I don't suppose you've managed to discover what's causing the trouble?"

"I have answers for the latest incidents." Xi strolled forward, halting next to the desk. "The collapse at the sanctuary happened when the wooden beams in the ceiling shattered."

The sanctuary had been Darcy's idea. She'd spent years barely scraping by, unaware why she was different from other people. She wanted a place for demons to go that would offer them food and a warm place to sleep, as well as protection from the more predatory creatures. Or even from humans, who had a tendency to kill what they feared.

A week ago, the old warehouse collapsed into a pile of rubble, wounding several of those seeking asylum. Darcy had been furious, and Styx had promised to get to the bottom of the collapse.

"Did someone tamper with them?" he asked Xi.

The Raven shrugged. "The damage was too great to determine if it was an accident or deliberate."

Styx was willing to bet it was deliberate. "And the others?"

"The fire at the Viper Club was caused by an electrical surge," Xi continued. "And the rampaging vampire that we captured claims he was kidnapped and injected with some unknown toxin that sent him into a psychotic episode."

It'd only been a night ago that Styx had received a frantic call that warned there was a crazed vampire destroying a human nightclub. The male was not only creating chaos, but he was threatening to expose the existence of vampires. Something that would be catastrophic for the entire demon-world.

Styx had personally gone to the club to capture the idiot and toss him into a locked cell. It was also when he'd suggested to Darcy that she might want to visit her sister. Anything to get her out of town.

"Where was he kidnapped from?" Styx demanded.

"In front of your lair."

Styx hissed in outrage. What demon had the balls to kidnap a vampire beneath the nose of the Anasso?

A dead one.

Grimly, he resisted the urge to push his fist through the wall. Now that he was king, he had to pay for repairs. It was insane what a good carpenter could charge.

"What was the vampire doing here?"

"He doesn't remember. All he can recall is leaving his home two nights ago to hunt for his dinner and being attacked by two Weres, who held him down and injected him with something. The next thing he knew, he was chained in your dungeon."

"Darcy doesn't like the word 'dungeon,'" Styx reminded his companion, his thoughts distracted. Had the vampire been kidnapped because he was coming to see Styx? Perhaps he knew something about the troubles plaguing the city. Or had he been kidnapped just because he happened to be near Styx's lair? Like a warning shot?

Impossible to know for sure.

"Holding center for disobliging guests," Xi offered in dry tones.

"That's better."

"If you say so."

Styx shrugged. He didn't understand his mate's distaste for the word "dungeon." There were cells that locked and guards to keep watch. You could call it the Four Seasons Resort if you wanted; it didn't change what it was.

"He was sure it was Weres?" he asked his companion.

"Positive. And I could smell the scent of dogs when I went to interview him."

Styx continued to tap his finger, his mind seething. Could the Weres be behind this relentless attack? The thought made his stomach clench with dread.

"I need to have a word with Salvatore." Salvatore was the King of Weres and Styx's brother-in-law. Yep, he could write the book on dysfunctional families. "Then I'll question our disobliging guest." He reached to touch the massive sword strapped to his back. For the past couple of weeks, he had never left his bedroom without it. Some people had therapy animals. He had a big, pointy weapon that could slice off a troll's head. Hey, it gave him comfort. "I might be able to prompt his memory."

"I'll continue to dig for information on the other disturbances," Xi offered, his expression even more stoic than usual, a certain sign that something was bothering him.

"You seem…"

Xi frowned. "What?"

"Troubled."

Xi hesitated. His emotions were always hidden, but they ran as hot as lava beneath his icy composure.

"The accidents could be random," he finally said.

"But?"

Xi shrugged. "But I don't believe in coincidences."

"Neither do I," Styx agreed. "See what you can find out. But be careful."

Xi arched his brows. Styx grunted, not having to guess why his guard seemed surprised. He sent his Ravens to deal with the most challenging, most dangerous tasks. They were a brutal weapon that he wielded without mercy.

He certainly never patted them on the head and told them to be careful. Styx twisted his lips. "There's a funky feeling in the air," he muttered.

Xi's brows arched even higher. Styx rolled his eyes.

"Go do your job," Styx growled.

A faint smile skimmed over Xi's lips before he turned and silently disappeared from the room.

* * * *

Brigette was on the hunt.

Gliding through the darkness, she crouched low to the ground as she followed the two intruders. She'd picked up their scents long before they'd actually entered the desolated grounds that surrounded her lair. A benefit of spending time alone in this remote part of Ireland.

Night after night, she prowled through the village, which was nothing more than shattered foundations and sorrowful ghosts. Or along the barren cliffs, listening to the waves crash against the jagged stones and breathing deeply of the salty breeze. She had nothing to distract her.

Well, unless you counted the thousand regrets that haunted her.

Regret for having betrayed her pack to join with the evil Beast who'd nearly destroyed her. Regret for having driven her wolf into hibernation. Regret for having wasted her opportunity to rewrite history.

She was lying in the ruins of her parents' cottage when she detected the icy power of an approaching vampire. With a fluid speed, she was on her feet and racing over the decaying ground to circle around the intruders.

Following behind them, Brigette took inventory of the two demons who were attempting to sneak along the edge of the cliff.

The vampire was a tall, slender female with pale blond hair pulled into a long braid. She was wearing a black turtleneck sweater and tight black slacks that made her look like she was stepping off a runway, not trudging through the tough heather and climbing over rocks.

The sight was annoying as hell.

Not only did she hate leeches, but she knew that, in contrast, she must look like crap. She was still wearing the same robe that she had been given in the dungeons beneath the mer-folk castle. Oh, she'd washed it, but it was threadbare and stained and should have been burned weeks ago. Plus she hadn't brushed her hair since...Hell, she didn't even know.

Long ago, her hair, the color of crimson, had been her pride and joy. She'd brushed the fiery curls until they tumbled down her back like a river of fire. Now she could barely bother to eat, let alone worry about the sheen of her hair.

Silently cursing at her stupid distraction, Brigette turned her attention to the vampire's companion.

A male Were.

Surprise, surprise. There might have been an uneasy truce established between the vamps and the pureblood Weres, but as far as she knew, it was rare for either species to tolerate each other, let alone willingly work together.

Her gaze skimmed over the male. He was large, with a shaved head that was currently coated with a fine mist. His body was bulked with muscles that strained against his flannel shirt and jeans. He had on a pair of hiking boots that crunched loudly against the stony ground, and she could catch the scent of metal. He was carrying a gun. Maybe more than one.

It was hard to make out his features in the thick fog that shrouded the area, but she sensed that he was younger than her. She also sensed that he didn't possess her strength. Not unless he shifted into his wolf, something she didn't intend to allow.

Coiling her muscles, Brigette soared through the air, landing in front of the Were. The male snarled, but before he could react, Brigette had her silver dagger pressed over his heart.

"If you so much as twitch, I'll slice open your heart," she warned.

The male stiffened, his eyes smoldering with a golden fire as his musk blasted through the air.

"Careful, female," he snarled, baring his teeth, "or I'll take a bite out of you."

She pressed the knife hard enough to slice through the flannel shirt and draw blood. "You wanna make this into a pissing contest, bruh?"

"Don't mind him. He's an idiot," an icy female voice drawled.

Brigette glanced toward the leech, careful to keep the knife poised to strike the killing blow.

"Who are you?"

"I'm Maryam." The female pointed toward her companion. "And this is Roban."

"A pureblooded Were and a vamp traveling together." A humorless smile curved Brigette's lips. "Has hell frozen over?"

Maryam's pale, beautiful face was set in grim lines. "Not yet, but it's coming."

"Really?" Brigette shrugged. "I didn't get the memo."

"I'm here to deliver it in person."

"Lucky me."

Maryam glanced toward the Were. "Can you release Roban? He's bleeding all over the place."

Brigette glanced toward the male, realizing she'd stuck the knife in deeper that she'd thought. The wound wasn't going to permanently injure him, but the silver in the blade kept him from healing. Which meant that the blood continued to seep through his shirt and dribble down his jeans. And, as a bonus, the silver would keep the Were from shifting into his wolf form.

"I could." She glanced back at the leech. "I won't, but I could."

"Even if I assure you that we come in peace?"

Brigette snorted. The leech sounded like a character from a cheesy horror film. "Especially if you assure me you come in peace." She pressed the knife a quarter of an inch deeper. The Were grunted in pain, droplets of sweat joining the mist coating his bald head. Brigette wrinkled her nose. He was all moist, and not in a good way. "I'm not asking again. Why are you here?"

Something flashed through the female's icy blue eyes. Probably fury, maybe heartburn. No. The Were was the one with heartburn. The leech was definitely furious.

Still, Maryam made a commendable effort to control her emotions. "I was looking for you."

Brigette scowled. There'd been a few brave souls who'd come to the remote village after she'd returned Chaaya and Basq back to Vegas, along with Levet to the mer-folk castle. She didn't know if they were there to pin a medal on her chest or chop off her head. And she wasn't going to stick around and find out.

This time, however, she was curious. She wanted to know why this odd couple had invaded her home.

"Did Ulric send you?" she asked.

"No. Although, your cousin is the reason I decided to make you an offer," Maryam told her.

Brigette narrowed her eyes. "Is it one I can't refuse?"

The vamp shook her head. "Nothing so dramatic."

"What's the offer?"

Maryam glanced toward the Were, who grimaced before nodding his head in some sort of silent agreement. The vampire turned her attention back to Brigette.

"I belong to Chiron's clan," she revealed.

"You're a Rebel?"

"Yes. I traveled with Chiron and Ulric after we were banished by the former Anasso," Maryam told her. "I considered them my family."

Chiron was a vampire who owned Dreamscape Resorts, a successful chain of human casinos around the world. He'd also taken over a clan of vampires who had been banished by the former Anasso when their leader, Tarak, had disappeared. Tarak had recently escaped his prison, and there was a new Anasso, and supposedly they'd all come together in one big kumbaya moment.

Ulric was Brigette's cousin who'd been taken by the goblin raiders that Brigette had led to the village and sold into captivity by the former Anasso. Chiron had rescued him, and they'd formed an unbreakable bond that had lasted the past five hundred years.

The fact that Maryam was a Rebel, however, did nothing to ease her suspicion. If anything, it intensified her distrust. Ulric had more reason than anyone else in the world to want her dead.

Ah, families...so much fun.

"Is there a point to this?" Brigette drawled. "Or are we just reminiscing about the good old days? I'll warn you, my good old days included lots of blood and screaming."

"I want you to know that I consider Ulric my friend."

"Good for you. He blames me for destroying our pack, so if that's all—"

"For centuries, the Rebels enjoyed the freedom to live as we please," Maryam overrode Brigette's words. "We didn't have a king, and we didn't need one."

Brigette rolled her eyes. A part of her had followed the intruders with the hope they might provide some entertainment. There was only so long a poor female Were could brood alone in the wilderness.

"That's your point?" Brigette didn't have to pretend her disappointment.

"In part."

"I'm rapidly getting bored." Brigette tightened her fingers on the hilt of the dagger. "And when I'm bored, things die."

The Were growled, and Maryam hastily lifted her hand in a gesture urging restraint. "You asked me to explain why I'm here. That's what I'm trying to do."

Brigette was pleased that the two obviously took her warning seriously. They should. She would kill Roban without a second thought.

"You're not explaining very well," she warned.

There was a distinct chill in the air, and a hint of fang, as Maryam struggled to contain her irritation.

"As I said, we were all doing fine without a king, and then Chiron betrayed us."

Brigette arched a brow. "Betrayed?"

"He bent his knee to the new Anasso."

There was a bite in the female's tone. As if Chiron had slaughtered babies instead of simply acknowledging Styx as the King of the Vampires.

"So?"

"We're now under the yoke of a power-hungry despot."

Brigette released a startled laugh. "Power-hungry despot? That's a little drama queen, don't you think?"

The air went from chilly to frigid. Maryam obviously didn't find any humor in her tragic overreaction.

"It's the truth." Her tone was stiff. "I have proof that Styx is plotting to enslave the Rebels."

Brigette frowned. Over the past centuries, she'd been more or less trapped by the evil Beast who'd threatened to destroy the world. But there had been times when she'd traveled away from her village. And in all those times, she'd never heard anything that would imply that the new Anasso was evil.

Indeed, most of the demon-world had celebrated when the old king had perished and Styx had taken the throne.

"Why would he do that?" Brigette demanded in genuine confusion.

"To punish us."

"Punish you for what?"

"For being rebels."

"Hmm." Styx could have punished the rebels the moment he'd become the Anasso, so why wait? She kept the question to herself. Instead, she turned her attention to Roban. "Why are you here?"

He bared his teeth, but she still had the silver dagger stuck in the center of his chest. "Because we've also discovered a plot to enslave the Weres," he grudgingly answered.

"That's a lot of enslaving."

The blue in Maryam's eyes frosted over. "It's been done before."

The leech had a point, Brigette silently acknowledged. Throughout the endless years, there had been countless tyrants who'd used their powers for evil. Including her former mistress.

Still, it all seemed sketchy to Brigette. "Where's your proof?"

"In Chicago."

"Convenient."

"Join us, and I'll show you." Maryam stepped closer, holding out a hand. "I swear no harm will come to you."

Brigette growled. It didn't matter that her wolf had turned its back on her. She could still do serious damage. Maryam froze before slowly and deliberately taking a step back.

Smart leech.

"What do you want from me?" Brigette demanded.

"There are rumors you have the power to defeat even the Anasso."

Ah. Brigette felt a ridiculous pang of disappointment. She didn't know why. The only reason anyone could possibly seek her out was to kill her, or in the hope they could use her evil powers.

Powers that she no longer possessed.

Brigette struggled to keep her expression calm. "Presuming the rumors are true, why would I use my powers to defeat the King of the Vampires?"

It was Roban who answered. "He intends to return the Weres to our prison camp in Italy. We nearly became extinct the last time we were trapped."

Brigette stifled a yawn. "And?"

The green eyes once again smoldered with the golden power of his wolf. "You don't care about your people?"

Envy seeped through her like poison. Christ, she missed her animal.

"I massacred my own family. What do you think?" she snapped, preparing to carve out the male's heart.

Chapter 2

"Brigette, don't," Maryam protested, genuine fear in her voice.

In contrast, the male merely glared at her, refusing to react to the dagger that was a breath from puncturing his heart.

"I told you this was a waste of our time, Maryam."

"It was worth trying." A tight smile curved the female's mouth. "I'm sorry you won't join us," she told Brigette. "If you'll release Roban, we'll leave, and you can return to…" She waved a hand around the village, which was grindingly bleak. "Whatever you were doing before we interrupted you."

If the leech had threatened her or physically tried to rescue the Were, Brigette would have destroyed them both. End of story. Instead, she found herself plucking the knife out of the male's heart and stepping back. She half-expected the two to attack her; instead, they turned and started to walk away.

Just like that.

Brigette scowled. She should let them go. She had no interest in their crazy fear that Styx was trying to enslave them. As long as people left her alone, the world could go to hell, right?

Besides, she couldn't give them what they wanted. Once the evil Beast had been locked back in her dimension, the dark powers had been stripped from Brigette. Now she was just a Were who couldn't call on her wolf.

Worthless.

"Wait!" she called out.

Maryam halted, glancing over her shoulder. "What?"

Brigette hesitated. She felt as if she was poised on the edge of a knife. Or maybe standing at a crossroads. One decision would turn her life in a different direction. So far, her decisions had been utterly shitty. The first had caused the destruction of her family. The second had left her alone in this grim, desolate place.

Ah, well. A wry smile twisted her lips. Three times was the charm, wasn't it?

"What's in it for me?" she demanded.

Maryam slowly turned to face her. "What do you want?"

"What I've always wanted. Power," Brigette admitted.

Maryam studied her with a narrowed gaze. "Your own pack?"

"Yes." Brigette smiled as Roban whirled around with a snarl of disbelief. "And money," she added. "Lots of money."

The leech nodded, ignoring her companion, who did nothing to hide his gut-deep disgust with Brigette.

"That can be arranged," the female promised.

"I want it up front."

Maryam gave a lift of one shoulder. "You have to wait until we get to Chicago."

"If this is a trick…"

"It isn't," Maryam interrupted Brigette's warning, holding up a slender hand. "Cross my heart and hope to die."

"Oh, you'll be hoping to die if you double-cross me." Brigette strolled forward to join them, blowing a kiss toward the snarling Were. "That's my promise to you."

* * * *

It took Levet a full hour to at last track down the Queen of the Mer-folk. The castle beneath the ocean was surprisingly large, but that wasn't the reason it was so difficult to find Inga. It was because she wasn't like a traditional queen.

She hated sitting on the massive throne, surrounded by marble and the exquisite murals she'd painted on the walls. Or in her private chambers, which looked like they'd been decorated by the architect who created Versailles. Only on steroids. Massive amounts of steroids.

Perhaps it was because Inga hadn't been raised to become the ruler of the mer-folk. She hadn't even known she was a mer-folk. She'd taken after her ogre father, with a large body that stood over six foot and was broad enough to plow through a horde of trolls. Her hair was red and grew in amazing tufts that refused to be tamed by a brush. Her teeth were pointed and her brow heavy. Only her eyes spoke of her mermaid mother. They were a pale blue, although they had a tendency to flash crimson when she was annoyed.

Which was most of the time.

Or perhaps it was because the mer-folk still hadn't fully accepted her as their leader. Unlike many other demon societies, the throne wasn't passed down from the mer-folk king to one of his children. It was the large trident that Inga was clutching in her hand that chose the current leader. The magic of the Tryshu not only revealed the king or queen; it also possessed the power to make the leader invincible. At least until it decided to choose a different leader.

The mer-folk were stuck with Inga, but they didn't have to like it. And there were many in the castle who enjoyed causing trouble for the current queen.

Following her scent into the weapons room, next to the dungeons at the very bottom of the castle, Levet waddled across the bedrock. Around him, a hundred tridents, shields, and armor made out of strange iridescent fish scales were stacked against the wall or hanging from the low ceiling. It wasn't until he passed through a narrow door, however, that he at last found his quarry.

"There you are, *ma belle.*"

Inga whirled around, the blousy material of her tie-dyed muumuu floating around her like a psychedelic tent.

"Oh. Levet." A relieved smile.

Levet would usually assume the smile was because she was pleased to see him. Granted, there were a few odd creatures who didn't appreciate a three-foot gargoyle with dazzling fairy wings and stunted horns, but overall the females adored him. And why not? He was charming, his magic was awesome, and he was a knight in shining armor who spent his nights saving the world from disaster.

All in all, an amazing creature.

But he sensed Inga's smile was simply relief that he wasn't one of the mer-folk. He stepped farther into the cramped space, which was more a closet than an actual room. "Are you hiding again?"

A flush crawled beneath Inga's cheeks. "Hiding? Don't be ridiculous," she scoffed, using the Tryshu to point toward the nearby shelves. Levet ducked, nearly knocked in the head by the butt of the massive trident. "I'm doing an inventory of our weapons."

Levet wrinkled his brow. "Is that not Rimm's job? He is the captain of your guards."

"He's in charge of the regular weapons, but I have turned this closet into a vault to hold Riven's collection."

"Ah." Riven had been the former king, who'd used a magical artifact to trick the Tryshu into naming him leader so he could rule with an iron fist. He'd been a collector of powerful magic. Most of it evil. "I thought your mother was studying them?"

"She has gone to speak with the ogres."

Levet widened his eyes. The ogres had not only killed Inga's father, but they'd tried to murder Inga when she was just a baby.

"After what they did?"

Inga shrugged, although her eyes flashed crimson. "The ogres seem to think that my blood means I'll be willing to give them a favorable trade deal."

"Trade for what?"

"Pearls, mainly."

Levet snorted. He'd never liked ogres. He liked them even less after he'd discovered how they'd hurt Inga.

"Did you tell them to stick the trade deal up their hot toddies?"

She blinked. Then blinked again. "Patooties?"

Levet waved a hand. "Same thing."

"I wanted to, but my mother convinced me that we can't afford to turn our backs on potential allies."

Levet pursed his lips. There were times when he forgot that Inga was a queen who had people who depended on her to make adult decisions.

"I suppose that makes sense," he grudgingly conceded.

A rare smile touched Inga's lips. "My mother is the wisest person I've ever known."

Levet reached to touch her arm. For centuries, Inga had believed she was a stain on her family. And that she'd been sold into the slave trade by her own mother. Now she knew that had been a wicked lie, and that she had a family who adored her. It was the one good thing that had come from discovering she was the queen.

"That doesn't explain why you are hiding in this smelly place," Levet said.

"I'm not hiding." Inga heaved a sigh. "Well, not entirely. I'm ensuring that no one has tampered with the magical items."

"Who would tamper with them? This castle is a fortress."

"A fortress?" Inga snorted. "Have you forgotten that, just a couple months ago, Brigette managed to escape from my dungeons and that crazy druid priestess opened a portal in my throne room?"

"True," Levet was forced to concede. He'd been kidnapped by Brigette and taken to a bizarre dimension where they'd nearly been killed. More than once. It'd been a grand adventure. "Is anything missing?"

"Not that I can tell. I really need to have Mother make an itemized list so I can be certain that we keep track of everything. Most of them are quite dangerous."

Levet stepped closer to the shelves. He could easily detect the sparkles that floated in the air, revealing a magical barrier to protect the items.

"Did you attempt to use any of these?"

Inga moved to stand next to him, the soft scent of an ocean breeze wrapping around him. Levet sucked in a deep breath. He loved how she smelled.

"My mother has." Inga pointed toward an object on the top shelf. It was hard and black, with a luminescent sheen. Like a black pearl. "This one forms a protective bubble that is impervious to everything but lava."

"Impressive." Levet nodded toward the large, golden medallion that was hanging from a leather strap. There were strange marks etched into the gold that he'd never seen before. "What about this one?"

"So far, all we've discovered is that it smells awful."

Instantly enchanted, Levet reached up a hand. "Really?"

Inga grasped his horn and tugged him back. "Absolutely not."

Levet didn't argue. He was already distracted by a delicate figurine that looked like a diamond chiseled into the shape of a swan.

"What about the sparkly one?"

"We're not sure. My mother could sense tremendous power, but she couldn't ignite the magic."

Levet pointed toward an object that looked like a plain pebble on one of the lower shelves. "I know what that one is."

"Really?"

"It is a doulas stone."

"What does it do?"

"It—" Levet was interrupted, as there was a knocking in his head. There was no other way to explain what he experienced. "Oh."

"What's wrong?"

"Someone is wanting in."

"In?" Inga's gaze darted toward the door, as if expecting an attack. "In where?"

Levet tapped a claw against his temple. "They wish to speak to my mind."

A portion of Inga's tension eased. "Who is it?"

"I'm not certain."

"I thought you could only speak telepathically with those whom you've made a mental connection with?"

He absently nodded. Inga was right. He had to have established a relationship with the creature who wished to mentally contact him. A good thing. Otherwise, every Tom, Dick, and Larry...no wait, hairy? Harry? Anyway, they would all come a-knocking on his brain.

"It is familiar," he murmured. "And yet strange."

Inga looked worried. "Don't answer it."

"I have no choice." Levet shuddered. "It will not stop. Thump. Thump. Thump. As if my poor head is a drum." Closing his eyes, Levet concentrated on the presence reaching out to him. "*Bonjour?*"

"At last," a female voice echoed through his mind.

"What do you mean 'at last'?" Levet mentally protested. "You are fortunate that I answered at all."

"Levet, I don't have time for your babbling."

"Babbling?" Levet furrowed his brow. The rich, powerful voice was familiar, but it wasn't until the female had used that particular word that Levet realized who was speaking. "Oh, Brigette."

"Yes."

Levet's wings fluttered with relief. Most people assumed that Brigette was evil and had done terrible, awful things, but Levet had glimpsed into her heart. The female Were genuinely regretted what she'd done and now spent her life punishing herself for her sins.

He'd been quite worried about her.

"How are you? *Non.* Wait. Where are you?" Levet demanded. "I have tried to search for you, but—"

"Levet, just hush up and listen to me."

Levet stiffened. "Rude."

"Oh, Christ." Brigette abruptly laughed. "I've missed you."

"I have missed you as well," Levet assured the Were. "Is there a reason you wished to speak with me?"

"I need you to get a warning to Styx."

"What has happened?"

"There's a group of rebels who are plotting a coup against him."

Levet frowned. Why would the vampires be plotting a chicken house against the Anasso? That didn't make sense. Oh, no. That was a coop. A coup was something to do with lopping off the king's head, right?

"Not Chiron?" he asked in surprise. He'd heard that the Rebels had made nice with Styx and they were all one big happy family.

Well, as happy as a bunch of arrogant, ill-tempered blood-suckers could be.

"No. They're not a part of the Rebel clan, they're just rebels. They hate Chiron as well."

"Who?"

"It's some vampire who calls herself Maryam and a pureblood Were named Roban," Brigette told him.

The names weren't familiar, but Levet preferred to avoid leeches whenever possible.

"Where are they?"

"In a section of tunnels beneath Chicago."

Levet jerked in shock. Styx's lair was in Chicago. Not to mention his besties Viper and Dante. Three of the most powerful vampires in the world.

"That is bold. And rather..."

"Suicidal?"

"*Oui.*"

"They have hundreds of warriors signed up for the cause."

A dozen questions buzzed through Levet's mind, but he forced himself to concentrate on the most important one.

"Including you?"

"I'm just here for the sightseeing," she instantly denied a loyalty to the traitors.

Levet breathed a sigh of relief. "What do you wish me to tell Styx?"

"They're plotting something big."

"Big? That is it?" Levet shuddered, easily able to imagine Styx's thunderous reaction. The Anasso was not only the leader of the vampires, he was also the most ill-tempered. "Could you be more vague, *mon amie?*"

"It's all I've got. At least for now."

"You are staying with them?"

"I don't have anything better to do."

Levet wasn't fooled. He might not understand how or why Brigette was with these new rebels, but he did know it wasn't because she was bored. Or at least not entirely. Now, however, was not the time to question her motives.

If there truly was danger in Chicago, then he had to get to Styx to warn him. Not that he cared about the overbearing leech, but Levet adored Styx's mate, Darcy. He would do whatever necessary to ensure she wasn't harmed.

"Be careful," he warned Brigette.

"Never."

The presence of the female Were abruptly disappeared, leaving Levet momentarily disoriented.

"You're leaving, aren't you?"

Slowly, Levet opened his eyes, discovering Inga staring down at him with a sad expression. He grimaced.

"It is my duty."

She nodded. Duty was the one thing that this female understood. "You'll come back?"

"Always."

Chapter 3

Xi traveled through the tunnels like a whisper. Barely stirring the air, he moved from shadow to shadow, observing the numerous demons who gathered in the massive cement tunnels that had once been a part of Chicago's reservoir plan. Logically, the vast cement passages would seem to be a perfect place to convert into lairs. They were dark and damp and well hidden from the crowded streets of the city. But most vampires preferred natural caverns. They weren't fans of the stark industrial stench of cement and rusty iron.

That reluctance might explain why there was so much rubbish tossed around. A vampire's meticulous habits could be damaged when they were stuck in a nasty environment. Or maybe the layers of trash were caused by the hundred or so demons that moved in and out of the tunnels. The gargoyle's warning had indicated that there were more than just a couple of rebels living beneath Styx's feet. Xi, however, hadn't expected such a diversity among the demons. It wasn't just vampires and Weres. There were fairies and brownies and several mongrels.

Why would they interest themselves in vampire business?

It was a question that Xi wasn't going to be able to answer by lurking in the shadows.

After a full twenty-four hours of watching the various creatures who lived in the hidden liar, Xi at last went in search of the female Were who'd sent the warning. He'd easily picked her out from Levet's description.

Watching her interact with her fellow rebels, he'd determined that she was kept at a distance by most of the demons, as if they hadn't yet decided whether or not to trust her. Or maybe they resented her presence because of her past. It was no secret that she'd sacrificed her pack and nearly overrun the world with a tide of evil to gain power.

Whatever the case, she didn't appear to be a beloved member of the group.

Moving in silence, he entered the side tunnel she'd claimed as her own. It was far enough from the others to offer the illusion of privacy. He glanced around the cramped space, which held a mattress tossed on the hard ground and a few clothes piled on a chair. That was it.

With his usual caution, Xi stepped into the space, already prepared for the rush of heat as the hidden Were leaped forward to press a silver dagger against his neck.

"Stop right there," Brigette warned.

Xi turned to glance at the female, who was glaring at him with smoldering eyes. And promptly froze in shock.

He'd seen her, of course, as he'd spied on the rebels. And a part of him had been captivated. Not by her slender curves or the pale perfection of her face, which was framed by a tumble of lush, crimson curls. Or even the dark eyes that contrasted sharply against her smooth skin. He was a vampire, not a human with an obsession with surface beauty. No, he was far more intrigued with the powerful grace of her body beneath her jeans and her chunky ivory sweater. She had a bold, in-your-face attitude that gave her a swagger as she moved past the disapproving gazes. It revealed a fierce spirit that was far sexier than the shape of her slender nose or the plush softness of her lips.

But seeing her at a distance and having her up close and personal were two different things.

Two *very* different things.

The eyes weren't just brown, but a rich, velvet darkness that lightened to gold at the center. And her skin wasn't pale; it was as creamy and soft as the petals of the chrysanthemums that he remembered from his homeland. Even her hair was more vibrant, with shades of copper and bronze and gold mixed with the red.

And her scent...warm and spiced with heather.

She was a sensual wonderland of erotic temptation.

For a long moment, they simply stared at one another, as if they were both knocked off guard by the meeting. Then the spell was broken as Brigette narrowed her eyes. Obviously, she was angered by her reaction.

"Who are you?" she snapped, pressing the dagger until he felt the silver sizzle into his flesh.

Too smart to try to jerk away from the lethal blade, he instead held himself perfectly still.

"I'm Xi, one of the Ravens. Styx sent me."

The dagger bit deep enough to draw a drop of blood before Brigette lowered her hand and stepped away.

"What took you so long?" she asked.

"I don't rush into situations." He glanced around to make sure that there was no one hiding in the shadows. Once assured that they were alone, he turned his attention back to the female. "The Anasso wants to speak with you."

She held the dagger loosely in her fingers, but she didn't put it away. A less than subtle warning.

"Then why didn't he come?"

"He assumed it was a trap."

She blinked, as if surprised by his blunt honesty. "If I wanted to trap him, I'd be a little more creative than mysterious rebels lurking in dark tunnels beneath his city."

Xi shrugged. "He'll meet with you at his lair."

Her brows pulled together, and he assumed she was going to argue. Most demons had an independent streak. And female Weres had a streak a mile wide.

But she surprised him, by slowly nodding her head. "First, I want to get something."

"What?"

She headed out of the side passage. "Follow me."

He reached to grasp her arm, spinning her back to meet his frown. "Not until you tell me exactly where you're going and why."

Her jaw tightened as she jerked away from his touch, but with a visible effort, she maintained her temper.

"The leader of this merry band of misfits has a stack of scrolls she claims were recently sent from Styx. She has them locked in her office."

Well, that wasn't what Xi had been expecting. "Scrolls?"

"Pieces of parchment with writing on them and rolled into cylinders. Some even have pretty ribbons."

"I know what they are." He did his own share of temper maintenance. "I also know that Styx has never used a scroll in his very long existence."

"How can you be sure?"

It was a legitimate question. It wasn't as if he'd spent every minute of every day with the Anasso. Xi, however, was confident that his master had an aversion to communication that could be traced by an enemy. Letters, texts, emails. And most certainly scrolls.

"If Styx has something to say to someone, he does it face-to-face. It avoids any misunderstandings."

"All the more reason to get the scrolls, so he can see them for himself."

Xi considered her words. He didn't think it was a trick. He'd been watching her long enough to have sensed a potential snare. But the night was swiftly passing, and as a vampire, he had a lethal aversion to the dawn. He wanted to get this female to Styx's lair as soon as possible.

His gaze skimmed over her face, taking in the stubborn line of her jaw. She wasn't leaving here without those damned scrolls. He waved a hand toward the opening.

"Lead the way."

Holding the dagger in a light grip, Brigette headed out of her private space and entered the large tunnel. They traveled a short distance before she crawled through a narrow vent that opened into an annex tunnel. This one wasn't nearly as large as the others, and worse, it had a groove running down the middle of the cement floor that was filled with stagnant water. The walls were covered with a greenish mold that filled the air with a pungent scent, and the ceiling was low enough to brush the top of his head, forcing him to walk bent over.

It was dank and cold and unpleasant, but walking directly behind Brigette, Xi found himself wrapped in the warm scent of heather. Suddenly, the tunnel wasn't nearly as unpleasant.

A delicious shiver raced through Xi.

He'd never been so vibrantly aware of another creature.

It was oddly exhilarating.

And dangerously distracting, he sternly reminded himself.

They walked in silence, both aware that voices would echo through the long tunnel. Even through the thick cement, he could hear the sound of voices seeping from other parts of the underground maze. At last, she reached another vent, and with a gesture to follow her, Brigette squeezed through. Xi swiftly followed, finding himself in a dark space that was filled with rubble. It looked like a dump space for the humans who'd constructed the tunnels. There was also a rusty set of rebar steps leading toward a heavy hatch in the ceiling. An emergency exit? Probably.

Brigette glanced over her shoulder. "Wait here."

"No."

She made a sound of impatience. "This isn't a trap."

"I wouldn't have followed you if I thought it was."

"Then why are you being a pain?" she snapped.

Xi shrugged. "I don't want you disappearing."

"Why would I disappear?" she asked in confusion. "I called to warn you guys, remember?"

Deep inside, Xi knew he wasn't being entirely reasonable. It wasn't like she could evade him. Now that he had her scent, he could track her anywhere in the world. But he couldn't shake the strange compulsion to keep her in sight.

"I'll go with you."

His tone was reasonable, but it was blatantly obvious he wasn't going to compromise. Brigette clenched her teeth, looking like she wanted to throat-punch him.

"Fine."

With a toss of her glorious hair, she turned to cautiously push open a door that had been carved into the cement. She paused, no doubt ensuring there was no one nearby before she stepped into the dark room. Xi was less than an inch behind her, his gaze quickly skimming over the large space.

There was a heavy mahogany desk in one corner, along with several file cabinets and wooden shelves that were stuffed with books. A large map of the world had been pinned to a bulletin board. There was also a heavy steel safe set next to a pile of weapons that ranged from wooden spears to AK-15s. Something for anyone, he wryly acknowledged.

"This is Maryam's office," Brigette absently explained, heading toward the safe. "Make yourself useful and keep watch while I open the safe."

During his earlier sweep, Xi hadn't managed to get this deep in the tunnels. The female vampire had been wise enough to travel with a full battalion of guards, including her pet Were, Roban. It hadn't been worth the risk of exposure. Now he realized he should have suspected that Maryam would have a hidden exit. A leader would have to be stupid not to have a back door for a quick escape.

He curiously watched Brigette punch in a series of numbers on the electronic pad. "You know the security code?"

The female concentrated on pulling open the door of the safe. "I was in the room when Maryam opened the vault. A sloppy mistake."

Xi arched a brow. "You memorized a key code with fifteen symbols after seeing it once?"

"I didn't see it. I heard the beeps. They're very distinct," she muttered, clearly distracted. "And I remember most things. Unfortunately."

Xi was impressed. That was the sort of talent that could come in handy. With a faint smile, he moved across the room to pull open the door that led to the main tunnel. He couldn't sense any demons in the area, but he didn't intend to be taken by surprise.

He heard the sound of rustling papers and caught the scent of parchment before the safe was closed with a soft click. A minute later, Brigette was standing at his side.

"I've got them," she murmured in a soft voice, holding up the lacquered wooden box she held in her hands. "How did you get in here?"

"This way."

He released his powers, muting his presence. It would also help to disguise Brigette's scent as long as she stayed near him. Then, heading down the tunnel, he led her to a side passageway.

She touched his arm. "Are you sure?" she whispered. "I've searched these tunnels, and this is a dead end."

"I have a portal waiting for us," he assured her.

She snorted. "Handy."

Xi continued through the labyrinth of tunnels, at last pausing as they reached the blank cement wall. There was nothing there to indicate a portal. At least not to him. Vampires had no ability to detect magic. But he'd made a precise mental note when he'd stepped out. He had no intention of fumbling to find his escape route. Not when he was in enemy territory.

Xi reached to grab Brigette's hand, despite the fact that she could no doubt see the opening. He didn't care. He wanted to touch her. It was that simple.

And that complicated.

Stepping forward, they were encased in darkness. Usually, traveling through the portal made Xi itchy. He hated magic. Any kind of magic. This time, he barely noticed the darkness or the weird prickle that crawled over his skin. The petty irritations were utterly overwhelmed by the explosive heat that seared through his skin and raced through his body.

He told himself that the intoxicating warmth was the result of touching a Were. They ran hotter than any other creature, including humans and fey. But that wasn't it. He could have shoved his hand in an oven and it wouldn't have caused such an intense reaction.

In the blink of an eye, they were stepping out of the darkness and onto the empty street in front of Styx's lair. Brigette tugged her hand free, but the motion was slow, almost reluctant. Had she been enjoying the contact as much as he had?

He thought he detected a faint shiver race through her body, but she hastily turned away from him, inspecting their surroundings.

"Where are we?" she asked, a hint of suspicion in her voice.

Xi didn't blame her. The elegant neighborhood, with ginormous homes and yards that looked like football fields, wasn't what most demons expected for the King of the Vampires.

Xi nodded toward the largest mansion, which rose from the surrounding gardens like a brick-and-mortar behemoth.

"That's the Anasso's lair."

She sent him a startled glance. "It must be nice to be the king."

"Not really. It's usually a pain in the ass."

Xi spent most evenings dealing with potential threats. Not only to Styx, but to the vampires in general. He'd recently returned from a remote island where a rare breed of sylphs were capturing vampires and sacrificing them to their god of fertility. It'd taken time, but he'd at last convinced them that the future of their small tribe depended on finding another way to have more children. But he'd been around Styx enough to know that his evenings were usually filled with tedious complaints from vampires who acted more like petulant children than masters of the night. Along with demands that he perform miracles.

Brigette shrugged. "Why are we out here? Why not open the portal inside his lair?"

"Styx doesn't allow magic in his house."

"Is he afraid?

"You can ask him yourself." Xi headed toward the mansion. "Although I wouldn't suggest it."

* * * *

Brigette stupidly assumed nothing could shock her. Not after the savage destruction of her pack, the bleak years as a servant to the evil Beast, and then being captured and thrown into the mer-folk dungeons. That didn't even include her last adventure traveling through various dimensions in search of a magical means to ease her guilt. But Xi had proven her wrong.

Wrong on an epic scale.

The second the tall vampire had stepped into her private space she'd been…rattled. She'd thought it was because she hadn't been able to sense him. No scent, no icy power, not even the sound of a footstep. He'd simply appeared as if by magic.

But it wasn't confusion or surprise that thundered through her as she'd taken in the stark perfection of his face and the fascinating tattoos on the sides of his skull. It wasn't even lust. She'd felt her first stirring of desire when she'd encountered the male Jinn a few months ago. Kgosi had managed to remind her that she was still a young female in her prime.

Nope, it was pure stupefaction.

There'd been something about the dark eyes. There were like deep pools of mystery. Yeah, it was hokey. But they really were deep pools. The sort that made female hearts flutter. Including her own. And the way he studied her, as if he was seeing the parts of herself she kept fiercely hidden. She was being stripped bare, and yet she hadn't felt exposed. Instead, she'd been...comforted. As if he'd seen her tainted soul and accepted her without judgment.

Then they'd stepped through the portal, and she'd been blasted by his icy power. It was like flipping a switch. One minute, there'd been nothing, and the next...bam. His energy had vibrated through her, sending shock waves of awareness detonating through her.

Suddenly, her breath had lodged in her lungs, and the most ridiculous certainty settled in her heart. It whispered that something fundamentally important had just occurred. As if her life could be divided in two. Pre-Xi and post-Xi.

Which was stupid, of course.

Nothing had happened, she sternly chided herself. The King of the Vampires had finally condescended to meet with her and sent one of his flunkies to collect her.

End. Of. Story.

She fiercely held on to that thought even as she trailed far behind Xi as he led her across the manicured lawn and through a side door into the house. No use being distracted by the searing sensation of his icy touch. Or the evocative scent of cedarwood. Right?

They moved through wide corridors with sparkling chandeliers and priceless works of art nailed to the walls. And by the time they reached the private study, Brigette was wondering if there was any marble left in Italy. There had to be acres of the stuff zigzagging through the endless hallways. Like a marble maze studded with gold.

No doubt, most creatures would find the place beautiful. And it was. But to Brigette it felt like a monstrous trap.

Life had taught her that nothing came for free. The cost this place must demand on a soul wasn't worth paying. At least not for her.

At last, she was standing in front of the male she'd been trying to reach for the past two days.

"So you're the King of the Vampires?" Brigette allowed her gaze to trail over the Anasso.

He was an impressive sight. His six-foot-five frame was incased in black leather, and his black hair was woven into a braid that fell to his lower back. His face was lean and bluntly carved, with eyes that held an ancient wisdom. At the moment, that face was lined with a weariness she assumed had something to do with Maryam and Roban's constant attacks.

"I am," he admitted in a deep voice.

She tilted back her head. At six foot, she rarely had to look up at anyone. Still, she wasn't going to let him intimidate her.

"I thought you would be bigger," she drawled. "With horns and a tail."

The ground trembled as Styx released a portion of his legendary power. Behind her, Brigette thought she heard Xi mutter something about stubborn idiots in low tones.

"And I thought you would be smarter. It's not the wisest decision to show your face after you tried to destroy the world."

Brigette's smile remained, although she covertly balled her hands into tight fists. She would endure endless torture before she'd reveal her raw regret for the past.

"Well, I've never been over-burdened with brains," she assured him.

Styx narrowed his eyes, but before he could continue the unpleasant conversation, there was a scent of granite, and a tiny shape appeared in the open doorway.

"*Mon amie.*" Levet moved forward, his fairy wings shimmering and a charming smile adding a beauty to his lumpy features.

Genuine joy melted Brigette's heart. This gargoyle was the only creature in the entire world who treated her as if she was more than a traitor who should be destroyed.

"Levet."

The gargoyle waddled forward, gently touching her arm. "I am so delighted to see you. I feared you might never leave that moldy village."

"So did I," she admitted.

"So why did you?" Styx asked.

Brigette had given some thought to her reasons. Her only conclusion was that it was complicated.

A part of her had been curious, a part had been aggravated, and another part had been bored and seeking a distraction from her self-imposed exile. Why not travel to Chicago and discover what was happening?

Then, after she'd arrived, she'd become caught up in her role as a spy. For the first time in five hundred years, she was thinking about something besides herself. And it'd been...exhilarating.

She chose the easiest answer. "I don't like people intruding into my territory and assuming they can manipulate me into using my evil powers for their benefit."

Levet frowned. "You no longer have evil powers."

Brigette shrugged. "That's not the point."

"If you were pissed, you could have run them off," the Anasso said, his voice edge with suspicion. "Or killed them. There was no need to travel all the way to Chicago."

"I wanted to see for myself what was happening. They claimed that the new King of the Vampires not only intended to enslave the vampires, but the Weres as well."

Styx grunted, as if her words had caught him off guard. "Why the hell would I enslave anyone?" He waved a hand around the office, which was stripped of most of the froufrou nonsense that filled the rest of the house. "If it weren't for Darcy, I wouldn't even have servants. I would live alone in my caves."

Brigette shrugged. "Roban also said you were going to send the Weres to Italy. Something about their old hunting grounds."

"They should be so lucky," Styx muttered. "Salvatore has done nothing but bitch and gripe about the weather in Kansas City. He would love to return to Italy, although I doubt he'd be willing to be confined to his old hunting grounds." Styx paused, as if struck by a sudden thought. "Still, I might consider the possibility. The mangy fur-bag too often forgets that I'm at the top of the food chain."

There was a glint in the Anasso's dark eyes. As if he was deliberately trying to provoke her. A wasted effort. She had no loyalty to Salvatore, the King of Weres. She'd never met the male and had no interest in being part of a pack. She'd given up any right to a family.

"Maryam has proof," she told the towering vampire.

"Show me."

Brigette held out the wooden box. "In there."

"Oh." Levet's wings fluttered. "A mystery box. Can I open it?"

Styx took the lacquered container, then, with a mocking smile, he shoved it toward the gargoyle. "Knock yourself out."

Levet wavered, clearly torn between his insatiable curiosity and the realization that there might be something dangerous hidden inside.

Folding his hands behind his back, Levet wrinkled his snout. "On second thought, you should have the honor."

There was a whisper of a chilled breeze as Xi stepped past her, in full Raven mode. Taking the box from his master, he flipped open the lid. Styx leaned forward, peering inside.

"Scrolls."

Brigette rolled her eyes at his puzzled tones. "Why are vampires so baffled by scrolls? My uncle devoted endless hours to reading and creating them."

"Only a fool writes down his private thoughts or secret plans," Styx informed her with an arrogance that set her teeth on edge.

"Really?" Brigette drawled. "Then why do they have your signature? And your fancy-ass official seal."

Xi took a scroll from the box and studied the wax seal before he unscrolled it. Was that what you did to scrolls? Unscroll them?

Whatever you called it, Xi handed the opened scroll to Styx. "She's right."

"Thanks, Captain Obvious," Brigette mocked.

Xi merely regarded her with a steady gaze, but the Anasso released a warning growl. "You do know I could kill you and no one would care?" the king demanded.

"I would care," Levet promptly protested.

Warmth stole through her heart even as Styx made a strangled sound of irritation. "You don't count, you chunk of granite," the vampire snapped.

Levet stuck out his tongue, but Brigette was already turning away. She'd finished what she'd come there to do. She didn't have to stick around to be insulted by a leech.

"Let them burn the world to the ground, I don't care," she said. "Enjoy the Armageddon."

"Stop."

She glanced over her shoulder, her steps never slowing. "You're not the boss of me."

"I'm...sorry."

The harsh words brought Brigette to an astonished halt. Slowly, she turned to confront the massive vampire.

"Excuse me?"

Styx looked as if he'd had a lemon shoved in his mouth. Or maybe up his ass. He was definitely puckering.

"I've been under a lot of pressure lately. It's made me a little..."

Chapter 4

"Grouchy? Crabby-pants? Homicidal?" Levet offered in sweet tones.

He'd stuck around the mansion in the hope of seeing Brigette. He'd been worried about the female Were since she'd wished him away from the mists that surrounded her homeland. The sight of her appearing healthy, quick-witted, and as feisty as ever eased the worry that had plagued him for the past few months.

Typically, the King of the Vampires ignored him, his gaze locked on the female Were.

"On edge," Styx grudgingly admitted. "Please tell me what you know about the vampire who is claiming I intend to enslave everyone."

With a concise efficiency, Brigette revealed the fact that the female vampire named Maryam had assembled a large collection of misfit demons who had little in common beyond their desire to create as much chaos as possible.

"Maryam." Styx furrowed his brow. "The name is vaguely familiar, but I don't recall ever doing anything to cause such animosity."

"You can annoy a creature without even trying. It is one of your greatest talents," Levet offered.

"You…" Styx took a step toward Levet before Xi smoothly distracted him.

"How could someone use your seal?" the Raven asked.

Styx closed his eyes, as if he was counting to ten. He did that a lot. At least when Levet was around. Darcy swore he wasn't so bad-tempered when they were alone. Levet wasn't sure whether to believe her or not.

With jerky motions, Styx moved to his desk and pulled open a drawer. Then, digging toward the bottom, he at last pulled out a small object with a wooden handle and a flat, golden tip.

"This is my official seal."

Xi moved to hold the scroll next to the seal, studying the design. "It isn't the same."

Styx leaned forward, his eyes suddenly narrowing. "No. That seal belonged to the previous Anasso. Darcy had a new one created on the off chance that I might need it. A waste of money."

Xi nodded, as if he'd already suspected the answer. "Who would have access to his belongings?"

Styx took time to consider his answer. "I presume there was one in his stuff that I left in the caves."

Xi's lips twisted into a humorless smile. "No one could get past the Ravens."

Levet pursed his lips. It was true. He'd tried a few times to sneak past the Ravens to investigate the caves. He was certain they were filled with all sorts of forgotten artifacts from the former Anasso. But he'd been blocked before he could even enter the caves. Annoying leeches.

"It's possible he had more than one," Styx pointed out.

They all looked at the scroll, but Levet didn't just look. He looked forward to take a sniff. There was something...

"Fish," he at last announced.

Styx looked confused. "What?"

"I can smell fish." Levet repeated slowly. Vampires weren't always the brightest crayons in the box.

Styx's lips parted, as if he intended to share one of his rude remarks. They were tediously predictable. But, snapping his mouth shut, he lifted the scroll to his nose. He sent Levet a glare before turning his attention to his Raven.

Aggravating leech.

"It's faint, but there's definitely the stench of fish, and it's old," Styx told his companion. "These scrolls were written centuries ago."

Xi glanced down at the box he still held in his hands. "Could Maryam have stumbled across a pile of old scrolls and decided to use them to her advantage?"

"That seems the most likely," Styx agreed.

"No." Brigette intruded into the conversation.

Styx arched a brow. "You sound certain."

"Not certain, but Maryam believes the scrolls came from you. The revolt she's leading isn't just a power grab. She sincerely fears you're trying to enslave the vampires."

For once, Styx didn't argue. Perhaps he sensed that Brigette was telling the truth. Or, more likely, he understood that the female Were was ready and willing to walk away to leave him to deal with the rebels.

As she'd said, this wasn't her battle.

Tossing the seal onto his desk, he considered her words. "If she believes the scrolls are real, that means she found them and assumed that they belonged to me. Or...someone is manipulating her."

Levet tilted his head to the side. "Who would want to manipulate her?"

Styx flashed a smile that had lots of fang showing. "That's what you're going to discover."

"*Moi?*" Levet folded his arms over his chest. "This is leech business."

"You're the hero, aren't you?"

Levet scowled at the arrogant vampire. His position as official knight in shining armor was supposed to impress and delight the females, not put him in constant danger. Clearly, he hadn't fully considered the consequences of the title.

"Why does being a hero suddenly seem like a curse?"

Styx shrugged his indifference. "All you need to do is travel to London and examine our old lair there."

Levet perked up. Usually his duties included creepy, slimy, evil places filled with muck, not one of his favorite places in the world.

"Why there?"

"For centuries, the Anasso lived in tunnels beneath the White Tower that stretched all the way to Billingsgate."

Levet had spent considerable time in London after his family had kicked him out of Paris. Indeed, he'd been watching as William the Conqueror had commanded the White Tower be erected. He knew the neighborhood well.

"The fish markets," he murmured.

Styx nodded. "Exactly."

Levet scratched his horn. That would certainly explain the lingering scent of fish on the scrolls. Back in the day, the area had a pungent aroma that wasn't for the fainthearted.

"What am I supposed to look for?"

"We had a hidden vault built beneath the Thames where the former Anasso kept his private papers," Styx told him. "I want you to discover if anyone has recently been snooping around there."

Levet scowled. As much as he enjoyed his little adventures, he wanted to return to the mer-folk castle. Inga needed him there to watch her very fine backside. *Non*, wait. Back. To watch her back.

Unfortunately, he'd spent too much time with the King of the Vampires to bother arguing. It would be easier to poop daisies than to convince the stubborn Styx to send someone else.

"You are going to owe me," he muttered, heading toward the door.

"Put it on my tab," Styx smoothly told him.

Levet snorted. "If you ever bother to pay that tab, I shall be as rich as King Midas." He paused to kiss Brigette's hand. "Goodbye, *mon amie*. And be careful. I would rather Styx be overthrown than for you to be injured."

She smiled with wicked amusement as Styx muttered a curse, and with an airy wave of his hand, Levet left the room.

* * * *

Brigette watched Levet disappear from the office, bothered by the thought that the tiny creature might be putting himself in danger. After all, Levet had many fine qualities, but common sense wasn't one of them. He followed his heart, not his head and would eagerly rush into disaster.

Just look at what had happened when they'd been together.

With a sigh, Brigette shook her head. There was no stopping the stubborn gargoyle. She might as well concentrate on her own lack of common sense.

As if reading her mind, Styx stepped toward her. "What about you?"

"What about me?"

"Are you returning to your home?"

"I have no home." The words were out before she could halt them, and Brigette felt a blush steal beneath her skin as Xi studied her with that knowing gaze. Dammit. There was nothing worse than a whiny Were. Especially one who deserved her bleak fate. She shook her head, thrusting away her bout of self-pity. "I'm going back to the rebels."

"Why?"

It was a legit question. Brigette had satisfied her curiosity. She knew the basics of Maryam and Roban's rebellion. And why they'd sought out her help. Someone else could figure out the details. Plus, there was always the real possibility that once the word of her arrival in Chicago began to spread, there would be Weres who wanted to punish her for her past. No one had forgiven or forgotten what she'd done.

The only intelligent thing to do was return to her homeland. So, of course, she was going to stay.

"They're plotting something big," she at last muttered.

"You don't have any details?" Styx demanded.

Brigette wrinkled her nose. She'd overheard bits and pieces, but she didn't think anyone but Maryam and, perhaps, Roban actually knew the full endgame.

"I think it might have something to do with the clan chiefs. I also heard Maryam mention Chiron. But I don't have any specific plans," she admitted.

Styx paused, his dark gaze studying her with an unnerving intensity. "What do you care? You turned your back on this world a long time ago."

She opened her mouth to tell him it was none of his damned business. He might be the King of the Vampires, but he had no right to question her. Instead, the truth spilled out.

"Ulric is the only family I have left." There, she'd said it. Ulric might never forgive her, but she couldn't bear the thought that he might be taken from this world. He was her only connection to the pact she'd destroyed. "And since he is a personal guard to Chiron, he's in danger. I'll be damned if I let that bitch do anything to hurt him."

She braced herself, expecting some snarky comment. Or even a refusal to believe she couldn't care about anyone but herself.

Instead, Styx planted his fists on his hips, silently considering his options. "The obvious choice is for us to storm the tunnels and clean out the vermin."

Brigette was shaking her head before he finished speaking. "They're expecting that," she warned. "I overheard Maryam tell Roban to double the number of triggers hidden in the tunnels."

"What kind of triggers? Magic or human technology?" Styx demanded.

"I'm not sure, but I would guess magic," Brigette told him. "Plus, Roban added that he'd heard from someone named Perez that the other surprises were now in place and waiting for her command to set them off."

Styx grimaced. "I'm assuming that means the mysterious triggers are someplace other than in the tunnels."

Brigette nodded. "That would be my guess. I'm hoping I can figure out what they are and where they've been hidden."

"Keep us informed," Styx commanded.

She nodded, turning back toward the door.

"I'm going with her."

Brigette froze in shock at Xi's soft words. The was the last thing she'd been expecting.

"No way." Whirling around, she stabbed the leech with a fierce glare.

"It's not a bad idea," Styx told her. "Xi can search in places you would never be allowed."

"How? Does he have mind control?" There were a rare few vampires who could not only enthrall humans, but demons as well.

Xi answered. "I can hide my presence."

She snorted, her gaze involuntarily absorbing the compelling beauty of his face before sliding down his slender body. A creature would have to be dead and buried not to notice this male.

"You're invisible?" she mocked.

"Not quite." Xi gave a lift of one shoulder. "But I can mute my powers and disguise my scent. You have to physically catch sight of me to know I'm there."

Oh. That explained how he'd managed to sneak up on her. And why she'd been astounded when they'd arrived in Styx's lair and she'd been hit by the full effect of his presence.

Brigette considered the possibility. It would definitely be handy to have someone who could move through the tunnels undetected, she silently conceded.

Not that she was going to let Xi know she welcomed his help. She was a lone wolf. Literally and figuratively.

She shrugged. "It's not like I can keep you away," she told the male.

"True." A mysterious smile touched his lips, as if he suspected there were a horde of butterflies fluttering in her stomach. "Are you ready to go back?"

Brigette folded her arms over her chest. It was one thing for Xi to be in the tunnels, doing his own thing. It was another for him to hover over her like some gorgeous, sexy, highly disruptive babysitter.

"I don't need an escort."

"You can't use the portal without Xi," Styx pointed out.

"Of course I can't." Brigette's jaw tightened. She could easily find her way back to the tunnels, but there would be no way to sneak back in without alerting Maryam. That would lead to questions she didn't want to answer.

She turned away.

"Brigette," Styx called out.

"What?" She marched toward the door. She wasn't going to be stopped again.

"Don't do anything rash." Styx's tone was stern. "If Maryam is as dangerous as you fear, we don't want her to feel cornered."

Brigette continued out of the office and through the maze of marble hallways. She didn't need to be warned about the female vamp. Maryam had been welcoming to Brigette, but there was no doubt that she was in charge of the ragtag group of demons. If one of them stepped out of line, they were taken into the private office, and when they returned, they had the look of a creature who'd walked through the fires of hell. Whatever happened in there ensured that no one questioned Maryam's orders.

Of course, Brigette had actually been in hell. It was doubtful the leech's threats would have the same impact on her.

She was crossing the yard when Xi moved to walk beside her, his long strides easily keeping pace. Childishly, she refused to glance in his direction, but she didn't need to. She was absurdly conscious of everything about him. The cool power that swirled around her. The tantalizing scent of cedarwood. The electric tingles that sizzled in the air between them.

And those aggravating flutters in the pit of her stomach.

They'd reached the street when Xi abruptly spoke. "Where did you get your weapon?"

Brigette scowled. She was annoyed. Not because Styx had sent along a babysitter. If she hadn't wanted the Anasso to interfere with what she was doing, she would never have contacted Levet to warn the male. She knew enough about alphas to realize he'd insist on having his own eyes and ears on the rebels. He'd be a fool to trust her for his information.

No, her annoyance was with herself. And those flutters in the pit of her stomach. As if she were a silly pup and not a grown-ass female who'd nearly destroyed the world.

"There's no need for chitchat," she muttered. "I prefer the silence."

"It's not chitchat. I have a matching one."

"A matching what?"

"A matching dagger."

Startled, Brigette turned her head before she could stop herself. Her eyes widened as he reached behind his back to pull a dagger from a hidden holster.

It looked to be almost an exact duplicate of her own. The same long, silver blade with a power that shimmered in the fading moonlight. The same heavy, black hilt. It even smelled the same. Exotic spice and mysterious power.

"How?" she demanded.

He twirled the dagger, revealing an expertise that matched her own. "It was created for me by a master in Jingzhou over two thousand years ago."

Brigette pulled her own dagger, finding comfort in the solid weight. The weapon had been a touchstone through the long centuries of darkness. A connection to her family.

"My father told me it'd been in our family since it was given as a reward to one of my ancestors," she said.

Xi arched a brow. "A priceless reward. Your ancestor must have performed a profound service."

Brigette abruptly shoved the dagger back in her holster as she was punished with the memory of her father staring at her with open disappointment.

"My father probably told me, but I wasn't interested in the stories when I was young," she retorted, vaguely aware that she was giving away far more than she intended.

"What were you interested in?"

"My own happiness."

Xi shrugged, his expression impossible to read. "Typical youth."

"Typical?" A strange anger blasted through Brigette. She didn't fully understand it. Shame, of course. It churned through her like acid. And something that she suspected was regret for lost opportunities. She needed this male to treat her with the same disdain that everyone else offered her. Otherwise, she might begin to believe that her awareness could become something more. The most dangerous thing in the world was hope. "I stole this dagger from my father just hours before I allowed a horde of goblins to destroy my pack. Don't ever call me typical," she snapped.

Xi came to an abrupt halt in the center of the street, his expression unreadable. "I stole a rare artifact from a rival clan chief just to show off my powers, and hours later, he massacred my entire clan. You don't have a lock on carrying around a shitload of guilt. Get over yourself."

The vampire didn't drop a mic, but he did step into the portal and disappear from view.

End. Of. Conversation.

Chapter 5

Levet loved seedy bars. The seedier the better. And the Bone-In Bar in Lower Thames was just that sort of place.

It wasn't the stench of fried onions and unwashed demon bodies that Levet enjoyed. Or the thunderous sound of shouting from a distant corner, where a crowd was watching two trolls arm-wrestle. Or even the food, which resembled something that collected at the bottom of a dumpster.

He loved them because everyone minded their own business.

No one cared that he wasn't the tallest gargoyle, or that his wings shimmered with color, or that his magic was a little…unpredictable.

Crossing the wooden floor, which was sticky from ale and whatever blood had been spilled earlier in the evening, Levet climbed onto a high stool next to the bar at the side of the cramped, smoky space.

One of Styx's minions had sent him through a portal to London. The sun had disappeared over the horizon, but it was still early enough for the streets to be crowded with humans. He preferred to wait a few hours before seeking out the former Anasso's lair. Besides, it had been years since he'd had the opportunity to spend time with his old friend Craddock.

The male was a mixture of demons. Hobgoblin, brownie, and some sort of fey sprinkled in. He was taller than Levet and twice as wide, with a square face and skin that looked like old tree bark. His head was bald, and his eyes were brown until he was angry. Then they turned a deep red. His pointed teeth had been coated in gold, and he liked to flash them whenever possible. He thought they made him look cool. Levet personally thought they made him look like a villain from a James Bond movie.

Still, they'd been friends for several centuries.

Turning to see who had entered the bar, Craddock's face creased into a smile. The male wiped his hands on his greasy apron before filling a tankard with a foamy ale and setting it on the bar in front of Levet.

"It's been a while." Craddock pointed out the obvious.

Levet took a cautious sip. His palate had changed since he'd resided in London. Viper's very fine collection of expensive tequila and aged whiskey had taught him to appreciate something beyond the swill that Craddock served. Not that Viper realized that Levet had a key to his precious cellars. What a leech didn't know didn't hurt him.

Or, at least, that had always been Levet's philosophy.

"*Oui*. I have been busy," Levet admitted.

Craddock pulled out a greasy rag to wipe the counter. "So I have heard."

"Did you?" Levet sat straighter on the stool, trying to keep his expression humble. Real heroes didn't gloat. A shame really. He had so much to gloat about. "Have there been bards singing songs of my many adventures?" he asked. "Or great works of art hanging in the museums?"

The bartender shook his head. "No bards, and I never visit museums, so I can't say if there's any pictures of you. But there was a merman in here the other night complaining about his new queen and the pesky stunted gargoyle who was hanging around the castle. I figured he had to be talking about you."

Levet scowled. Since Inga had taken over the throne, she'd encouraged her people to travel throughout the world. They'd been trapped in the castle for a millennium. First, by Inga's grandfather, who'd been terrified of dragons, and then by Rivan, who'd held them captive with brutal force. And this was how they repaid her kindness. By insulting him.

Thankless inmates. No, wait. Ingrates.

"Stunted." Levet sniffed, taking another sip of ale. Maybe by the third or fourth tankard, the vile stuff would start to taste better. "I am compact, not stunted."

Craddock shrugged. "Whatever lets you sleep."

Levet scowled, but before he could convince the fool that size didn't matter, the scent of fruit swirled through the air. An imp. And the sheer pungency of the scent meant it could only be one particular imp.

"*Non*," Levet muttered. "It can't be possible."

The bartender looked confused. "What can't be possible?"

"I smell…" Levet sniffed the air. "My nemesis."

Craddock glanced around the crowded room, appearing more confused than ever. "There's no platypus here. Course, I'm not exactly sure what one looks like, so it might have snuck in when I wasn't looking."

Levet rolled his eyes. "Not a platypus. I adore them. So tiny and cute. "

"Then what are you complaining about?"

"My nemesis." Levet waved his hands in exasperation. "The Brutus to my Caesar."

Craddock shrugged. "Yeah, I have no idea what that means."

"Just look for a six-foot imp with long red hair and hideous taste in spandex," Levet snapped.

Craddock's eyes abruptly widened. Obviously, he'd at last spotted Troy. "Bloody hell. He's…"

"A pain in my derrière," Levet muttered.

"Levet. It's been a while. How is my favorite lump of granite?"

The deep, rich voice swirled around Levet, even as Troy, the Prince of Imps, came into view. Levet pursed his lips, understanding Craddock's stunned expression.

Troy was always flamboyant. Tonight, however, he was over the top, with his long, brilliant red hair pulled into a complicated knot on top of his head and his tall, muscular body hidden by a floor-length cape made entirely of pure white feathers.

Levet wrinkled his snout. "Were you eaten by an ostrich?"

Troy smiled, running his hands down the feathers with sensuous pleasure. "Isn't it divine?"

"You look like a Cirque du Soleil reject."

Troy clicked his tongue. His arrogance was impervious to insults. Probably because his features were flawless and his eyes as brilliant as emeralds. He was a gorgeous male, and he knew it.

"Jealousy is never attractive, *mon ami*," the imp chided.

Levet folded his arms over his chest. He wasn't jealous. He was… annoyed. For months, Inga had allowed this oversized buffoon to offer her advice on how to be a queen. As if she needed to change anything. She was perfect. And now he was popping up in places he shouldn't be.

Like the black plague.

"What are you doing in London?" Levet demanded.

Troy leaned against the bar. "Searching for you. Unfortunately."

"Why?"

"The Queen of the Mer-folk was concerned about you."

A sudden warmth filled Levet's heart. "Inga sent you?"

"She mentioned your latest escapade when we were chatting," Troy said in dismissive tones. "I knew she would be fretting until someone she trusted arrived to keep you out of trouble."

Levet's brief joy at Inga's concern was squashed by the imp's rude words. "Trouble. *Moi*? That is absurd. I am never in trouble."

Troy laughed. "Dude, it's a weekly event. Do you want me to list the disasters you've caused?"

"I am a hero." Levet sniffed. "You cannot make pancakes without cracking eggs, right?"

"Something's cracked," Troy mocked.

Levet glared at the aggravating creature. "Why were you talking to Inga at all? I thought you'd left the castle."

"I stopped by to say hi. She depends on my sage advice."

"Fah. She tolerates you because she is too nice to tell you to go away."

Troy's smile widened. They both knew that Inga had often turned to Troy when she was feeling uncertain in her position as queen. The knowledge was like a burr beneath Levet's thick hide, constantly rubbing.

Thankfully, the imp didn't press the sensitive issue. "Tell me why you're in this nasty bar."

"Hey," Craddock protested, proving he was blatantly eavesdropping on the conversation.

"If I'm not honest with you, you can't improve, right?" Troy told the bartender in patronizing tones.

"I…"

"Shoo." Troy waved a contemptuous hand. Craddock frowned, but with a muttered curse, he turned to shuffle away. Troy waited until he was out of earshot before he studied Levet with a searching gaze. "Why are you here?"

Levet wanted to tell the imp that it was none of his business, but he knew Troy well enough to accept that the stubborn creature wouldn't go away until he had his answers.

"I'm on a secret mission for Styx."

"Secret mission?"

"*Oui*. Now, go away."

Troy leaned against the bar, his expression curious. "I assume this has something to do with the evil dog you adopted? Inga said she'd mentally contacted you before you left the castle."

Levet stiffened in outrage. "Don't call Brigette a dog."

"But she is evil."

"Not anymore," Levet protested. "She is attempting to redeem herself."

"And her redemption has something to do with you being in London?"

Levet clicked his tongue. He wasn't comfortable discussing Brigette and her inner motives. She was like him. Complicated. Misunderstood. A misfit who was often shunned by society.

What would a male like Troy know about such things?

"If you must know, I am searching for Styx's old lair to discover if a bunch of smelly scrolls have been stolen from his hidden vault."

Troy arched a brow. "Well, that makes zero sense."

"Good." Levet waved his hand. "Go away."

"Ah." Troy heaved a dramatic sigh. "If only it was possible."

"It is."

"I promised Inga. Until you return to the mer-folk castle, the two of us are partners."

Levet's heart sank to the tips of his sharp claws. Troy was a flighty, self-absorbed horse's patootie. But a promise was a promise. No demon would break one.

Which meant they were well and truly stuck together.

"As long as I am the one giving the orders."

Troy's lips twitched. "Do you know the definition of partners?"

"*Oui*, it means you do what I say."

"Or?"

"Or else."

"That's your snappy comeback?" Troy demanded.

"Argg." Levet jumped off the bar stool and waddled toward the door "Let us get this over with."

"The sooner the better," Troy added, his cloak billowing behind him as they headed toward the door.

* * * *

Xi was still in the main tunnel when he sensed Brigette approaching. He'd made a meticulous search of a few of the side shafts, but the place was like a labyrinth. Each branch had new branches, and there were dozens of manholes that opened into caverns beneath the main tunnels. It was going to take weeks to meticulously inspect each one.

Waiting in the shadows until the female was just a few inches away, Xi stepped forward. Brigette yelped at his sudden appearance before sending him a frown that warned him not to smile at her startled reaction.

"Have you found anything?" she snapped.

"Not yet." He glanced around, his lips curling in disgust. There were layers of rubbish that had been dropped and left in place. Bones, torn clothes, empty containers. "Nothing beyond trash."

"Yeah, tidiness isn't high on the list for the rebels." She shuddered before turning on her heel to retrace her steps. "It's almost dawn. You can stay in my room."

"An invitation?" Xi asked, readily following behind her.

"Get over yourself."

Xi smiled as Brigette tossed his words back in his face. He wanted her to be sassy. He knew from experience that it was all too easy to self-destruct from guilt. His hand lifted, as if he intended to brush his fingers down the ivory silk of her throat, but instead he grabbed her arm and pulled her into the darkness as the sound of footsteps echoed in the distance.

Shockingly, Brigette didn't fight against his hold. Instead, she pressed close, as if realizing his ability to mute his presence would help to disguise her own. Smart wolf.

The footsteps came closer before fading into a lower tunnel, but Brigette remained close enough for her heat to sear through his clothing. Xi's fangs lengthened as her musky scent teased at his senses, stirring a reaction that wasn't entirely unexpected.

She was a beautiful female, with a lush sensuality that would attract any male. Or female. But while most creatures no doubt allowed her past to mar their opinion of her, it only emphasized Xi's fascination. He saw beyond the pretty surface to the raw, vulnerable female she kept hidden.

The musky scent deepened, as if Brigette was struggling to leash her own awareness. Then, sucking in a sharp breath, she pushed him away.

"The rebels aren't all vamps, but they tend to roam the streets at night and return to the tunnels during the daylight. We need to move."

In silence, they flowed through the darkness. Brigette took the lead, using her familiarity with the maze of tunnels to avoid the demons, who were noisily returning to their temporary lair.

At last, they entered her rooms and propped a wooden slab across the entrance. It was heavy enough that only a handful of demons had the strength to move it.

"Do the other demons have private spaces?" he asked.

Brigette moved to perch on the edge of the narrow cot that was pressed against the far wall. It was the only actual piece of furniture beyond a wooden chair and a small wooden trunk that he assumed held Brigette's few personal items.

It looked exactly what it was. An underground cement tunnel.

"Many of the lesser demons sleep together in a side passageway," she told him. "They feel more comfortable in groups."

"And safer."

"Yes," she agreed. "There's a lot of predators in here."

Xi hadn't actually seen many demons since they'd been out and about creating chaos, but he'd caught scents of mongrel trolls and orcs and even hellhounds. The sort of aggressive creatures that enjoyed causing pain to the fragile fey.

"What about Maryam and Roban?" he asked.

His last few hours had discouraged any hope that he might discover clues just laying around. There might be plenty of trash, but there was no indication of what they might be plotting. Or any mystery mastermind pulling strings from the shadows.

If there was information in the tunnels, it had to be in Maryam's possession.

She shrugged. "They usually rest, then a few hours before the others begin to stir, they have a private meeting."

"In the office?"

"No, in Maryam's private quarters."

"Where's that?"

"It's at the opposite end of the tunnels and hidden behind an illusion."

Ah, well, that explained why he hadn't managed to track down the female vampire. He had no ability to see through magic.

"Guarded?"

Brigette sent him an "Are you stupid?" glance. "The female is as paranoid as a dew fairy at a goblin convention. Her rooms are guarded twenty-four/seven."

"I don't suppose there are any secret passages that would allow us access?"

She was shaking her head before he finished his question. "Not that I've discovered. Plus she has layers of magic protecting the tunnel. There's no way to get close without setting them off."

He didn't bother to ask about the spells. Instead, he considered their limited options. "Then we need a distraction," he at last decided. "Something that will get everyone out of the tunnels so we can search her rooms."

"Easier said than done," Brigette warned. "The rebels are constantly expecting to be betrayed. And I'm certain Maryam would have traps waiting for anyone who entered while she was gone."

There was the heavy sound of footsteps in the outer tunnel, and they fell silent as a crowd passed. Brigette glanced toward the entrance, her body tense as if expecting someone to try to force their way into her private space. Xi studied the purity of her profile and the muscles that were coiled, ready to launch her into attack. A sleek animal posed to strike.

Beautiful.

His fangs once again lengthened, along with other parts of his body, and he had to battle against the urge to cross the narrow space and tumble her back onto the cot. The fact that he didn't know if she would melt beneath him or try to rip out his throat sent a tingle of excitement down his spine.

It was odd. Over the past centuries, he'd avoided conflict. His past mistakes taught him the risk of seeking foolish thrills.

Now, he couldn't deny a bourgeoning addiction to Brigette's compelling combination of danger and brittle frailty.

Unnerved by the sheer intensity of his awareness, Xi forced himself to concentrate on the reason he was in the nasty tunnels. Once they'd discovered who was manipulating Maryam, he could return to the serene privacy of his lair.

Somehow, the thought didn't offer the serenity he'd expected to feel.

"Tell me what you've discovered so far," he commanded.

"Not many of the demons are willing to talk to me." She pushed herself onto the cot to rest her back against the wall. "Even the rebel riffraff have decided I'm too evil to be a part of the Scooby gang." A humorless smile twisted her lips. "But I've overheard snatches of conversations. I'm not invisible, but I'm good at finding hidden passages."

"What did you overhear?"

"Most of the demons that Maryam has collected are misfits," she told him.

"Mongrels?"

"I'm not talking about their species. I mean that, for one reason or another, they were shunned by their own people," she corrected him. "Or they left because they didn't fit into their family."

Brigette's tone was indifferent, but Xi wasn't fooled. This female had been an outcast for five hundred years. She understood these rebels better than most demons.

"Like you?" he asked.

"I was never shunned," she snapped.

Xi arched his brows at her sharp tone. What was she going to think when he told her that he'd been shunned? And how much did her reaction matter to him?

Questions for another time.

"But you didn't fit in?" he instead pressed.

She shrugged. "I thought I was special. As if whatever I wanted should be handed to me on a silver platter."

Xi could easily imagine her as a spoiled, petulant pup. No doubt, she had been beautiful, intelligent, and highly rebellious. It would give her the power to manipulate others at a very young age. Power she didn't have the maturity to handle.

"And that made you an outsider?" he asked.

Brigette stilled, eyeing him with a suspicious expression. "Where are you going with this?"

"Do you sympathize with the rebels?" he bluntly demanded.

"Once evil, always evil, eh?" Her eyes flashed with instant fury. "You're just like everyone else."

He leashed his urge to smile. She cared about his opinion. If she didn't, she would dismiss his words with the flippant indifference he'd seen before.

"I'm like no one else, Brigette," he insisted. "And I'm not judging you. But as someone who was once driven from my home, I can understand the need to search for a new family and a common goal."

She glanced away, as if she was about to shut him out. Then, with a visible effort, she forced herself to turn back to meet his steady gaze.

Did she realize that she needed his help?

"I would sympathize if they'd come together to create their own family," she said. "Most demons feel safer when they travel in packs. But it wasn't enough for them." She waved a hand toward the covered entrance. On the other side, the scurry of demons continued to echo through the tunnels. "They allowed themselves to be convinced they have to burn down the world to get what they want." She paused, her hands curling into tight fists. "I'll die to stop them."

Xi jerked, as if he'd taken an unexpected blow. "No."

She looked surprised by his fierce tone. "Excuse me?"

"You're not dying." He instinctively pulled back his lips to reveal his fangs. Not a warning. A pledge. "Not as long as I'm here."

Chapter 6

Surprisingly, Brigette slept for six solid hours. Climbing off the narrow cot, she told herself it was because she hadn't slept well since arriving in Chicago. She was bound to crash and burn eventually. But, deep inside, she knew that the reason had something to do with the large male vampire who had just silently pushed aside the heavy wooden board that covered the door and slipped out of her private room.

Having him so near had offered a rare sense of protection while she slept. As if she had someone to watch her back for the first time in over five hundred years.

Brigette stomped toward the wooden chest and opened it to pull out some of the clothes that Maryam had offered the night they'd arrived in the tunnels. She wasn't going to start thinking of Xi as a partner. He was a temporary weapon she was utilizing to halt the rebels.

A gorgeous, astonishingly sexy weapon who…

No, no, no. Shutting out the image of Xi's pale, perfect face, Brigette hurried to the makeshift shower that had been set up in an abandoned pump station. At this hour, it was empty, giving her the perfect opportunity to scrub herself from head to toe.

Then, pulling on jeans and a soft sweater the color of the buttercups that bloomed in spring, she pulled her damp hair into a braid. At last, she shoved her feet into a pair of leather boots and headed out to do a quick recon.

Less than five minutes later, Xi silently appeared at her side. He didn't look as if he'd spent the day standing guard. His glossy hair was as smooth as silk, the buzzed sides revealing the odd tattoos, which shimmered even in the darkness. His jeans and T-shirt were wrinkle-free. And his dark eyes smoldered with an intense energy that hummed through the air.

Everything about him was sleek and immaculate. And overall…lethal. Like an elegant samurai sword.

An unfamiliar excitement raced through her, an electric current that was sparking long-forgotten nerves back to life.

Thankfully unable to read the weird-ass thoughts floating through her mind, he glanced around the tunnel, making sure they were alone before speaking.

"Where are you going?"

"To search Maryam's office again," she told him.

"For more scrolls?"

Brigette shook her head. "I've done a quick look through the desk and the safe, but it's possible there's evidence hidden behind an illusion. Perhaps even an opening to another tunnel. Plus I want to take another look at the map she has on the wall."

"I'll go with you."

She sternly ignored the flutter of pleasure at his offer. She was an evil bitch who'd nearly destroyed the world. She didn't flutter.

"I thought you were going to do your Batman thing?"

His lips twitched. "Batman?"

"You know. Creep through the shadows and attack without warning." She ran a slow glance over his lean body. "Plus there's that whole black vibe you've got going on."

"At least I'm the hero, not the villain."

She snorted. "It depends on your point of view."

He blinked, as if caught off guard by her response. "That is remarkably profound."

Her face blazed with a sudden heat. Was she blushing? Christ. First flutters and now blushing. She was going to get kicked out of the evil bitch club if she wasn't careful.

She headed down the tunnel. "Let's go before the others start stirring."

"Right behind you."

He didn't have to tell her. Despite the fact that he had a talent for disguising his presence, she was acutely aware that he was just inches away. Was it because she knew he was there? Or was the answer something far more dangerous?

With a shake of her head, she led Xi into the hidden passage. Then, reaching the small chamber, she sucked in a deep breath. Her wolf remained in hibernation, but she was capable of smelling any demon in the vicinity. Nothing.

Pressing open the door, she slipped inside, closely followed by Xi. It was pitch-black, with the outer door shut, but neither of them needed light to see as they circled the office. Brigette concentrated on searching for any illusions. They were easy to overlook, especially if they'd been bewitched to encourage creatures to avoid them, but there was usually a shimmer of magic that gave away their location.

At last accepting there was nothing to find, Brigette moved to stand next to Xi as he studied the large map.

"Do you see a pattern?" she asked, keeping her voice pitched low. The maze of tunnels created massive echo chambers.

Xi folded his arms over his chest. "Vampire strongholds."

Brigette reached out to touch the closest pin pushed into the map. "Chicago," she murmured.

"Styx's lair," Xi said.

Her finger moved across the map. "Vegas."

"Roke."

"Or Chiron," Brigette added. "Maryam was banished along with him, but they parted ways at some point. She might resent him for kicking her out of his clan."

"True."

Brigette continued to draw her finger across the map to the next pin. "London."

"Victor."

"I assume he's the clan chief?"

"Yes."

She touched the last pin. "Ireland, although I don't see any nearby city."

"Cyn," Xi swiftly guessed. "He's the local clan chief. Or perhaps Tarak. He was Chiron's clan chief before he was kidnapped by the merman."

Brigette slowly nodded. "Maryam claimed she was focused on removing Styx since he threatened to enslave both vampires and Weres, but it's been obvious since I arrived in Chicago that the rebels are more intent on overthrowing the establishment than protecting demons. It makes sense that they would attack the clan chiefs around the world." She turned her head, discovering that Xi was smiling. "What's so funny?"

"Styx would have a panic attack if he heard himself described as establishment," Xi retorted.

Brigette was bemused by the unexpected glimpse of humor. It would be easy to dismiss the Raven as a mere pawn in Styx's army. But, with every passing hour, she was discovering more and more about the complex male. He was loyal, of course. And a powerful warrior. Those were expected. But he was also willing to accept her suggestions without the usual arrogant assumption that he knew what was best. And when he looked at her, he didn't seem to see a worthless traitor who deserved nothing but contempt.

Plus he was sexy as hell.

Now she had to add in the fact that he had a charming sense of humor.

Dangerous.

She cleared the strange lump from her throat and forced herself to speak. "Why would Styx have a panic attack? He's the Anasso. That's establishment, isn't it?"

"Styx likes to think of himself as a badass warrior, not a dull bureaucrat."

Brigette's lips twisted. When she was young, she'd resented the leader of their pack. He'd been a scholar, not a fighter, preferring to hide in a remote area rather than joining the other Weres in their ancient hunting lands. She thought it made their pack weak. It wasn't until too late that she realized that anyone could flex their muscles. A true leader was more concerned with the security and happiness of their family.

"And what about you?" she asked.

Xi arched a brow. "What about me?"

"Do you consider yourself a badass warrior?"

"I'm a warrior. I prefer not to be a badass."

Brigette tilted her head. There was a hard edge in his voice that spoke of secrets he held deep inside him.

"Really?"

The dark eyes became even more mysterious than usual. As if bleak memories were swirling in their depths.

"I joined the Ravens to ensure peace, not to indulge a lust for violence."

She believed him. The words sounded more like a pledge than political correctness. The knowledge only intensified her fascination.

Awkwardly, she turned her attention back to the map. "What do you think this means?"

"I'm not sure, but I don't think it's good."

"No." They both stiffened as the air prickled with a sudden chill. "Someone's coming."

Xi pulled back his lips to flash his fangs. They were impressive. Long and lethal, and oddly sexy.

"The vampire," he warned.

Brigette glanced toward the door leading to the hidden tunnel. "Wait for me out there."

He frowned. "What are you going to do?"

"I want to talk to Maryam."

He looked like he wanted to protest, but as the chill in the air thickened, he grudgingly headed out of the office. A second later, the outer door was pressed open, and Maryam stepped inside.

The female looked as elegant as always, with her pale hair pulled into a knot at her nape and a red silk jumpsuit covering her slender body. She looked like she was headed to dinner at some fancy-schmancy restaurant, not running a demon rebellion.

"Brigette." Her expression was suspicious, although she clearly wasn't surprised. She would have caught Brigette's scent long before she opened the door. "What are you doing in here?"

Brigette shrugged. "Waiting for you."

Maryam took a cautious step forward, her gaze darting around the office. Once assured that Brigette was alone, she moved to take a seat behind her desk.

"What do you want?"

Brigette strolled until she was standing directly in front of the desk. "You made several promises when you came to my home and asked me to join your little rebellion."

The aquamarine eyes flashed with anger, but her expression never changed. She was a master at controlling her emotions.

"I gave you the reward you asked for," she reminded Brigette.

There had been a thick roll of cash in the bundle of clothing that had been left in Brigette's room.

"Money." She curled her lips, revealing her lack of interest in the small fortune. "You promised a pack."

The female tapped a long fingernail against the arm of her chair. It was painted red and looked like a dagger.

"That's not something I can just hand over," she informed Brigette. "You'll have to be patient."

"I'm not particularly good at that. Just ask my parents."

"Until the revolution has started, I have no power to grant your wish."

Brigette made a sound of impatience. She didn't have to imagine how she would behave if she were a part of an evil pack to take over the world. She had firsthand knowledge.

"Exactly when will this revolution begin?" she snapped.

The temperature in the room dropped. "Soon."

"That's sort of vague."

The nail continued to tap against the arm of the chair. A staccato warning that this female might appear calm but there was a fierce emotion smoldering inside her. Why else would she start a rebellion?

"Revolutions rarely come with a timeline."

"Maybe not, but I do." Brigette planted her hands flat on the top of the desk and leaned forward. Maryam believed that she was there for her own personal gain. She had to keep up the act or the female would become suspicious. "Things need to get rolling before I die of boredom."

Hoping to provoke the female into revealing something about her plans, Brigette found herself caught off guard when Maryam's expression softened.

"So much like your cousin," she murmured.

Brigette stiffened. "Ulric?"

Maryam nodded. "Like you, he was brash. Outspoken. Impulsive."

Unexpected pain sliced through Brigette's body. This vampire had spent more time with Brigette's only family than she had. And she had no one to blame but herself.

"Why did you leave Chiron?" she abruptly demanded.

Maryam sat back in her chair, turning her head to gaze at the map on the wall. "Chiron left. I stayed."

"Stayed here?"

"St. Petersburg."

"Not a bad place to get left behind," Brigette murmured.

A reminiscent smile touched Maryam's face, emphasizing her exquisite beauty. "It was a dazzling city, and I was a favorite with the czar."

"I can imagine." Brigette had no doubt that this female had the entire Russian court enthralled. Beyond her physical attraction, she possessed a compelling charm. It was one of the reasons she'd so easily managed to collect her large band of misfits. "That still doesn't explain why you didn't stay with Chiron."

"Because he was constantly traveling. We would barely settle into a home before he was ready to move on."

"And you were ready to settle down?"

"Yes."

Brigette wasn't convinced. Many demons created permeant lairs or dens to settle in, including Weres. But vampires preferred to travel. Not only because they mixed with humans who would notice they weren't aging, but they possessed a restless urge for fresh adventures. Unless...

"You found your mate," Brigette said, the words a statement not a question.

"Yes."

"What happened to him?"

"Her. Ulita. She was the clan chief of St. Petersburg."

"What happened to her?"

The emotion that was kept tightly leashed shimmered in the aquamarine eyes. A dark, profound loss.

"She had a bounty put on her head by the previous Anasso."

"Why?"

"She didn't believe the vampires needed a king." Maryam's slender fingers suddenly clenched the arms of the chair, her knuckles turning white. "And she was very vocal about her opinions."

Brigette studied the vampire. There was something personal in the female's sizzling fury. As if she held herself responsible for her mate's death.

"Surely she wasn't the only one?" Brigette asked. She'd never paid much attention to vampire politics. She was too self-absorbed with her own evil plans.

"No, but she was the chief of a very large, very powerful clan," Maryam explained.

"So he destroyed her?"

A raw pain twisted the female's features. "Along with most of her clan."

Brigette winced. Xi had asked her if she sympathized with the rebels. She didn't. She'd never been a victim, so she couldn't possibly appreciate the sense of betrayal they felt. But she admired Maryam's fierce need to battle against a tyrant. Even if she was being manipulated.

Of course, she wasn't about to reveal anything but a shallow impatience to get her promised reward.

"So much for your noble claim that you're trying to overthrow the Anasso to keep us all from being enslaved," she drawled. "This is nothing more than pure vengeance."

Maryam frowned at Brigette's mocking words. "No. "

"Hey, I'm not judging." Brigette shrugged. "'An eye for an eye' is my motto."

"This isn't revenge," the vampire insisted. "The old Anasso has already been destroyed. I'm preventing the past from repeating itself."

"Yeah, okay. Whatever you say."

With a swift movement, Maryam was on her feet. Her features were wiped of all expression.

"You've made your demands. Now it's my turn."

"Your turn for what?"

"You need to prove you can provide something to the cause."

Brigette continued to pretend boredom as she inwardly cursed. She'd known that this moment was inevitable, but she'd hoped she could put it off until she knew more about Maryam's plans. Or at least had a clue as to who was controlling the rebellion from behind the scenes.

"You want me to release the darkness?" She shrugged, holding up her hand in a dramatic gesture.

Maryam jerked back. "Not here."

"Then where?"

"The Viper Club."

Brigette lowered her hand. She didn't have to pretend her confusion. "Never heard of the place."

"It's a demon club in downtown Chicago."

"Why there?" Brigette demanded. She'd expected the woman to order her to attack Styx's lair.

A grim smile curved the female's lips. "Let's just say it will strike at the very heart of the Anasso."

"Okay." Brigette conceded to the inevitable. "I'll rest up, and then tomorrow—"

"Tonight," Maryam commanded.

Crap. "Tonight?"

"Is that a problem?"

Accepting that she had one last chance to figure out what the hell the rebels were plotting, Brigette sent the older woman a suspicious glare.

"Yeah. If we strike at the Anasso, he's going to come here and squash us like cockroaches." Brigette pursed her lips. "Unlike the rest of you, I'm here for profit. I have no intention of taking one for the team."

Maryam paused, studying Brigette with an icy expression. "How would he know we're here?"

Brigette snorted. "You have dozens, if not hundreds, of demons in and out of here each night. Do you truly trust all of them?"

"No. I trust no one. Which is why I have..." The word trailed away, as if Maryam had abruptly recalled that Brigette wasn't on the need-to-know list. "... protections in place."

"What protections?"

"Nothing for you to worry about." There was an edge of warning in the vampire's tone. She wasn't going to answer any questions. Period. "You just take care of your business."

"You do know I can't actually control how far the darkness will spread?" Brigette warned.

A humorless smile curved Maryam's lips, revealing her snowy-white fangs. "Let the chaos begin."

Yikes.

Chapter 7

Xi used the hidden tunnel to return to Brigette's room. Dusk was swiftly approaching, and the demons were beginning to roam the labyrinth of passages. Less than five minutes later, Brigette entered, her expression one of extreme frustration.

"So I guess that's that," she muttered.

Xi shook his head. From the second that Maryam had mentioned the Viper Club, he'd been working on a plan.

"Not necessarily."

She scowled. "Even if I was willing to infect the Viper Club—which I'm not—I can't do it. The darkness was locked away with the Beast."

"You don't actually have to do anything," Xi pointed out, pleased by Brigette's outrage. She didn't want him believing she was the same female who was willing to sacrifice her own pack. That meant he mattered to her, right? "We just need Maryam to *believe* you did something."

A portion of her defensiveness faded as she watched him move toward the opening and cautiously peer into the outer tunnel.

"How are we going to do that?"

"We're going to see Viper," he said, waiting until the nearby demons headed toward the exits before leading her through the abandoned tunnels.

Styx had paid the local sprite tribe a fortune to keep a hidden portal open 24/7. Just in case of an emergency. Xi hadn't taken it as a lack of faith in his abilities. They both had been around long enough to know that whatever shit *could* go wrong *would* go wrong. Especially in a battle.

"What's a viper?" Brigette demanded once they were far enough away from the populated passages.

"Not a what, a who." Xi ignored the stagnant water that gathered in greenish pools. It smelled better than the trash littering the main tunnels. "The clan chief of Chicago."

"I assume he's connected to the Viper Club?"

"The owner," Xi clarified. "We also need to warn Styx that we haven't managed to discover the hidden snares."

Brigette leaped over a puddle. "You think he might attack them?"

"It depends on the provocation," Xi admitted. "He would never take unnecessary risks with his soldiers, but he's not going to ignore a full-out assault on his city. I don't want any unfortunate mistakes."

They reached the end of the tunnel, and trusting that the magical portal was waiting for him, Xi walked straight forward. Thankfully, a darkness surrounded him, and by his third step, he was magically whisked out of the tunnels and to an empty parking lot. He didn't see the sprite holding open the portal, but he could catch the scent of lemons coming from a nearby tree.

He barely waited for Brigette to step into the lot before he grabbed her hand and pulled her down the dark side streets. They moved too fast for the human eye to track their passage, but that wasn't the reason for his speed. Maryam had managed to gather hundreds of demons in the tunnels right beneath Styx's feet. That meant she was not only a persuasive leader, but that she was extremely clever.

Just because she'd sent Brigette out to cause chaos didn't mean she didn't have a dozen other attacks planned. He wanted to speak with Viper as quickly as possible so he could return to Styx's lair. The Anasso was different from most leaders. He had no interest in personal power and detested being treated like a king, but he was fiercely protective of his people. If the aggravating diversions turned into mass causalities, he would go into the tunnels with guns blazing.

Figuratively and literally.

Brigette seemed equally anxious to reach their destination. Either because she wanted to discover his plan, or because she was ready to get back to the tunnels and get rid of him. He was hoping it was the first reason.

Minutes later, they reached the club, which was hidden behind a subtle glamour. Most humans would walk right past the brick building, which looked as if it was impatiently waiting to be condemned. As they stepped through the magical barrier, however, the full glory of the place was revealed.

The lobby looked like a Grecian paradise, with white marble on the floors and a coved ceiling that was encrusted with fist-sized diamonds.

Fluted columns lined the hallway leading into the club, where a demon could sate any hunger. Sex. Blood. Ambrosia. And gambling.

Everything but fighting. Viper did bad, bad things to anyone who unleashed violence at his properties.

Brigette's eyes widened as Xi led her up a curved staircase to the private balcony, which offered a stunning view of the club below them.

In the very center of the room was a large fountain that sprayed water toward the massive chandelier. Music drifted from a string quartet; the musicians were clustered on a small dais, while fey creatures in gauzy gowns twirled between the numerous tables, sparkles drifting through the air as they passed.

"Wow," she breathed. "This is…"

"Over the top?"

"Impressive."

Xi assumed she was talking about the club, although it might have been the slender vampire who rose to his feet as they stepped onto the balcony.

Viper, clan chief of Chicago, was a stunningly gorgeous male. Or at least that was the opinion of most females. They claimed his long hair was as pale as moonlight and that his eyes were as dark as a midnight sky. And, of course, he had the perfect features that all vampires possessed. Tonight, he was wearing a long, white, velvet coat with ruby buttons and satin knee breeches. Viper didn't follow fashion; he had his own unique style.

"I see Styx released the Ravens," the older male drawled, strolling to stand in front of Xi. "Is he fumigating the caves?"

Xi smiled. Unlike some of his brothers, he'd discovered that the best way to deal with Viper's mockery was just to ignore it.

"Something like that," he murmured.

"And you brought a guest."

Xi snapped his fangs together, caught off guard by the vicious flare of fury that raced through him as Viper made a slow, thorough survey of Brigette. What was wrong with him? Not only was Viper mated, but Xi had no right to react to a male appreciating Brigette's beauty.

Not yet, a voice whispered in the back of his mind.

"This is Brigette," he said.

"Brigette?" Viper flicked up a brow. "That Brigette?"

"Yeah, that one," Brigette answered in overly sweet tones.

Viper glanced toward Xi. "Does Styx know she's in town?"

Brigette snorted. "I don't answer to the leeches."

"We need to speak in private," Xi said, feeling the air prickle with a sudden heat. Brigette might have a smile pasted on her lips, but it wouldn't take much for her to go for Viper's throat.

Viper waved a hand toward the table set near the edge of the balcony. "No one will bother us here. Have a seat." They moved to settle on the sleek leather chairs. Viper grabbed a cut-crystal decanter. "Brandy?" Xi and Brigette shook their heads, but Viper poured a large shot of the amber liquor into his glass. "I think I'm going to need one," he muttered before he settled back in his seat and eyed them with a curious gaze. "Tell me why you're here."

Xi nodded toward Brigette, who seemed surprised that he expected her to take the lead. He shrugged. This was her story to tell.

In concise detail, she revealed Maryam and Roban's arrival in Ireland and her past few days in the tunnels beneath the city. Viper listened in silence, sipping his brandy as he absorbed her words.

Once she was done, Viper set aside the brandy, his expression stark. "That explains the mysterious fires, explosions, and cave-ins we've been experiencing over the past few weeks."

"Yes," Xi agreed. "In a way, it's a relief. If they're coming from one source, they're easier to contain."

Viper didn't look particularly relieved. "Then why aren't we containing it?"

"Because Maryam and her merry misfits are prepared to be attacked," Brigette answered.

Viper shrugged. "And?"

"And we're not ready to reveal that Styx has discovered the presence of her rebellion," Xi added.

"What are we waiting for?"

"It's possible there's a puppeteer pulling the strings from the shadows," Xi said.

"Of course there is." Viper shook his head in disgust. "I've fought next to Styx too many times to think anything can ever be easy. Who's on the hunt?"

Xi's lips twisted. "Are you sure you want to know?"

"I asked…" Viper's words trailed away as his eyes widened in horror. "Oh hell. Is that chunk of rock involved?"

"He does have a unique talent for stumbling into trouble," Xi said in his usual understated way. The truth was that the gargoyle plunged from one disaster to another, usually managing to come out unscathed. "If anyone can draw the demon out of the shadows, it will be Levet."

"And if the demon eats the aggravating creature, it's no loss," Viper drawled.

"True," Xi agreed.

"Hey, he's my friend," Brigette snapped, her eyes flashing with anger. "My only friend."

Viper sent Brigette a startled glance at her outburst before returning his attention to Xi. "What is it with that gargoyle and females?"

Xi shrugged. He'd never paid much attention to Levet, but he'd been vaguely aware that Styx's mate, Darcy, had been enchanted by the strange creature.

"You're asking the wrong vampire."

Brigette made a sound of disgust. "He has something you'll never have."

"And what's that?" Viper asked.

"A heart."

Xi exchanged a glance with Viper. There was a hint of respect in the older vampire's eyes. As if he hadn't expected Brigette to possess the courage—or perhaps the desire—to stand up for her friend.

"She does have a point," Xi murmured.

"Hmm." Viper shrugged away the insult. "I assume there's a reason you came here tonight?" He turned back to Brigette. "Unless you're seeking entertainment. For the right price, I can fulfill your deepest fantasy."

She rolled her eyes. "Doubtful."

Xi gripped the arms of his chair as an intense emotion jolted through him. It wasn't anger, although he wasn't happy with Viper's lingering gaze. No, it was a shocking desire to know Brigette's deepest fantasy.

And then satisfy it.

Over and over...

It was, at last, the realization that his chair was coated in a layer of ice that forced him to squash the erotic images that flooded through his mind and concentrate on the reason they were at the club.

"We need your help," he told Viper.

Viper sprawled back in his chair. "I have endless talents. What do you require?"

Xi once again glanced toward Brigette, silently urging her to reveal why they'd traveled to the club. Her jaw tightened, as if she was preparing herself for Viper's disgust.

"Maryam sent me here to spread my infection."

Viper looked confused. "Infection?"

"The darkness of the Beast," Brigette clarified.

The silver-haired vampire froze, his eyes narrowing. "You can do that?"

"Not anymore."

"But Maryam believes she still has the power," Xi told Viper.

"Ah." Viper nodded. "That's why you were invited to join the rebels."

"It wasn't my charming personality," Brigette said in dry tones.

Viper flashed a wicked smile toward Xi. "She's feisty."

Brigette growled low in her throat. "Feisty?"

"I have a plan," Xi intruded into the brewing argument.

"You always do." Viper waved a slender hand. "Tell me."

"We need to convince Maryam that your club has been infected." Xi told his companion. "How many customers are here this evening?"

Viper glanced over the bronze railing to the crowd below. "It's a slow night. Less than a hundred."

"How many do you trust to keep a secret?"

"Five." Viper considered for a second, as if running through a mental list of his various employees. "Maybe six."

"Any witches?"

Viper narrowed his eyes. "For the right price."

"Good."

Viper abruptly leaned forward. "Tell me your plan."

Xi was a master tactician. He could plot out a full battle strategy with a dozen contingency plans in less than an hour. Or discover a means of overpowering an enemy even with inferior troops. But he rarely had to devise diversionary tactics. He was a warrior, not a magician.

"You pay the witch to create a cloud of darkness, then have the demons that you trust begin a stampede to send the others into a panic," Xi said as he revealed his hastily concocted scheme. "Then you lock down this place as if it's been hit by the plague."

Viper stared at him for a long moment. "Let me see if I have this right," he finally said. "You want me to pay a witch an obscene amount of money to terrify my customers into fleeing from my club. Then I lock the doors for some unspecified length of time?"

"Yes."

Viper appeared genuinely horrified. "Do you have any idea how much money that's going to cost me?"

"Less than it will cost you if Maryam isn't convinced that the evil has been spread. She's determined to hurt Styx and cause as much destruction as possible," Xi reminded him. "The next attempt might destroy you."

Viper scowled. "I hate when people are reasonable."

"And right," Xi added.

"I'm sending the bill to Styx." Viper muttered, lifting his hand to gesture toward some unseen creature on a balcony across the club.

Xi's lips twitched as he imagined Styx's reaction to receiving a bill. The Anasso was a dedicated, loyal, ruthlessly fair leader, but he was notoriously tightfisted with his massive fortune. It would be easier to capture a unicorn than to get him to open his treasure box.

"It's your death warrant," Xi murmured.

Viper didn't bother to answer as a tall, bone-thin vampire stepped onto the balcony. The female was stunningly gorgeous, with thick black hair that tumbled over her shoulders and a pale face dominated by brown eyes the precise shade of aged cognac. She was wearing a red satin gown that clung like a second skin, stopping just short of her ankles and shoes with four-inch heels. Xi, however, wasn't interested in her physical appearance. He was judging the power that throbbed around her with a physical force.

He hadn't seen her around Chicago before, and she had the strength of a clan chief. So why was she working for Viper? An intriguing lesson for later.

"Ah, Satin," Viper drawled. "I need you to discretely locate any clan members in the club and ask them to come to the office."

Satin appeared curious, but, obviously accustomed to odd requests from her employer, she merely nodded.

"Oh, and find the most powerful witch in the place," Viper continued. "If there is one here."

"There is."

"Good. Bring her to see me."

Satin waited a second; then, when it was clear that Viper was done, she bowed her head and turned to leave as silently as she had arrived.

Viper leaned back in his chair and reached for his brandy. "All I want is a few decades of peace. Is that so much to ask?"

Xi offered a rueful smile. "You have been blessed to live in interesting times."

Viper swallowed the brandy in one gulp. "Blessed or cursed?"

Chapter 8

Levet wrinkled his snout at the pungent scent of mold that coated the floor and walls of the underground passages.

The lair wasn't like many of the caves and tunnels vampires usually preferred. It was paved with cobblestones, and the walls were coated with a stucco that was peeling in weird patches. Like a snake shedding its skin. Plus there were large rooms with heavy wooden furniture that had provided a comfortable place to gather, along with several smaller chambers for each vampire to have their own space. This hadn't been a temporary lair. The previous Anasso had created a home.

Unfortunately, time hadn't been particularly kind.

"Tell me again why we're strolling through these nasty tunnels instead of enjoying the many delights that London has to offer?" Troy drawled.

The oversized imp had left his feathered cape in the bar, revealing the poison-green spandex jumpsuit he was wearing beneath it. The feathers had been awful. The spandex was enough to blind a poor gargoyle.

"I told you. I am searching for clues," Levet snapped.

"Like Scooby Doo?"

"*Oui.*" Levet's wings fluttered at the comparison. He adored Scooby Doo. What could be better than a funny dog who solved mysteries? "Only without the yummy snacks," he added with a small sigh. "A shame. I do enjoy a snack. Even one that is not a Scooby."

Troy sauntered down the wide hallway, halting now and then to peer into one of the shadowed rooms.

"And what do clues look like?"

"Styx claims that the old Anasso had a secret vault hidden down here where he kept his private scrolls."

Troy sent him a confused glance, the top of his manly man-bun nearly brushing the low ceiling.

"So the clue is in the vault?"

Levet rolled his eyes. "You will never be a member of the Scooby gang."

"Is that supposed to make me sad?"

Levet shook his head. Perhaps he shouldn't be so grumpy. Not everyone was blessed with his own clever brain. Obviously, he needed to speak more clearly. Or perhaps more slowly. Imps could be quite stupid.

"Styx wants to know if anyone has recently been down here and if they managed to open the vault to steal the scrolls inside it."

"Ah." Troy stifled a yawn, already bored with the explanation. "Now the deeper question. Why?"

"Why what?"

"Why are you the one who is searching for signs of an intruder in this moldy crypt?" Troy clarified. "Shouldn't it be the responsibility of the vampires?"

Ah, indeed. That was a question that Levet often asked himself. It was not as if he was a member of their clan. Thank the goddess. He had no desire to be an unofficial vampire. And yet they always sought him out in times of trouble.

"They do not have my specialized skills."

"And what specialized skills are those?"

"I can see through illusions. Smell magic. Follow a trail that not even a hellhound can detect." Levet happily shared his awesome abilities. Not that he should have to. Troy had seen him in 3Z...no wait...3D action before. "Why are you asking?"

The imp shrugged. "Inga is concerned. She believes you were sent here because it is dangerous and the vampires don't want to put themselves at risk."

"That is probably true." Levet's wings drooped. He wasn't so stupid that he didn't realize that the leeches would happily sacrifice him. Of course, on the plus side, it was pleasant to know that Inga was worried about him.

Troy sent him a curious gaze. "Then why are you here?"

"Because it is my duty."

They turned into a narrow passage that led toward the back of the lair. From overhead, Levet could catch the scent of mud.

They were at the edge of the River Thames.

"Duty to whom?" Troy inquired. "You were kicked out of the Gargoyle Guild, weren't you?"

Levet scowled. "You don't have to remind me."

"So who are you trying to impress?"

The passage narrowed even further, and the air seemed oddly thick, as if it was trying to push them back. Levet grimly pressed on.

"None of your business," Levet muttered.

"If you're hoping to convince Inga you are a male of worth, you don't need to bother," Troy drawled. "For whatever reason, she believes you are some sort of hero."

"I am a hero." Levet puffed out his chest. "I have saved the world on three separate occasions."

Troy held out his hand, as if feeling the air. Did he sense the thickness that was swiftly becoming oppressive?

"So you claim," he murmured in absent tones.

"Do you not believe me?"

Troy clicked his tongue with blatant impatience. "It doesn't matter what I believe. Inga simply wants you to stay out of danger. Is that so much to ask?"

Levet's breath was squeezed from his lungs at the thought of Inga. The female was three times his size, with a magical trident that could destroy large cities, but in many ways she was vulnerable. His place should be standing at her side, offering her comfort and, occasionally, his sage advice.

But here he was, trudging through the abandoned lair instead of comfortably settled in the mer-folk castle. It wasn't that he didn't care about Inga. Just the opposite. But he was compelled to complete his mission.

Levet hunched his shoulders. "As I said, it is my duty."

"Duty to who?" Troy wrinkled his nose. "Or is it whom?"

"Duty to *moi*."

"Why?"

Levet glared at the imp. It was time to turn the...What was the word? Chairs? Sofas? Tables?

"Why are you assisting Inga to become a proper queen for the mer-folk?" he demanded of the imp.

Troy widened his eyes, as if confused by the abrupt question. "Am I? How tedious of me. No one should be proper."

"Fah." Levet's tail twitched around his feet. A sure indication of his annoyance. "That is not an answer."

They walked in silence, as if Troy was considering his words. "Boredom," he at last admitted. "Plus the pleasure of tweaking your nose. Oh, and watching the mer-folk squirm." A humorless smile twisted his lips. "The arrogant little twits deserved to be punished for treating Inga like an interloper."

Levet believed him. Troy was the sort of imp who enjoyed being as annoying as possible. But that didn't fully explain his fierce devotion to ensuring that Inga was accepted as Queen of the Mer-folk.

"And?" Levet pressed.

Troy shrugged. "And the desire to accomplish something meaningful in my rather meaningless existence."

His words perfectly captured that nebulous hunger that drove Levet to charge into danger.

"*Oui*. That is why I do it as well."

Troy glanced down, and they shared a long, rather rueful glance. "We have more in common than I originally suspected." He released a sharp laugh that echoed through the empty passages. "A horrifying thought."

"Truly horrifying." Levet shuddered, although it wasn't so much a reaction to Troy's words as the sense of dread that was beating against him like a physical force. "Wait," he muttered.

The imp came to a sharp halt. Troy might enjoy pretending to be a buffoon, but he was a stunningly powerful male who possessed magic that could make grown trolls tremble in fear. More importantly, he was smart enough to accept Levet's ability to sense danger without question.

"What is it?"

"A tingle in the air," Levet muttered, rubbing one of his stunted horns as he was buffeted by a wave of revulsion. As if some unseen force was trying to physical shove him out of the lair. "Do you sense it?"

"Yes. An illusion," Troy murmured. "This way."

The larger male turned to walk down a side passage; his steps were slow and deliberate, as if he was battling against the same desire as Levet to flee the area. Levet followed behind, using Troy's larger body to shield him from any unpleasant surprises. Hey, he might be a hero, but he wasn't stupid.

After what felt like an eternity, they at last reached the end of the passageway. Halting, they studied the heavy steel door, which was coated in rust.

"This must be the vault." Troy said, cautiously reaching out his hand, as if he was searching for hidden booby traps.

Levet wasn't nearly so cautious. He didn't like the icky magic that clung to his skin, as if he'd been dipped in goop. He wanted to see what was in the vault so they could get out of there. Lifting his hand, he used his powers to create a large fireball. It flared to life and then sputtered like it was about to go out. Levet clenched his teeth, consumed with a horrifying fear that he might not be able to perform while Troy was watching.

Then, much to his relief, the flames returned to dance cheerily in the palm of his hand. Whew, that would have been embarrassing. Lifting his hand, Levet launched the burning ball directly at the door.

There was a sizzling sound as it flew through the air, quickly followed by a splat as it hit the rusted steel. Troy gasped when he realized what was happening, but even as he hurriedly wrapped his arms over his face, a loud explosion echoed through the lair.

Levet winced. He hadn't intended to be so noisy. Or so...dusty. Still, as the cloud of decimated stucco and mold settled, it revealed that his magic had done its job. There was now a large hole in the center of the door.

Coughing, Troy turned his head to glare at Levet. "Damn, gargoyle, be careful. You nearly singed off my man-bun."

"Don't be a baby." Levet hopped through the jagged opening, glancing around the rectangular space.

It was nearly empty. In one corner were a few swords and a spear, and a handful of old coins were scattered across the floor. Closer, however, there was a shelf that held dozens of scrolls.

Levet cautiously moved forward. His explosion had not only opened the door, but it had also broken whatever magic was creating the reluctance to approach the vault. That didn't mean, however, that there weren't a few nasty surprises hidden in the shadows.

He reached the shelves and grabbed one of the scrolls, studying the melted seal that held it shut.

"This is the same as the scroll that Brigette brought from the rebels." Levet glanced back toward the door, his brow furrowed. This lair had belonged to the previous Anasso. "The question is how did the rebels acquire them?"

"A good question," Troy murmured. "That illusion wasn't just to hide the opening to the safe. It was also laced with a powerful magic that would have discouraged most demons from even entering the passage."

"*Oui*, I felt it." Levet shivered. Revulsion spells were the worse. "So whoever took the scrolls knew they were down here."

"That someone." Troy moved toward the shelves, bending down to point at a footprint outlined in the dust.

Levet moved to squat beside the imp, studying the clue. He sniffed. He could catch the lingering scent. A vampire. But the size of the print was too large to have been the female rebel who'd given Brigette the scroll.

"This has been here less than a year," he murmured, noting the thinner layer of dust in the middle of the track.

"Agreed," Troy said.

About to straighten, Levet's attention was captured by a glimpse of bronze beneath the shelves.

"What is this?"

Crawling forward, Levet reached beneath the shelf to pull out a small, bronzed medallion in the shape of a raven.

"An amulet of some sort," Troy murmured.

Levet wrapped his fingers around it. He was still holding the scroll he'd grabbed in the other hand. "I have seen one like it before."

Troy sent him a startled glance. "Where?"

"Styx."

* * * *

Brigette watched from the shadows as the last of the demons ran screeching from the Viper Club. She didn't know precisely what sort of spell the witch had used, but there'd been lots of boiling black clouds and a vile odor that had her and Xi retreating, along with the rest of the customers.

Of course, as nasty as it was, it couldn't compare with the true darkness of the Beast. Brigette had spent over five hundred years enthralled by the toxic evil. The smothering malignancy had nearly destroyed her. In fact, once she was in the dungeons of the mer-folk, she'd prayed that she would die. Anything to forget the grim years.

Clenching her hands into tight fists, Brigette silently reminded herself that this was nothing more than smoke and mirrors. The Beast was locked away, along with her evil. There was no reason for her palms to sweat and nausea to roll through her.

She sucked in a deep breath, battling back the sickness. Then, without warning, Xi stepped next to her, running his fingers down her back.

"This should be fairly convincing," he murmured.

Oddly, the cool touch eased the tension clutching her body, as if a vise had just been loosened. She instinctively leaned closer to the hard comfort of his body, watching Satin urge the nymphs away from the cloud of darkness that billowed out the front door. The elegant vampire was also using her phone to capture the stampede of demons. No doubt she was going to post it on social media. Smart. It would add to the rumors that something terrible was happening.

"At least for a few days," Brigette agreed, turning to face Xi. Concentrating on his gorgeous face allowed her to forget about the dark cloud surrounding the club. "Of course, Maryam might become suspicious if the darkness doesn't start spreading through Chicago."

Xi nodded. "I'll go speak with Styx. We can use the other Ravens to share stories of an evil plague attacking other parts of the city."

"You're going to see Styx now?"

"I want to tell him about the map we saw in Maryam's office," Xi told her. "And warn him that the rebellion is more widespread than we first assumed."

Brigette's knees suddenly threatened to buckle. She told herself it was her lingering reaction to the witch's potent spell. She had…what did the humans call it? PTSD? Yeah, that was it. She was going to need time to recover from the trauma of being in the clutches of the Beast. But the panic churning through her had nothing to do with fear. It was a sense of loss. As if she'd momentarily touched something glorious, only to have it slip away.

Stupid.

Brigette shook away the irrational thoughts. Nothing was slipping away, because she'd never had anything to begin with, right?

She forced a stiff smile to her lips. "Thanks for your help."

She was walking away when Xi spoke. "I'll be returning to the tunnels."

Brigette froze, stunned by the relief that cascaded through her. Slowly, she turned back. "Why?"

He stepped forward, allowing his cool power to wash over her. Brigette shivered in pleasure.

"Until we've discovered who is ultimately behind the attacks, someone must keep an eye on Maryam." His dark gaze swept down her body before returning to rest on her upturned face. "Besides…"

"Besides what?"

His smiled revealed a hint of fang. "Besides, I intend to keep an eye on you."

More shivers raced through Brigette, along with a white-hot anticipation that clenched her stomach. She tried to hide her fierce reaction behind a pretense of indifference.

"I've told you guys I don't need a babysitter."

His smile widened. "Babysitting is the last thing on my mind."

For a breathless moment, Brigette's gaze was mesmerized by the sight of those razor-sharp fangs. She'd always been isolated. First, by her overprotective pack, and then by the curse of the Beast. But she'd heard stories about what a vampire could do with his bite. The pleasure was supposedly so intense a creature could become instantly addicted.

Did she want to find out for herself?

Oh, yeah.

Desperately.

Not trusting herself to speak, Brigette spun away from Xi and hurried away from the club. It wasn't that she was opposed to exploring the desire that simmered between them. After so many centuries of denying herself the smallest sensual pleasure, she was acutely hungry for the touch of a male. But while it might have been a simple matter to find a willing partner to scratch her itch, she sensed that nothing would be simple if that male was Xi.

The sensations that buzzed between them were more than just lust. They were two magnets being drawn ruthlessly together. There was no reason to it. No chance to deny or avoid it.

Just...fate.

And right now, Brigette wasn't ready to be swept up in some epic, tidal wave of destiny.

Not when she was trying to prevent a revolution.

Reminded of her self-imposed task, Brigette picked up her pace as she scurried through the dark streets. Maryam would have someone watching to tell her when Brigette returned to the tunnels.

Entering the secret hideout through a side tunnel, Brigette had barely managed to reach the main passage when a hand reached out to grab her arm. Roban. Brigette growled, spinning to kick the idiot in the balls. Roban muttered a curse, barely jumping out of the way of the painful blow.

"Careful, bitch," he snapped.

Brigette narrowed her eyes. "Grab me again, and I'll rip out your heart and stuff it up your ass. Got it?"

The male Were ignored the threat, pretending he wasn't intimidated as he smoothed his hands down the flannel shirt he wore, along with a worn pair of jeans and heavy boots. He made an effort to look like a badass. Something that wouldn't be necessary if he actually was a badass.

"Well?" Roban demanded.

Brigette folded her arms over her chest, meeting him glare for glare. "Well, what?"

"I'm waiting for your report."

Brigette deliberately glanced around the empty passage before returning her gaze to the Were.

"I don't answer to you."

"I'm Maryam's partner."

His eyes glowed with the power of his wolf, and a soul-deep envy punched Brigette directly in the gut. Swallowing her snarl, she twisted her lips into a humorless smile.

"More like her lapdog."

Roban growled low in his throat. "I warned her it was a bad idea to allow you to join us."

"Allow? You begged me to come."

Heat vibrated in the air. Weres were naturally aggressive, and the fact that they were suspicious of each other made the sparks fly.

"Once a traitor always a traitor," Roban snarled.

Brigette laughed. She could care less what this male thought of her. Xi, on the other hand...

No, no, no. She wasn't going to let thoughts of the delicious vampire distract her.

"Do you know the definition of hypocrite?" she drawled. "Look it up."

"We're saving the demons from their oppressors."

She laughed at his fierce claim. "There might be some demons in this rebellion who are doing the saving, but it isn't you." Flicking her gaze up and down his body, Brigette wrinkled her nose in disdain. "You're hiding in shadows while creatures with actual courage are out there fighting on the front lines."

Roban flinched, as if she'd managed to hit a raw nerve. Did he fear he looked like a coward? Or was he frustrated that he wasn't allowed to fight?

"Every army needs servants to do the dirty work," he struck out.

"Just as they need a fall guy," she shot back. "If things start going south, trust me, you're going to be the one who pays the price. Styx isn't going to be very happy when he gets his hands on you."

Roban's expression hardened. He might be impatient to enter the battle, but he was ruthlessly loyal to Maryam. He would never believe she could betray him.

"You're delusional."

"Once upon a time, I was delusional, but never again. Only an idiot trusts anyone. Usually a dead idiot." She sent a finger wave in Roban's direction as she continued down the passage. "Have a nice day."

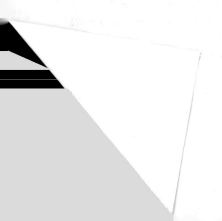

Chapter 9

Xi wasn't sure what he expected when he arrived at Styx's lair, but he certainly wasn't prepared for the king to grab his arm as soon as he stepped over the threshold to drag him into the massive house.

"Good," Styx snapped. "I'm glad you're here."

Xi allowed himself to be hauled through the wide hallways. "Are you okay?"

Styx grimaced. Although the male was wearing his usual leather and his hair had been pulled into a tight braid, there was a frazzled impatience that sizzled around him.

"I've been better, and, unfortunately, I have a fear it's going to get worse before it gets better," the king muttered.

Xi's lips parted to ask if something had happened, but he was distracted by a familiar scent.

"Why do I smell granite?"

"The gargoyle's here," Styx revealed, pushing Xi into his office before he had an opportunity to escape.

"The gargoyle has a name." A tiny voice came from across the study. "It is Levet."

Xi sent Styx a puzzled glance. "I thought he was in London."

Styx looked pained. "He was. Then, a couple minutes ago, he was banging on my door, demanding to be let in."

Levet sniffed. "I have returned with clues, but if you are going to be a poopy-head I will leave."

Xi arched a brow. Levet was always mouthy, but he wasn't usuall suicidal. "Poopy-head?"

"Don't encourage him," Styx muttered.

Levet flapped his wings, an expression of impatience on his ugly features. "Do you wish to know what I have discovered or not?"

Styx leaned against the desk. "Tell me."

Levet cleared his throat, clearly enjoying his moment in the spotlight. "As you requested, I traveled to the old lair in Billingsgate." The gargoyle wrinkled his snout. "You really should send one of your Ravens to give it a good cleaning. I'm coated in mold. I had to polish my tail three times to get the grime off."

The lights flickered as Styx struggled to control his temper. "I could rip it off, and you wouldn't have to worry about it."

"No need to be so grumpy," Levet complained. "I am the one who has been crawling through moldy tunnels that smell like dead fish while you have been in this mansion as snug as a roach in a rug."

Styx stiffened in disbelief. "Did you just call me a roach?"

"I think he meant snug as a bug," Xi hastily prevented the king from crushing the creature beneath his massive feet.

Darcy would never forgive her mate. And, besides, they needed Levet's information.

Apparently coming to the same conclusion, Styx grimly leashed his anger. "Did you find the vault or not?" he asked the gargoyle.

"*Oui.*"

"And?" Styx prompted.

"There were scrolls that looked exactly like those Brigette brought from the rebels. They even smelled the same."

"Anything else?"

Levet nodded. "There were footprints in the layers of dust that coated the vault. As I said, the place is a mess. Perhaps you should—"

"Could you tell how recent?" Styx interrupted.

Levet shrugged. "Within the past year. I cannot be more specific."

"Did you try to track the intruder?" Xi asked.

"I intend to return and follow the trail. But, first, I want you to see what I found," Levet said.

Styx waved an impatient hand. "Show me."

Levet stepped forward, holding out his hand. Then, with the dramatic flair of a dew fairy, he peeled open his fingers one by one.

"Ta da."

Styx made a strangled noise as he studied the small bronze amulet that had been carved into the shape of a raven. Then, with a stiff motion, he reached to pluck the piece of metal from Levet's hand.

"Where did you find this?"

"Inside the vault."

Xi grimaced. The insignia looked similar to the one that Styx had given him when he'd become a Raven, although there were subtle differences. Just like with the seal.

"The previous Anasso offered these to his most loyal servants," Styx said, confirming Xi's suspicion.

"It was his lair, right?" Xi said. "It wouldn't be unusual to find personal belongings."

Levet shook his head. "There was no dust on it. It'd been left there at the same time as the footprints."

Xi grimaced. "A vampire."

The lights flickered again, before shattering into a thousand shards. Xi had no idea how many bulbs the king went through each month, but it had to cost him a small fortune.

"One of my brothers," Styx rasped.

Xi sensed Styx's smoldering fury that the brewing rebellion had been stirred to life by a former brother.

"Can you tell which one?" he asked the older vampire.

"No." Styx slid the amulet into the front pocket of his leather pants, turning his attention to the gargoyle. "You need to return and see if you can follow the trail."

"Of course I do." With a sniff, Levet waddled toward the open door. "As always, it is my duty to save the world. Let us hope that flighty imp is holding open the portal."

Xi watched the gargoyle disappear before glancing back at Styx. "What imp?"

Styx shrugged. "I didn't ask."

Xi briefly considered following the tiny creature to discover who was working with him, only to dismiss the impulse. He had more important matters to consider.

"What about you?" he asked his king.

Styx tapped his fingers on the edge of the desk, his thoughts obviously focused on the amulet that had been discovered.

"I'll start contacting my former clansmen."

"That's going to take time."

Styx shook his head, an ancient sorrow darkening his eyes. "Not as long as you would think. Many of them have perished over the centuries." His jaw tightened. "Eventually, I'll figure out who is so eager to overthrow me."

"Whoever it is should have asked for the throne. There was no need for such an elaborate plot to overthrow you." Xi deliberately lightened the mood.

With Darcy still in Kansas City, it would be easy for Styx to become mired in his regrets of his past. They needed him sharp-witted and prepared to make difficult choices if they were going to survive the rebellion.

Styx snorted, a hint of rueful amusement dispelling his air of gloom. "No shit. I would have handed over the throne on a silver platter." He sent Xi a questioning gaze. "Are you going back to the tunnels?"

"Yes. I want to discover what nasty surprises they have hidden and, more importantly, uncover what new chaos they're plotting."

Styx arched a brow. "New chaos? Is there something I should know?"

Xi offered a concise account of the evening's events, including a request that Styx send the other Ravens to spread rumors of an evil darkness invading the city. Styx listened in grim-faced silence. At last, he shook his head in weary frustration.

"At some point, I'm going to have to stop playing defense and go on the offense," he warned in dark tones.

"Unfortunately, I don't think the rebellion is restricted to Chicago."

"What do you mean?"

"Maryam has a map in her office with several places marked on it," Xi told the older vampire. "Chicago, Vegas, Ireland, and London."

Styx frowned. "That's a little vague."

"I would assume they're target sites."

"Damn." Styx scrubbed his face with weary hands. The Anasso might have been an unwilling king, but he'd readily shouldered his duties, along with a fierce determination to protect his people. The past weeks of covert attacks and mayhem had taken their toll. "I just asked Darcy to come home. Maybe she should stay in Kansas City until we find out who's behind this madness."

"Right now, I'm not sure that anyplace is entirely safe," Xi warned.

Styx lowered his hands to study Xi with a wry expression. "And people claim I'm a Debbie Downer."

"You are," Xi told his companion. "I'm a realist."

"Go." Styx waved a dismissive hand. "Do your thing."

Xi nodded, heading out of the mansion. He was anxious to return to the tunnels...

No, that wasn't true. It was his duty to return to the tunnels, but any eagerness to return was entirely due to Brigette. Being parted from her for even an hour was causing something very close to physical pain.

The sensation should have baffled him. Why the hell would he feel such an intense need to be near a female he barely knew? Especially a female who was as troubled and broken as Brigette. But he wasn't baffled.

An instinct as old as the beginning of time was stirring inside him. And there wasn't a damned thing he could do to stop it. Even if he wanted to.

A smile spread over his face as he left Styx's lair and headed toward the nearby portal.

* * * *

Levet located Inga in her grand throne room. She wasn't seated on her throne, although it was the hour she was supposed to be hearing petitions from her people. Instead, she was crouched in the back, intently painting a fresco on the wall.

The newly crowned Queen of the Mer-folk wasn't the prettiest demon. Not even on a good-hair day. And she wasn't the friendliest. In fact, a rabid hellhound possessed more charm.

But she possessed a heart that was bigger than the ocean, and an artistic talent that was stunning to behold.

Stepping around the dais, Levet watched in silence as Inga completed a brilliant blue fish that was darting among the coral painted along the baseboard. It looked so real that Levet expected it to leap off the wall.

Sucking in a deep breath of the soft scent of a salty breeze that swirled around Inga, Levet forced himself to break the peaceful silence.

"Ah, *ma belle*. I thought I might find you here."

Inga blinked, as if she'd been miles away. "Levet." Rising to her feet, she tossed aside her paintbrush and smoothed her hands down her floppy muumuu. Levet thought he could see paint stains on the material, but it was hard to tell against the vivid pattern of lemons splotched over a purple background. "Have you already completed your quest?"

"*Non*, but I have discovered a clue."

"What sort of clue?"

Levet shared the details of his latest adventure, taking care to reveal his courage in traveling to London and discovering the hidden lair. He wanted the female to be properly impressed by his skills. And then he finished with his return to Styx's office, where the Anasso confessed that the amulet Levet had discovered belonged to one of the old Ravens.

"Wait." Inga scowled, a hint of crimson shimmering in the depths of her blue eyes. "There is some sort of rebellion against the King of the Vampires, and you believe the mastermind is a brother to Styx?"

Levet sniffed. "Not surprising, really. There is nothing more dangerous than family."

Inga glanced toward the double doors that were firmly closed. "I can't argue with that."

"Then you understand that I must see if I can track down the vampire." Inga snapped her attention back to Levet, her expression hard with annoyance. "No, I don't understand. It sounds like leech business to me." Levet wasn't angered by the female's sharp tone. In fact, he struggled to hide his smile of satisfaction. He wanted her to be afraid that something might happen to him. It was the only way he could tell that she cared at all.

"If there is a vampire war, then we will all be swept into the bloodshed," he pointed out in gentle tones.

She planted her hands on her hips, the hideous gown pulled tight over her impressive bosom.

"Not down here. I can close the barrier, and nothing could get into the castle."

Levet took a second to appreciate the sight of her flushed cheeks and crimson eyes before he heaved a small sigh. She truly was a magnificent female, but as much as he longed to remain trapped in this castle with her, it was an impossible dream.

Moving forward, he grabbed one large hand and squeezed her fingers. "Your grandfather tried that. You cannot stick your head in the sand like a chicken."

"Ostrich," she muttered, staring down at him with an expression that tugged at his heart.

She looked...lost.

He sent her an encouraging smile. "We are all in this together, are we not?"

She refused to be comforted. "Why you? There are other demons who could track down the vampire. Including Styx's mate. Isn't she a pureblooded Were?"

Levet held onto her fingers. The scent of scorched salt was thick in the air. "Why did you accept the Tryshu?"

Inga's anger faltered as she studied him with a puzzled gaze. "I didn't accept it. Fate shoved the stupid thing into my hands."

Levet nodded. He'd been there during the final battle against Riven. The massive trident had wrenched itself from the merman's grip and literally flown across the floor toward Inga. She would have been skewered if she hadn't caught the magical weapon.

"Exactly," he said.

Their gazes entwined, and the sheen of crimson in her eyes faded to leave them a crystal blue. She started to bend forward, almost as if she intended to kiss him, and Levet's wings fluttered in anticipation. She was plus-sized yumminess wrapped in a lemon muumuu and an ocean breeze. And he wanted to topple her over so he could kiss her from the tippy-top tufts of her hair to the tips of her toes.

But even as Levet was braced for her long-overdue kiss, she was abruptly straightening and moving toward the dais.

"Fine." She grabbed the Tryshu, which was leaning against the throne. "Then we'll do this together."

Levet blinked, his stomach sinking. What did a male have to do to get this female to enjoy some cuddle time? Then, he heaved a sigh. Now wasn't the time to think of such things.

But later...

"You know it is not possible, *ma belle.* Your place is here with your people." He sent her a wry glance. "Why else would you curse me with that aggravating imp?"

She clenched the huge trident, knowing he was right. "Where is Troy?"

"Waiting in the old Anasso's vault for my return," Levet said. Troy had been less than pleased when Levet insisted on returning to the mer-folk castle on his own. Levet, however, had insisted. He did not enjoy watching the too-handsome imp flirting with Inga. Especially when he couldn't be certain that the ogress didn't enjoy the other male's attentions. "He is ensuring that nothing creeps through the portal to attack while I am preoccupied."

She nodded, and it was impossible for Levet to detect whether or not she was disappointed not to have an opportunity to spend time with the imp.

"Why did you come here?"

"Along with the amulet I discovered in the old Anasso's lair, there was also a footprint that we believe belongs to the traitor. I intend to use it to track down the mystery vampire, but I'm going to need assistance."

Inga looked confused. "None of my warriors possess your skills in following a trail."

"*Non,*" Levet agreed. He wasn't boasting. Not on this occasion. There were few demons who possessed his exceptional tracking skills. Not even vampires. "But you do possess an amulet that can amplify my ability," he told his companion.

"Me?" Inga shook her head. "What are you talking about?"

"The doulas stone."

It took a second for Inga to figure out what he was talking about. Then she lifted her shaggy brows.

"Do you know how to use it?"

Levet cleared his throat. He didn't want to lie to this female. She was too important. But then again, he wasn't above taffying with the truth. *Non*...fudging the truth.

"I know the basics," he vaguely assured her.

"It could be dangerous."

"I will be fine."

There was a long, painful pause as Inga studied him with a worried gaze. "You promise?" she at last demanded, her voice harsh with concern.

Levet sensed a warm rush of...something. It tingled and swirled and made him feel almost giddy.

Reaching out, he brushed his claws over her hand, careful to avoid the Tryshu. The weapon would shatter him into a pile of rubble.

"I promise."

She nodded. "I'll take you to the vault."

Chapter 10

Brigette paced her cramped room. There was a voice in the back of her mind, whispering that she needed to rest while she had the opportunity. If life had taught her nothing else, it was to be prepared for anything. Evil beasts from another dimension. Crazy-ass druid priestesses. Three-foot gargoyles with fairy wings. And part of being prepared meant that she wasn't exhausted.

But there was no way she was going to sleep.

Not now.

She did halt her pacing long enough to release her hair from the tight braid and brush out the long, crimson strands. Having it pulled back was giving her a headache. Or maybe the stench from the tunnels was the cause. Or…

Her thoughts were interrupted as the makeshift door to her room was shoved aside and Xi stepped inside. It'd been less than a couple hours since she'd last seen the vampire, but something inside her eased. As if a weight had just been lifted from her shoulders.

Was she relieved to have him back? Or just eager to hear what he'd discovered?

She was going with the theory that she was eager to hear what he discovered. It was a nice, straightforward explanation for something she was beginning to suspect was quite complicated. Or maybe primitively simple.

"Did you speak with Styx?" she demanded.

Xi nodded as he replaced the barrier. "And Levet."

Brigette blinked, caught off guard. "I thought he was traveling to London."

"He returned to tell Styx that he'd confirmed that the scrolls in Maryam's office came from the previous Anasso's lair."

Ah. Brigette felt a twinge of satisfaction. She'd known the scrolls would be a valuable clue when Maryam had revealed them. And because of her suspicions, the vampires would have a place to start the hunt for the traitor lurking in the shadows. It was oddly nice to do something that gave her a sense of pride instead of shame.

Hoping that Xi couldn't read her ridiculous thoughts, she cleared her throat. "So how did the scrolls get to Chicago?"

"There's a possibility that it's connected to one of the older Ravens," Xi told her.

Brigette made a choked sound. She wasn't intimately familiar with vampire politics, but she did know that the Ravens were the most trusted and loyal servants to the Anasso.

"One of you?"

Xi shook his head. "One of the guards for the previous Anasso."

Brigette shoved aside her shock. She, better than anyone, knew that loyalty could be purchased for the right price. And at least the suspect pool would be fairly small. How many Ravens could there be?

A few dozen?

"You believe the Raven is working with Maryam?" she asked Xi.

"I think it's more likely that he's manipulating her."

Yeah, that's what she thought too. Maryam's fierce assertion that she was a savior was too sincere to be an act.

"Why?"

"My first guess would be to take the throne from Styx."

"If he wants the throne, why not challenge him directly?"

Xi looked genuinely surprised by the question. "You've met Styx."

Brigette shrugged. The Anasso was thunderously powerful, and he no doubt had weapons he kept hidden. But he wasn't an army.

"Okay, maybe no one would be stupid enough to confront him in a fair fight, but they have hundreds of demons gathered down here. Not even the Anasso could defeat them all if they decided to attack."

Xi's expression tightened with frustration. "That's the question I'm asking myself."

"You have a theory?"

"Not really a theory."

"Tell me," she urged.

Xi paced across the room, following the same path she'd been using. Brigette hid a smile. It was nice to know that she wasn't the only one who paced when she was trying to work through a problem.

Yet another thing they had in common, a voice whispered in the back of her mind.

"If I was attempting to remove Styx from his throne, I might try to make him appear to be a weak king who is incapable of protecting his people," Xi slowly spoke his thoughts out loud.

"But?"

He smiled toward her as she easily sensed that he didn't believe that theory. "But it's a sketchy tactic. Not only do you risk being discovered and crushed by Styx, but there's no guarantee that it would actually work." He shook his head. "Who would go to such an effort without a guaranteed payoff?"

He was right. At first, Brigette had assumed that they were using the tactics of anarchists. The sort of small, bloody attacks that would eventually topple the ruling elite. But if there was a hidden player who intended to take the throne, then Maryam and Roban's strategies were baffling.

She watched Xi pace from one end of the cramped space to the other. "What would you do?"

"If I had this group?" Xi halted, glancing toward her as she nodded. "I'd hit him swiftly and cause as much damage as possible before he knew what was happening," he told her without hesitation. "Then I'd start making examples of any vampire who dared to challenge my authority. There's nothing like a few heads on a pike to convince demons to accept new leadership." He paused, his lips twisting with frustration. "This petty stuff is annoying, but it's really accomplished nothing more than to alert Styx that someone is plotting against him."

His words perfectly captured Brigette's own dissatisfaction. None of this made sense. "I agree."

They shared a glance. Then, without warning, Xi's expression softened, and he slowly moved to stand directly in front of her.

"I thought you would be sleeping." He reached to brush his fingers through her hair, his rich male scent teasing at her senses. "You must be exhausted."

She tilted back her head, meeting his searching gaze. Less than a day ago, she would have destroyed any male who dared to touch her without invitation. Now she shivered with an exquisite sense of anticipation. She wanted those cool, clever fingers exploring more than her hair. She wanted them traveling down her body, removing her clothes, and discovering the erotic spots that she'd forgotten she possessed.

The room filled with the earthy scent of her musk, but Brigette pretended she was indifferent to the lingering stroke of fingers through her hair. She was good at pretending.

"I am exhausted, but I can't sleep," she confessed.

His face instantly hardened with concern. "Has something happened?"

"Nothing I can pinpoint, but there's a change in the air," she said, leaving out the fact that she'd been too worried about whether or not he'd return to the tunnels to sleep. That was on a need-to-know basis. And right now, he didn't need to know. "Can you sense it?"

"A vampire can't feel magic."

"It's not magic. It's..." Brigette didn't have the exact words to explain the tingle that vibrated through the tunnels. "A buzz, as if there's a new energy." She grimaced. "I can't explain it."

He closed his eyes, as if using his powers to try and detect the mystery buzz. At last, he gave a shake of his head and opened his eyes.

"The only thing I can sense is the coming dawn."

She forgot the strange tingle, instantly intrigued by his words. "What does it feel like?"

"Heavy. As if the air is pressing down on me."

That made sense. Vampires would need to have an early-warning system in place to protect them from the sun.

"I can't feel the dawn, but I can smell it," she murmured.

He arched a brow. "It has a scent?"

Brigette was confused by the question. "Everything has a scent."

"What is it?" he asked, his fingers tracing the line of her jaw.

"Dew-sprinkled grass and a sun-kissed breeze."

A slow, heart-stopping smile curved his lips. "You're a romantic at heart."

Brigette swayed forward, mesmerized by his soft caress. He was barely touching her, but the brittle shell she'd used to protect herself was shattering as if it were as fragile as glass.

Christ. How had she survived so long without feeling his fingertips stroking over her skin. Or the icy breeze wrapping around her like an embrace?

It was the sheer intensity of her hunger that had her sharply pulling away. This need couldn't be natural, could it? It felt like she'd been bewitched.

She moved to press her back against the wall, needing as much space as possible between them. It was either that or she was going to throw him onto the nearby bed and ensure there was absolutely no space between them.

"I'm not a romantic at heart. I'm evil," she rasped. "Or have you forgotten?"

Xi watched her with dark, unfathomable eyes, his hands clenching as if he was forcing himself not react to her fierce rejection.

"You make sure I never forget," he told her. "Why is that?"

She hunched a shoulder. "Just stating a fact."

"No, you're trying to push me away."

"Not very successfully," Brigette retorted, knowing, as the words left her lips, that they were unfair.

Hadn't she reached out to Styx? And hadn't she made it clear that she expected to be included in any investigation? That wasn't even to mention the fact that she'd melted with blatant pleasure each time Xi was near.

Xi, thankfully, didn't point out her hypocrisy. Instead, he continued to study her with a somber expression.

"I'm stubborn enough to decide for myself who I desire as a friend."

It wasn't what Brigette was expecting him to say. Her defenses faltered in confusion. "A friend?"

"It's a place to start," he murmured.

"To start what?"

His lips twitched, then he clearly refused to be lured into discussing the magnetic tug of awareness that sizzled between them. No doubt, he sensed she was ready and eager to shut down that particular conversation.

"Why did you bond with Levet?" He abruptly changed the subject. "He's not the easiest creature to like. In fact, he's a pain in the ass."

Brigette hesitated, then shrugged. She'd rather discuss Levet than her uncomfortable emotions.

Hell, she'd rather discuss beheadings, rabies, or projectile vomiting.

"We have a lot in common," she said.

Xi grimaced. "I can't imagine anything you have in common."

Brigette might have agreed when she had first encountered the tiny demon. Levet had latched onto her when she was trying to escape the mer-folk castle, and she would have killed him if she'd known how. But as they'd traveled through the strange dimensions together, she'd discovered that the gargoyle had suffered far more than any other demon she'd ever met. And yet he was always positive, always eager to help others. He'd changed something deep inside her.

Something that made her…a better female, and a better Were.

It was because of him that she'd come to the tunnels to discover what was happening. In the back of her mind, she knew he would expect her to do the right thing.

"We're both exiled from our people," she told Xi. "Although Levet is treated as an outcast because he looks different, which isn't fair."

Xi was shaking his head before she finished. "Don't let his act of martyrdom fool you. He might be exiled by the gargoyles, but he's managed to worm his way into the affections of every demon female he encounters. Including Darcy, Styx's mate."

Brigette searched Xi's exquisitely carved features. "And that bothers you?"

"It didn't. Now I have an unreasonable desire to strangle him," he admitted in self-derisive tones.

"Why?"

He stepped toward her, his eyes narrowing. "I'll answer your question after you answer mine," he promised.

"What question?"

"Why do you try to keep others at a distance?"

Brigette sent him an annoyed glare. "I thought I made it clear that I don't want to discuss it."

He took another step forward. Not close enough to touch her, but easily wrapping her in the comfort of his icy power.

"Are you afraid of hurting others, or afraid of them hurting you?"

Brigette turned her head away. She didn't want him to the see the wounds that were opening deep inside her.

"I'm not afraid of anything," she muttered.

"Fine." There was a long pause, and Brigette could feel his gaze skimming over each line and curve of her profile. As if searching for the truth etched on her face. "Why do you insist on reminding me you're evil?"

She kept her head turned away. "I can't let myself forget."

"Forget what? Your family?"

She clenched her teeth. Nothing could make her forget her family. Her memories of them were seared into her soul. No. They weren't what she was afraid of forgetting.

"That I hate myself," she breathed.

Xi made a sound deep in his throat. As if he'd taken a punch to the gut. "How long are you going to insist on this self-imposed punishment?"

With an effort, Brigette turned back to meet his smoldering gaze. "Forever."

Chapter 11

Levet reluctantly returned to London with the doulas stone clutched in his hand. Stepping out of the portal, he glanced around the shadowed vault, where Troy was standing guard to ensure nothing could creep through the opening.

At least, he was supposed to be standing guard. Instead, Levet discovered the troll sprawled in a corner, snoring loudly enough to wake the dead. Really. Levet's tail snapped around his feet as he marched forward. So much for the frivolous creature having his back. This imp would have slept through an entire horde of trolls marching into the lair and through the open portal.

Which meant that he had put not only Levet in danger, but Inga as well. That was unforgivable.

Halting next to the imp, Levet kicked him in the leg. "Wake up."

Troy opened his eyes, glaring at Levet. Then, with a sinuous motion, he stretched his arms over his head and yawned.

"Couldn't you see that I was sleeping?" Troy groused, without apology, as he shoved himself to his feet. "Or at least I was, until you so rudely interrupted my dreams. And they were some very fine dreams. There was this exquisite harpy who held me captive during her breeding season who—"

"Not now," Levet interrupted, turning to head across the vault. "I have important matters to attend to."

"How long are you staying in this smelly lair? It's going to take an eternity to get the fishy smell washed off my skin."

Levet wrinkled his snout. The imp wasn't wrong. Dead fish was the sort of stench that tended to linger. And not in a good way. He'd need a good scrubbing to get rid of it.

"*Oui*, it was not pleasant. I was very stern with Styx," Levet assured his companion. "He needs to have the lair thoroughly cleaned. Perhaps fumigated."

Troy laughed. "I'm sure he was delighted to be chastised for his lack of housekeeping skills."

He should have been, Levet told himself. How could the king know what needed to be done if he wasn't told? But, as usual, the leech had been utterly ungrateful for Levet's assistance.

"To be honest, he is a grumpy pants." Levet shrugged. Styx's default setting was grumpy, but now he was uber-grumpy. "Still, he has agreed to contact his brothers to discover which one left his amulet behind in the vault."

Troy strolled to stand next to Levet. "Then what are you doing?"

Levet squatted down, his gaze locked on the footprint. "There is more than one way to pet a cat."

"To what?" Troy made a sound of impatience. "Never mind. Tell me your plans."

"I'm going to use one of the artifacts that was collected by Riven to help me track down the owner of this footprint."

"Really?" Troy knelt beside Levet, his expression suddenly interested. "I've studied the collection, but I've never been allowed to use them. Which artifact do you have?"

Levet held out his hand to reveal the small pebble balanced on his palm. "The doulas stone."

"Of all the powerful items, that's the one you chose?"

"*Oui.*"

Troy snorted. "It looks like something I shook out of my shoe."

Levet clicked his tongue. "Appearances are always deceiving when it comes to magic." He ran a dismissive gaze up and down Troy's spandex-covered body. "Usually, the flashier the object, the less power it possesses."

Troy ignored the blatant insult. His arrogance was far too thick to be dented by the jab.

"What does it do?" he instead asked.

Levet forced himself to shake off his annoyance. It was going to take all his concentration to use the unfamiliar power of the stone.

"It will..." He struggled the think of the proper word. ". . . latch onto the essence of a person and lead me to them."

Troy straightened. "Does it use your magic to make it go?"

"In part."

"Damn."

Levet tilted back his head to study Troy's worried expressions. "What is wrong?"

"Don't take this wrong, but your magic is like a powder keg that explodes without warning and usually does the maximum amount of damage."

Levet clicked his tongue. "You are the rudest imp I have ever known."

Troy shrugged. "Well, it's nice to be the best."

Levet turned back to concentrate on the footprint, carefully laying the stone in the center.

"Stand back," he warned in absent tones.

Troy scurried across the vault. "If you kill me, I'm going to haunt you for the rest of eternity."

Stuck for the rest of eternity with this imp? Levet shuddered. He'd received many threats over the long centuries. But none of them had ever sent a chill of terror down his spine.

* * * *

Xi leaned against the wall, studying the beautiful, stubborn Were stretched on her narrow bed. She had her arms folded behind her head and her eyes closed, but he knew she wasn't asleep. There was an energy that hummed around her like a jet engine about to take off. Still, for the past hour, he'd allowed her to pretend.

It wasn't just because he'd sensed she needed time to gather her composure. He'd poked and prodded until she'd confessed ancient wounds she'd kept buried for centuries. Of course, she wanted some space from his prying. But her silence gave him the opportunity to consider what she'd confessed.

It was one thing to battle against Brigette's belief that she was impervious to the need for a pack. She'd been alone for a long time, and it would be only natural that she would be wary of letting anyone get close.

But now Xi understood that it was far more complicated than that.

She didn't push people away because she was scared of being judged for her past. She did it to punish herself.

So how could he convince her that she'd suffered enough?

He wasn't sure that he knew how. Unlike Viper, or even that ridiculous gargoyle, he wasn't really a people person. He'd spent long centuries wandering the world alone. Then several more centuries as a Raven. It made him a formidable warrior, but he sucked at social skills.

Dwelling on a way to convince her that it was possible to overcome her grinding sense of guilt, Xi stiffened as Brigette slowly opened her eyes.

"I can feel you staring at me," she said in dry tone.

Moving forward, Xi perched on the edge of the bed. "What will you do when we've defeated Maryam?"

She scooted to a seated position, her back pressed against the cement wall. "You sound very sure that we'll succeed."

"I don't doubt it for a second."

Her lips twitched. "Arrogant."

"Confident," he corrected her. "So what will you do?"

"Return home." She shrugged. "It's not like I have anywhere else to go."

"That's what I used to think. Until Styx."

She hesitated, and Xi feared that she would ignore the opening he'd offered her. Then curiosity overcame her reluctance to offer him encouragement.

"Because of your past?" she asked.

Xi nodded, hiding his relief. He hoped that revealing his own journey to redemption, Brigette might see a future that didn't involve endless penance for her sins.

"Like most newly turned vampires, I was heady with my power," he admitted.

Brigette rolled her eyes. "As I said. Arrogant."

"Perhaps," he conceded. The truth was that he'd been puffed up with conceit. He'd truly believed that he was blessed above all other vampires. A blood-sucking superstar. "At first I didn't fully understand my unique skills. I knew I could easily hide from others and sneak up on my prey."

She tilted her head, her hair shimmering like fire despite the darkness that shrouded the room.

"Is it like a damper spell?" she asked.

Xi turned to fully face her, his hip pressed against her thigh. The heat of her skin seared through his jeans. Delicious.

"It's hard to explain. Just as you can smell the dawn without thinking about it, I can draw my presence deep inside me."

She arched a brow. "Like a turtle?"

"That's as good an analogy as any other." He smiled before his amusement faded. He never discussed the past. Not since he'd become a Raven. What good did it do to dwell on things that couldn't be changed? But he'd do whatever was necessary to prevent Brigette from spending the rest of eternity alone in her festering village.

"As I gained command over my powers, I realized that I could become virtually invisible," he continued.

"I knew you were Batman."

Xi touched the marks on the sides of his head. They weren't traditional tattoos. Instead, they'd appeared shortly after he'd been turned into a vampire. His sire had claimed they were the souls of his ancestors and that they offered him their protection. He thought it was more likely they were a visible display of his talents.

He could travel through the world as silent and deadly as a snake.

"Not as cool as Batman, but my clan chief often used me to spy on rival clans or to rescue prisoners being held captive," he told her. "I swiftly earned a place of honor among my people."

She studied him, the tension easing from her beautiful face as she became lost in his story.

"You make it sound like a bad thing."

"It only made me cockier."

"Shocking."

"My sire warned me that my belief that I was impervious to danger would bite me in the ass." He shook his head in resignation. His sire had been a unique male. Not only did he take in the children he created, but he'd personally trained them to become warriors for his clan. He'd been as close to a father as a vampire could get. "And he was right."

Brigette, surprisingly, didn't take the opportunity to make another dig at his conceit.

"You said you snuck into a rival clan?"

"A stupid stunt. But looking back now, I realize I was manipulated by a traitor."

"Another vampire?"

Xi clenched his hands. The familiar pain rushed through him as he remembered that fateful night. He'd been strolling through the massive castle that served as their lair, looking for entertainment. When he wasn't on guard duty, it was all too easy to become bored.

A fatal failing when combined with his oversized ego.

"A beautiful vampire named Emeline," he forced himself to continue. "She dared me to bring her the crown from the rival clan chief."

Brigette parted her lips, but whatever she was about to say was forgotten as she was struck by his words.

"Vampire clan chiefs wear a crown?"

Xi shuddered. Anyone who tried to stick a crown on Styx's head would find himself nailed to a tree and left for the sun.

"Only Drayson," Xi assured her. "He used to host massive banquets just so he could prance around with his golden crown and fortune in jewels attached to various parts of his body."

"He sounds...flamboyant."

"He was an egotistical prick, but he was also a brutal leader with a cunning ambition." Xi's jaw tightened. When he was young, he was stupid enough to judge a demon by his appearance. He'd allowed Drayson's outrageous behavior to lull him into a false sense of security. "I was a fool to underestimate him."

She studied him with an unreadable expression. "You decided to steal the crown to impress Emeline?"

He jerked, caught off guard. Brigette had never met Emeline or she wouldn't ask that question.

"No."

"But you said she dared you."

"She did. But I had no interest in her."

Brigette narrowed her eyes. She clearly didn't believe him. "Even though she was beautiful?"

Xi shuddered. "She was also a cold, humorless bitch who made my flesh crawl from the night she arrived in the lair."

Brigette's long lashes lowered over her eyes. Was she trying to hide her emotion? Before he could decide, she was glancing back up at him.

"So why did you do it?" she demanded.

He didn't want to answer. Not just because the memory of that night still haunted his dreams, but because he was ashamed.

"My bloated pride," he grudgingly forced himself to admit the truth. "I thought it was a game to pillage objects from various demons. Over the years, I'd stolen treasure chests filled with rubies from a troll chieftain, bags of gold from a band of goblins, and an enchanted sword from the local tribe of wood sprites. My increasing mound of loot impressed my clan and frankly kept me entertained. When Emeline challenged me, it never occurred to me that it was a trap."

"Were you captured?"

Xi's fangs ached. He would never forget the moment the silver leash had been snapped around his neck. Or the faces of the bastards who'd tied him behind a horse to drag him miles across the frozen ground. The fact that he'd been denied his revenge only made the memory more difficult to bear.

"Yes." He managed to keep his lingering fury out of his voice, but nothing could hide the ice that was crawling over the cement walls. It wasn't hard to determine a vampire's mood. Ice bad. No ice...well, there's a chance no one is about to die. "I barely reached the edge of our territory when I was ambushed. And chained to a tree."

She hesitated, as if debating whether to probe for more details of his capture. Then she shook her head, no doubt sensing that the memory still caused him pain.

"That doesn't explain how you were responsible for your clan being destroyed."

"Emeline told my chief that she'd witnessed me being kidnapped. She implied that if they hurried, I could be rescued." Another layer of ice coated the walls. "My sire sent his warriors to rescue me."

"Leaving your lair unprotected."

"Exactly. By the time the warriors realized they'd been lured away, it was too late." The words threatened to stick in his throat. Possibly because he'd never said them out loud. "They returned to find our lair burned to the ground, along with their mates and our sire. They had no choice but to accept defeat."

"Did they release you?"

"No. I managed to escape."

"You didn't return to your clan?"

He had. After he'd escaped, he'd been forced to find a nearby hovel to hide for the day and heal. But once the sun had set, he'd raced back to the castle. At the time, he had no idea his people had been attacked, not until he'd arrived at a smoldering pile of rubble. Wandering through the wreckage, he'd struggled to imagine what had happened. Finally, one of the warriors who'd managed to survive the battle revealed the brutal truth.

Because of him, the clan had been destroyed.

"They didn't consider me a member any longer," he said. "In fact, they insisted I leave. I don't blame them."

"I do." Astonishingly, Brigette reached out to lay a hand over his clenched fist. Heat blasted through him, easing the agonizing ache at the center of his soul. He desperately wanted to grasp her hand and press it to his lips. Or tug her closer so he could wrap her in his arms. Thankfully, he was a skilled hunter. This was the first time she'd initiated a touch, and he wasn't about to do anything that might cause her to pull away. "It wasn't your fault," she continued. "Emeline was the traitor."

"It was my arrogance that allowed her to so easily dupe me. A better vampire would have ignored her dare. Or recognized her danger to the clan," Xi insisted.

"Say whatever you want. It wasn't your fault."

His lips twitched at her stubborn insistence. He'd ripped open the wounds of his past to prove that the worst sins could be overcome. The last thing he'd expected was to have Brigette lessen the guilt that still gnawed deep inside him.

"You sound like Styx," he murmured.

"I just know the difference between poor decisions and betrayal."

"Intent doesn't matter. The outcome was the same." He leaned toward her, absorbing her rich musk. The scent was intoxicating. "The past is the past."

She scowled, but she didn't argue. And even better, she didn't pull her hand away. "Did Styx tell you that?" she instead asked.

Xi shoved away the dark memories of his former clan and instead recalled his meeting with Styx. The huge warrior hadn't been the Anasso yet, but his thunderous power had made him a natural leader. He'd taken in Xi when he'd been lost and broken, keeping him under his wing until Xi was strong enough to stand on his own.

It was a gift that Xi could never fully repay.

"No. He said to get my head out of my ass and start doing something productive with my life," Xi said dryly.

"That's when you became one of his Ravens?"

"No, that took much longer." Xi had pledged his life to Styx centuries ago, but it hadn't been until the previous Anasso was destroyed that he had asked Xi to become one of his private guards. "Only his most trusted warriors are allowed to join the Ravens."

She slowly nodded, easily sensing how much it had meant to Xi to be a part of the elite guards.

"So now you have a new clan," she murmured.

"More importantly, I have a new family. We might be occasionally dysfunctional—"

"Occasionally?"

"Okay, we're often dysfunctional," he conceded. He wasn't so blinded by loyalty that he was immune to the provocations, outrageous dares, and sporadic squabbles between the Ravens. You couldn't have a group of alpha warriors working together without a few broken bones. And sometimes a cracked skull. "But being a part of Styx's clan has healed a part of me that I thought had been destroyed forever."

She turned away, sliding off the bed. Xi would have been disappointed if he hadn't seen the aching loss that darkened her eyes.

She longed for a family. Even if she refused to admit it, even to herself.

"Most of the demons should be settled for the day," she said in gruff tones, heading for the door. "Time to return to the hunt."

Chapter 12

For Brigette, the day proved to be another frustrating search through the endless sprawl of tunnels. She could smell activity in a few of the side passages, but whatever had been done was now tightly wrapped in layers of illusion. Without the help of a fey creature, it was impossible to know what was hidden.

Of course, she didn't need any help in sensing the tingle of electricity in the air. It was as if the demons were suddenly on edge. The question was, why?

The frustration, combined with her hyperawareness of the potential for danger, had Brigette fully focused on her surroundings. No doubt a good thing. The last thing she wanted was the opportunity to dwell on the tall, gorgeous vamp walking soundlessly at her side.

It would be all too easy to lie to herself. To pretend that Xi's past gave him an insight into her treachery. And that his determination to see the good in her somehow washed away her sins.

It's what she wanted to do. How wonderful would it be to believe that her past could be washed away and she could just be a normal female in lust with the sexiest male she'd ever encountered? Maybe she could even consider leaving her blighted village and…

No. She abruptly slammed shut the mental door on the images of her and Xi together in a cozy cottage. Even if she wasn't damned for her betrayal, there was no way she was going to have a happily-ever-after with Xi. He was a Raven. A devoted personal guard to the King of the Vampires. He wasn't searching for a mate and a quiet existence in some remote lair. And neither was she.

Was she?

Threading their way back through the side tunnels as the sun set and the demons began to stir, Brigette halted when she noticed something off about the area.

Tilting back her head, she took a deep sniff. Nothing. She stepped back, peering down the nearest tunnel.

There was an icy breeze as Xi moved to stand next to her. "What's wrong?"

"The warriors that usually block this area are gone."

"Is this where Maryam's rooms are?"

"No. I'm not sure what's in there. They were always careful to keep it heavily guarded."

Xi nodded. "A perfect opportunity to see what they're hiding."

She grabbed his arm. "Or a trap."

"Quite likely." He tried to pull his arm from her grasp. "Stay here."

"No." She dug in her fingers.

He glanced down, obviously puzzled by her refusal to leap at the golden opportunity. "There had to be a reason Maryam kept it guarded. We need to find out why."

Any other night, Brigette would have agreed. She'd strolled through this intersection of tunnels a dozen times, hoping to get a peek at what they were hiding. Now she stubbornly shook her head.

"It doesn't feel right."

"Magic?"

She sniffed the air. Most spells had some sort of scent. Still nothing. "I'm not sure. It's just…" She hunched her shoulders. "Funky."

"Funky." He ached a brow. "Is that a technical term?"

"It's a frustrating, what-the-hell-is-going-on term."

Xi glanced toward the shadowed tunnel, his brief amusement fading as he used his own powers to search for danger. At last, he firmly pulled away from her grasp.

"As I said, there's only one way to find out. Stay here."

Brigette made a sound of annoyance. "You're not in charge, vampire."

"No, but I'm the sensible choice," he insisted. "I can be in and out before anyone realizes I'm there."

"You can't sense magic. We both go." She stepped forward, convinced that she'd made her point.

The aggravating leech stepped directly in her path. "One of us needs to keep watch in case things go south."

Her lips parted, but she couldn't deny the truth of his words. Someone had to signal an alarm if the guards returned. Or, worse, to go for help if this turned out to be a trap.

"You are..."

He stepped forward, cupping her face in his hands. "I know. It's part of my charm."

"That's not what I was going to say."

He gazed down at her upturned face, his attention lingering on her parted lips. "Then it's a good thing I did."

Brigette told herself to yank herself away from his cool touch. Or knock away his hands. Or even step backward. Instead, she swayed toward his hard body, as if she was drawn there by some unseen magic.

It was those dark, mysterious eyes, she silently acknowledged. They captured and held her like a magnetic force.

"You're trying to distract me."

A teasing smile curved his lips. "No, if I was trying to distract you, I'd do this."

Brigette's heart thundered in her chest as she watched his head slowly lower. The glow of distant lights filtered through the tunnel, emphasizing the stark perfection of his features and glinting off the sharp tips of his fangs.

"Xi." His name tumbled from her lips in a soft plea.

"I'll be back," he murmured, brushing his mouth over her forehead and down the length of her nose.

The cool caress sent a shiver a pleasure through Brigette. With an effort, she lifted her hands and pressed them flat against his chest. There was a voice whispering in the back of her mind that they were risking exposure with each passing second.

"Go."

His lips moved to the corner of her mouth, the edge of his fang pressing against her soft flesh. The icy male scent of him swirled through the air, cloaking her in temptation.

"I'm going," he whispered.

Her fingers curled to press her nails into his flesh. With one good push, she could have him pinned to the wall and his clothes stripped off his slender body. Then, wrapping her legs around his waist, she could ride him while those fangs sank deep into her neck...

"Xi," she groaned.

"I'm gone," he said, pressing a lingering kiss on her lips.

It was more than a promise of pleasure to come. It was a pledge of possession. As if he was claiming her as his own.

Or maybe that was just her befuddled imagination, she acknowledged, as Xi turned to silently disappear into the nearby tunnel. Maybe she wanted to be claimed by the fascinating vampire.

Dangerously lost in her troubled thoughts, Brigette nearly missed the scent of an approaching demon. With a muttered curse, she turned to head away from the opening, blocking Roban's path. The male Were might not be able to smell Xi's presence, but he could see him if he happened to peer into the tunnel.

Roban came to a startled halt, his green eyes flashed with the gold. "Female," he growled.

Brigette folded her arms over her chest. The male was larger than her with the power of his inner wolf, but he didn't intimidate her. He thought he was a badass with his shaved hair and the leather pants he was wearing, but he'd never confronted true evil.

Just another poser.

"I have a name." She stepped toward him. "Use it."

He ignored her command. "I've been searching for you."

"Why?"

A humorless smile twisted his lips. "Maryam has started preparations for the next phase of our grand plan."

Brigette snorted, her expression mocking. Inside, however, a tingle of alarm spread through her. This male detested her. More than that, he resented the fact that she wasn't prepared to become a martyr to the rebellion. If Maryam was going to send someone to include Brigette in the plans, it wouldn't be this male.

So what the hell was he up to?

"You mean there's more to the grand plan than a bunch of ragtag demons setting fires and collapsing roofs?" she taunted.

He bared his elongated teeth. "Those have been nothing more than the prelude."

"A prelude to what?"

"To our true purpose."

Brigette rolled her eyes. "Is that purpose to bore me to death?"

"The end of the ruling elite," he snapped.

As much as Brigette wanted to remind the idiot they were supposed to be preventing the demon-world from being enslaved by the evil Styx, not making a sleazy power grab, she forced herself to swallow her words. She'd already sensed the buzz in the air. As if the horde of demons were starting to prepare for something. Something big. She couldn't let her desire to aggravate the male overcome her need to discover what was happening.

"How do you intend to do that?" she demanded.

"Come with me, and I'll tell you."

Brigette hesitated. Roban wasn't subtle. The invitation might as well have *trap* written all over it. But she couldn't deny his request without creating suspicion. Plus, there was the danger that Roban might begin to question what Brigette was doing in this isolated area of the tunnels.

She needed to get the Were away so Xi could continue his search.

"Okay." She waved toward the passage behind him. "Lead the way."

He glanced over her shoulder, almost as if he was wondering why she was so anxious to head in the opposite direction. Then he shrugged and turned to lead her through the darkness.

Brigette's instinct was to walk several paces behind the male. She wanted plenty of opportunity to react to whatever nasty plan he'd devised. Unfortunately, the only way to probe for information was to pretend that she had no idea she was strolling into a trap.

Walking next to Roban, she pretended to smother a yawn. "You're supposed to be telling me about your plans."

"Maryam's plan," he sharply reminded her. "The rest of us are just her disciples."

Disciples? Yeesh. The female vampire was letting this rebellion stuff go to her head if she'd started referring to her collection of outcasts as disciples.

"Whatever." Brigette shrugged. "What's the plan?"

Roban glanced in her direction, his expression impossible to read. "We have spent the past few weeks importing large quantities of C-4."

Brigette furrowed her brow. She'd spent centuries rarely leaving the isolation of her abandoned village. It left large gaps in her knowledge of the current culture. But even as her lips parted to demand an explanation, she realized that she'd heard the term before.

"Isn't that some sort of human explosive?"

"Yes."

Brigette's brow remained furrowed as they turned into a passage that was thick with mold, as if no one had been through here in years.

"Explosions won't kill most demons," she pointed out the obvious.

His expression was complacent. "We've had them...enhanced."

"I don't know what that means."

Roban clicked his tongue, as if she was unbearably stupid. "The only way to truly ensure we got rid of our oppressors was to create a weapon they couldn't fight against."

Brigette shoved her hands into the front pockets of her jeans. It was that or punch the male in the throat.

Until this moment, she would have bet good money that nothing could be more annoying than spending five centuries confined with an evil beast from a hell dimension. But Roban was proving she was wrong. You didn't have to be a malevolent spirit to be a gigantic pain in the ass.

"You intend to blow them up?" she asked between clenched teeth.

He rolled his eyes. "Nothing so mundane."

"Then why do you want C-4?"

"We've wrapped the explosives in a powerful mortem curse." His voice was smug. "When the C-4 goes boom, it will spread the hexed shards. Any creature inside or near the lair will be destroyed."

His words chilled Brigette to the bone. After spending time with Maryam in the tunnels, she'd started to hope that the woman was all talk and no action. It was easy to hide in the tunnels and send out small bands of demons to create chaos. It was another to strike out and incur the wrath of the most powerful vampires in the world.

But Roban's words proved that she not only intended to try and take down the clan chiefs, but that she had a sophisticated plan already in place. A powerful curse could destroy any demon, even a vampire. And to have it attached to a combustible object that could spread it through the air...

She had never heard of combining human technology with magic, so she couldn't begin to calculate how many lives would be snuffed out.

Too many.

She swallowed the sudden lump in her throat. "How are they triggered?"

Roban shrugged. "Magic."

They turned into a passage that was barely more than a hole dug in the earth. There was no cement and less than a handful of timber supports to keep it from collapsing.

Brigette, however, ignored the tons of dirt waiting to fall on her head. She was far more concerned with how she was going to halt the potential apocalypse.

"What kind of magic?" she demanded.

Roban managed to look even more smug. As if he was personally responsible for the lethal devices.

"That's the beauty. Each lair has been planted with explosives that are wrapped with different spells," he told her. "Some are designed to explode when a word of power is spoken. Others are set to explode on a certain date and time. The ones that guard these tunnels are designed to be triggered by intruders. Or by Maryam leaving the lair."

She sent him a sharp glance. "She's left before, and nothing exploded."

"The layers of magic were a recent addition. *Very* recent."

Brigette suddenly realized what was behind the illusions that she could sense throughout the tunnels. Crap. Where was Maryam and just how soon was she planning to leave?

"So what's the next phase of the grand plan?" Brigette demanded, her thoughts churning through various strategies to get to Xi and escape the tunnels without being noticed. "Am I supposed to set the bombs in Styx's lair?"

"The bombs are already set."

Brigette blinked. She'd overheard both Maryam and Roban whisper about triggers and surprises and vague threats to the clan chiefs. She'd even seen the map in Maryam's office. But to be told in gloating tones that countless vampires and lesser demons were about to be massacred was like a physical blow.

Suddenly, the need to escape from the tunnels wasn't just about survival for her and Xi. It was about being able to warn Styx that they were in danger.

"They're set to go off?" she forced herself to ask.

"Of course. We have them spread around the world. Along with a very special one for Chiron. As soon as Ulric walks through the door of his Vegas casino..." Roban smiled, spreading his hands as he made the sound of a massive blast. "Boom."

"Why Chiron?" Brigette demanded. She already knew the answer, but she had to keep the dog talking long enough to formulate a way to get away from him and locate Xi.

"He turned his back on the rebels."

"Maryam told me it was her decision to leave Chiron."

"She still considered herself a rebel, until Chiron agreed to kiss Styx's ass. He betrayed everyone who'd suffered at the hands of the Anasso."

"The old king is dead."

"It doesn't matter." Roban slowed his pace. "They're all the same."

"Even the King of Weres?"

A low growl rumbled in Roban's throat, a sudden heat blasted through the air. Was he nursing a personal grudge against the King of Weres? Or just a general hatred toward authority?

"Especially the King of Weres," he snarled.

Hmm. That seemed personal.

About to demand to know what his problem was with their king, Brigette belatedly realized they'd come to the end of the passage. In front of them was a dead end.

"Why are we here?"

He turned to face her. "I have something you need to see."

"Careful, dog." Brigette narrowed her eyes, pulling her dagger from the holster at her lower back. It never occurred to her that Roban might a physical threat to her. "You show me anything I don't want to see, and I'll chop it off."

He wrinkled his nose, as if he was morally offended by her words. "Relax, female, I don't screw traitors."

The sneering words rolled off Brigette. She couldn't care less about his opinion. Of course, she wasn't above taunting him with his hypocrisy.

"You know why you hate me so much, don't you, Roban?" she drawled.

"Because you betrayed your pack."

She waved her dagger beneath his nose. "Because you're afraid you are just like me."

The musk of his wolf choked the air a second before his hands reached up to shove her backward.

"I'm nothing like you, bitch."

Caught off guard, Brigette stumbled backward. She expected to slam against the dirt wall and instinctively braced herself. Once she regained her balance, she fully intended to carve the male into tiny bits of Were. She'd learned all she needed to know about the rebels' ultimate plan. Now it was time for the traitor to die.

But she didn't slam into the wall. Instead, she continued to tumble backward, landing flat on her back in the middle of a cage. The wall of the passage had been an illusion disguising the shallow alcove where the cage had been tucked away.

Shit. She'd known this was a trap, and yet she'd allowed herself to be led to it like a lamb to the slaughter.

The air was knocked from her lungs as she gazed up at the silver bars above her head. Struggling to breathe, Brigette forced herself to her feet even as Roban slammed shut the door of the cell. He smiled, reaching into his pocket to pull out a small box that he attached to the lock.

"What are you doing?" she snapped, trying to pretend that panic was thundering though her.

Roban eyed her through the bars, clearly pleased to see her caged. "Making sure you don't have the chance to stab Maryam in the back."

"Does she know that you're doing this?"

Roban shrugged. "Maryam, on occasion, allows her heart to rule her head. That's when I need to step in and protect her."

"Typical male," she jeered. "Thinking you know what's best for a female."

His jaw tightened, as if she'd touched a nerve. A minor victory as he stepped back and flashed a taunting smile.

"I've sacrificed everything to be with Maryam as she leads this rebellion. One way or another, I intend to see her succeed." He eyed her behind the bars. "Starting with ensuring a quick trip for you to the netherworld."

Brigette shuddered. Roban knew nothing of the netherworld. Or the grinding agony of being trapped in the evil darkness that had held Brigette captive.

"I've survived worse."

He smiled with an evil anticipation. "I put a bomb on the door, so if you open it, you'll die. But if you don't open it before Maryam leaves the tunnel, you'll die. I win either way." He gave an airy wave of his hand before he headed down the passage. "Bye, bye, Brigette. The world will be a better place without you in it."

Her heart sank to her toes as she glanced toward the small box attached to the lock.

"Bastard."

Chapter 13

Styx stepped out of the portal and glanced around the remote landscape. He'd never been in Iceland, but he realized that the rugged terrain, with its sharply angled mountains and impressive glaciers, was a perfect spot for a vampire who wanted to live in seclusion. Plus there was a stunning view of the nearby bay.

Cautiously allowing his senses to spread outward, Styx made sure there were no hidden dangers. The scent of ice sprites floated in the air, along with a nearby den of minks. And, more distantly, the scent of copper.

Ah. Just what he was hoping to smell.

Turning his head, he spoke to the imp on the opposite side of the portal. "Leave this open," he commanded, his gaze skimming over the craggy rocks and tufts of purple flowers that filled the cracks between them. At the top of the nearest hill, he could see a narrow opening. "There's a better-than-average chance I'm going to have to make a quick getaway."

Confident his servant would keep the portal ready for a speedy retreat, Styx adjusted the large sword strapped across his back and started to climb the rocks.

Over the past hours, he'd visited two of his former brothers. One in Taiwan and another in Peru. Neither had been able to shed light on who might be responsible for manipulating Maryam into creating a rebellion. On the other hand, he'd been able to scratch them off the list of possible suspects.

Now on to the next.

Reaching the opening in the volcanic rock at the top of the hill, he squeezed into the barren cave, a task that would have been easier if he wasn't so wide. Or so tall. And didn't have a sword the size of a javelin.

Scraping his leather pants and detaching patches of skin, Styx at last stood in the middle of the cramped space. He could still smell copper, which meant he was in the right place, but there was obviously an illusion that covered the opening to the male's hidden lair.

"Locke," he called out, although he didn't doubt for a second the vampire had sensed his arrival the moment he stepped out of the portal.

His suspicion was confirmed when a low, husky male voice floated through the darkness.

"Take one more step and you're trespassing."

Styx held up his hands in a gesture of peace. "I'm just here to ask a few questions."

"Not interested."

"It will only take a minute."

"Not. Interested."

Styx shook his head. The only thing his former brothers had in common was the fact that they were as stubborn as hell. Oh, and epically lethal.

"I'm afraid I'm going to have to insist," Styx said, the ground trembling beneath his feet as he released a hint of his power.

There was the sound of a footstep, and Locke stepped through the illusion at the back of the cave.

The ancient vampire was shorter than Styx, and less broad through the shoulders, but physical size had no bearing on the power a vampire possessed. The very air snapped and sizzled with electric shocks as Locke entered the space.

Styx shivered as the unseen current crawled over him. It didn't hurt, but it was a warning.

Lowering his hands, Styx studied his old friend. Locke had been with the former Anasso before Styx had joined the clan. The older male had always been standoffish, preferring to spend long chunks of time by himself. Styx assumed it had something to do with the star-shaped burn on the side of his neck. It was whispered among the Ravens that Locke's sire had enjoyed torturing his children by leaving them tied to the floor and opening tiny holes to let in sunlight. And that the former Anasso had rescued him.

That would certainly explain the male's devotion to the King of the Vampires, even when it became obvious the king had rotted his brain to a deranged mush.

Beyond the scar, however, he was as perfect as every other vampire. He had dark gold hair that was chopped at his shoulders and pale blue eyes rimmed with gold. His features were pale and sharply carved. He was dressed in a black Henley and jeans, along with heavy black boots.

"You think because you crowned yourself the Anasso you can come here and order me around?" Locke demanded, strolling forward.

"I'm not here as the Anasso. I'm here as your brother."

Locke arched a brow. "A little late, isn't it...brother?"

Styx nodded without hesitation. He had a thousand reasons for not reaching out to the former Ravens.

He'd been overwhelmed by his new duties. He'd taken a mate who was deliciously distracting. He was mourning the loss of their former master... blah, blah, blah.

The truth was, he'd been ashamed. Not for killing the Anasso. The bastard had gone beyond the point of salvation. But for not having had the balls to destroy him sooner.

It would have saved a lot of pain and distress for all of them.

"Yes." He resisted the urge to reach out. "It is late. I'm sorry."

The older vampire made a sound of disgust. "Are we supposed to kiss and make nice now?"

"You try to kiss me and my mate will rip out your heart and eat it. But we could make nice."

The electricity sizzled over Styx, but his attempt to lighten the mood had at least eased the promise of death from Locke's expression. Progress, right?

"Why are you here?" the male asked.

Styx went straight to the heart of his concern. There was no need for prolonged explanations. Locke wouldn't be interested.

"There's someone who entered our master's old lair in London to steal the scrolls he kept in his vault."

"Why would anyone steal the scrolls?"

"They're passing them off as proclamations from me," Styx explained.

"Why?"

Styx felt a stab of annoyance. He wasn't a perfect king. Honestly, he didn't even want to be king. But he wasn't crazy, or cruel, or even greedy. It was freaking aggravating to have a horde of demons lurking in the tunnels and plotting to dethrone him.

Or worse.

"I suspect they're being used to fuel enough anger against me to start a revolution."

Locke blinked. Obviously, he was caught off guard by Styx's words. Then he shrugged. "Am I supposed to care?"

"Probably not, but I'm hoping you can help me figure out who could have gotten into the vault."

There was a long, tense silence. Styx stiffened, prepared for the lightning strike that Locke could create with his power. Thankfully, there was nothing more than a prickle of pain as the male controlled his burst of anger.

"Are you asking if it was me?" Locke finally demanded.

Styx shook his head. He'd already gone to the two most likely vampires to betray him. Now he was seeking information.

"No, you aren't subtle, Locke. If you wanted me off the throne, you would walk up to my lair and chop off my head."

The vampire considered Styx's words. "I'd be more likely to put a stake through your heart. Your neck is as thick as a tree trunk. I'm not sure I have a long enough sword."

Something deep inside Styx eased. After the death of the Anasso, he'd slammed shut the door on his past. He didn't want to drown in the memories of all he had lost. Besides, with Darcy at his side, he was far more interested in his future.

But a part of him missed the males he'd considered his family. It was as if a piece of himself was missing.

He was careful to keep his inner thoughts to himself. This wasn't the time to hope for more than information.

"Which other brothers might want me destroyed?"

"Lago. He hated everyone."

That had been Styx's first guess as well. The younger vampire had been a fiery, reckless warrior who'd worshipped the previous Anasso. And he'd personally blamed Styx for the king's death.

"I just left his lair," Styx said.

"And?"

"He followed in the path of our master."

Locke stiffened at Styx's grim tone. "He's dead?"

"Worse. He succumbed to madness after feeding from the veins of drug users." It was the one way a vampire could feel the effects of drugs or alcohol. Unfortunately, it also putrefied their brains. "He's now sealed in a cage and kept alive by a handful of devoted servants."

Locke grimaced. "Harsh."

It was, but it was also the only way to keep the vampire from going on a crazed rampage.

"I also visited Adolfo," Styx said. Adolfo hadn't been as rabid in his devotion to the previous Anasso, but he'd never made a secret of the fact that he thought he should be next in line for the throne. Even if that meant sacrificing Styx. "He has a new mate and the start of a clan in Peru. He seems content with his life." Styx held Locke's gaze. "Anyone else that might want me dead?"

The male started to shake his head, then seemed to be struck by a sudden thought. "Ian."

Styx made a sound of surprise. The massive, brutally violent vampire would have been first on his list of suspects if he hadn't received word a year ago that the male had perished in a battle with a tribe of trolls.

"I thought he'd been destroyed."

"So did I. It was a rumor his servants put out, but six months ago, he arrived here—uninvited, I might add—wanting to talk," Locke said.

A thick dread crawled through Styx. Of all the brothers, Ian was the most unpredictable. He'd been unstable for centuries, and it was only because he was a ruthless fighter who had no fear that the old Anasso had allowed him to remain in the clan.

"Talk about what?"

"I don't have a clue." Locked folded his arms over his chest. "I told him to go away."

"Did he?"

"Yep." A humorless smile twisted Locke's lips. "Unlike some vampires, he didn't intrude where he wasn't wanted."

Styx shrugged. "I've intruded a lot of places I wasn't wanted."

"Truer words have never been spoken."

Styx ignored the insult. "Ian would have the motive to knock me from the throne. He never forgave me for killing our master."

"No. He was very vocal about his desire to put a stake through your heart," Locke readily agreed.

Styx grimaced. Why the hell had he agreed to become the Anasso? Being the leader was nothing more than a pain in the ass. Plus, the pay sucked. If he had any sense at all, he'd pack up Darcy, and they'd head to some remote cave. Maybe here in Iceland...It was isolated enough, and the views were spectacular.

The thought of Darcy sliced through his heart. He wasn't walking away from the throne. His sense of duty wouldn't let him. So the sooner he could deal with this latest disaster, the sooner he could have his mate back in his bed.

"Do you know where I can find him?"

Locke shook his head. "After the death of the Anasso, he moved from one lair to another."

Of course he did. Styx ground his fangs together. "Great."

Locke held out his hand as Styx turned to leave. "There was one thing."

Styx glanced over his shoulder. "What?"

"He told me to prepare."

"Prepare for what?"

"The resurrection."

Styx frowned. "The resurrection of what?"

"I have no idea."

The two males exchanged a long glance, and Styx felt a pang of regret. Until this moment, he hadn't realized how much he missed having this vampire in his life.

"Locke."

"What?"

"It was good to see you," Styx murmured. "My door is always open."

Some undefinable emotion darkened the pale eyes. Then, with a sharp shake of his head, Locke stepped back and disappeared behind the illusion.

"Goodbye...brother."

Styx turned to leave.

He still needed answers. And he wasn't going to find them standing around.

* * * *

Xi flattened against the wall as he came to the end of the tunnel. So far, he hadn't discovered anything that might require guards to keep it protected. Of course, if there was some sort of magical artifact, or if it was hidden behind an illusion, he wouldn't be able to sense it.

Now, however, he'd at last found something of interest. Peering through the opening at the end of the tunnel, he could see a wide octagon with a ladder in the center of the cement floor. Above the ladder was a large grate that offered an access point for human workers.

Standing in the center of the space was a large mongrel female. She was the size of a troll with broad shoulders, but her features were oddly delicate, as if she had some fey blood. She was dressed in black from head to toe. Was she hoping to fade into the shadows? Good luck with that. As Xi watched, the creature turned when a female male vampire entered the open space.

Maryam.

Xi tightened his power around himself, ensuring that his presence was hidden. This was a perfect opportunity to discover what the female was plotting.

"Have you seen Roban?" Maryam demanded as she came to a halt in front of the ladder. Like the mongrel, she was dressed completely in black, with her blond hair pulled into a tight braid. "He was supposed to meet me here as soon as the sun set."

"He said he had something to take care of."

The temperature dropped as Maryam struggled to contain her temper. Xi silently watched the ice crawl across the floor, creating fractures in the cement. Damn. The female vampire was more powerful than he'd expected. He needed to warn Styx.

"One of these days, I'm going to wring that dog's neck," the vampire muttered.

The larger female took a careful step to the side to avoid the layer of ice. Clearly, she was accustomed to dealing with Maryam's temper.

"Do you want to delay the evacuation?"

"No." Maryam planted her hands on her hips, tapping a polished nail against her belt. "We need to get started. Tell the first group that's headed to the airport to be ready to leave by midnight. They should all have their tickets. I staggered the flights depending on where their target is located, but I want them all at the terminal. The next group needs to wait thirty minutes before they leave. Once those who are flying to their destination are gone, I want the first group of drivers to start leaving. The cars I rented are parked in the empty warehouse near the wharf, with the keys under the seats. Those who will remain on foot will be the last to leave."

The larger female made a sound of impatience. "Is it really necessary to stagger all the groups? It's going to take hours to get everyone out."

Another layer of ice formed, creating more fractures in the cement. Xi stepped back. He didn't want to be close to enough to get trapped in a cave-in.

"We've been over this plan a dozen times," Maryam snapped.

"Yes, but…"

"You don't think the Anasso or one of his goons is going to notice if a couple hundred demons come streaming out of the tunnels at the same time?"

The mongrel hunched her shoulders. "It's too late for him to do anything about it."

"Only an idiot would underestimate Styx," Maryam snapped. "A dead idiot. Follow the plan, or I'll find someone who will."

The mongrel offered a hasty bow. She might be six inches taller and a hundred pounds heavier, but she was no match for a vampire.

"Yes, master."

Maryam whirled on her heel and retraced her steps back to the tunnel. Xi watched her disappear from view, debating whether to follow her. If he could destroy the female now, it might halt the rebellion. Then he shook his head. The evacuation had already been ordered. He didn't know what that meant, but he was certain it couldn't be good. Besides, there was a weird urgency to return to Brigette that was gnawing at him. It was like an itch he couldn't scratch.

Turning, he silently made his way back down the tunnel, sensing Brigette's absence before he reached the spot where he'd left her. Confused, he halted, testing the air. A growl rumbled in his throat at the scent of male dog.

Roban had been here. Standing close to Brigette.

So where had they gone?

Grasping the hilt of his dagger, he yanked it from the leather sheath and followed the fading trail. He ignored the distant sound of footsteps and the scent of various demons leaving their private spaces. He didn't care who happened to appear in the tunnel. Keeping his presence hidden was no longer a concern. All that mattered was finding Brigette.

Turning into a narrow passage, Xi picked up his pace. He was getting closer. He could feel Brigette's heat. Which meant that she was still alive.

The tightness in his chest eased, but his pace never slowed. The urgency to reach her continued to thunder through him. A primitive pulse that came from deep inside him.

He swerved into the secondary passage, bending over to avoid thumping his head against the low ceiling. It was barely more than a narrow channel that had recently been carved through the earth. He was guessing it had been done by the demons, not the humans.

Not that it mattered. His only interest was in the glint of the silver bars he could see just ahead. Slowing his pace, he peered through the darkness. He wouldn't be able to help Brigette if he ran headfirst into a trap.

When he was sure that Roban wasn't hidden in the shadows and that he hadn't left behind any dangers, he cautiously moved to stand in front of the cell built inside a shallow alcove.

"Brigette."

There was a soft rustle, and Brigette appeared behind the bars. She looked flushed with anger, and there were streaks of dust on her lovely face, but she was unharmed.

"Xi."

"What happened?"

Her jaw tightened. "Roban showed up just after you headed into the passage. I thought I could let him lead me into his trap without getting caught." Heat prickled in the air. "Obviously, I'm not as smart as I thought I was."

Roban. Xi swallowed a growl. He was going to take great pleasure in skinning that varmint when he got his hands on him.

"We'll deal with him later. For now—" He stepped forward.

"No, Xi, you have to get out of here."

He didn't bother to acknowledge her soft plea. The pits of hell could open up and he wouldn't leave without her. Instead, he reached toward the door of the cage. The silver bars would hurt like a bitch, but one good yank and he could have it opened.

"Stop!" she cried out, halting his hand an inch from the bars. "The door is triggered with explosives."

Xi cursed, his gaze locking on the tiny box that was hanging from the silver lock. It didn't look big enough to do much damage. Certainly not to a pureblood Were.

"What kind of explosives?"

"The kind that sends a lethal curse through the air."

Xi leaned forward, studying the box. He could smell the C-4 inside, but he had no way of sensing the magic. Which made it even more dangerous. Vampires were as vulnerable to an imp's curse as any other demon, but it was usually an up-close and personal sort of exchange. One imp tossing a curse at one opponent. There weren't many imps who had the balls to stand in front of a vampire and try to use his magic. The likelihood of launching the spell before the vampire ripped out his heart was less than zero.

To use human technology to spread the curse was a maniacal stroke of genius.

In silence, he studied the box, searching for a way to remove it without disturbing the C-4. There was no obvious means. At least none that he could accomplish without help.

"Xi, listen to me. You need to get out of here. Now." Brigette stepped close enough to the bars for her skin to turn red from the silver. "The tunnels are rigged with these bombs. They're set to go off as soon as Maryam leaves."

Xi once again ignored her, his concentration focused on the box. "It was created by an imp?"

"I suppose so. It doesn't matter. Did you hear me? You have to get out—"

"Smell it," he interrupted.

She made a sound of frustration. "Excuse me?"

"Smell the bomb."

"Did you take a blow to the head?"

Xi glanced up, sending her an impatient frown. Every passing second increased the danger. Not only for Maryam to leave and set off the curses, but for someone to wander by and catch sight of him.

"Brigette, tell me if you can recognize which imp created the curse," he commanded in stern tones.

She pressed her lips together, clearly resisting the urge to share her opinion of males who tried to order her around. Then, with an obvious effort, she forced herself to respond in a calm voice.

"Lynx."

Xi nodded. "Are there any other scents?"

She cautiously leaned forward, sniffing the box. "Just human and Roban."

"So no magic beyond the curse?" he pressed.

"No."

"Where can I find Lynx?

She straightened, scowling at him. "He'll be leaving with the others."

"Not yet. They're doing a staggered evacuation."

"How do you know?"

"I overheard a conversation between Maryam and a mongrel female who seemed to be in charge of getting the demons sent to their proper locations."

"That must be Naven."

Xi wasn't interested in the female mongrel. Not unless she got in his way. Then she was dead.

"Where can I find Lynx?" He repeated his question.

Brigette heaved a resigned sigh. "He stays with the other imps in a tunnel near Maryam's office. They depend on her to protect them from the predatory demons."

Xi nodded. That made sense. It was odd to have so many diverse demons living in the same space. There would be a constant struggle for supremacy between the species. And casual killings when a predator felt the urge to spill blood.

Only a leader who held an iron grip on her underlings could prevent it from becoming a mêlée.

"What does he smell like?" Xi demanded.

"Cloves."

He carefully reached between the silver bars to brush a finger down her cheek. "Don't go anywhere."

Her features appeared to melt, as if his touch had eased the fear she was desperately trying to hide. Xi hissed, slammed with the primitive impulse to remain and offer her comfort. It was only the clock ticking in his head that forced him to turn and rush down the passage. Each second he wasted edged them closer to disaster.

Turning toward the vampire's private office, he didn't bother to waste his energy on hiding his presence. It no longer mattered. Besides, there was new...emptiness in the tunnels. Obviously, the evacuation had started.

The thought propelled him even faster, and he was little more than a blur to the unsuspecting sprite who was strolling toward him. Coming to an abrupt halt, Xi grabbed the male by the collar of his long robe and lifted him off the ground.

He wasn't trying to frighten the creature. That would take too long, and it risked the creature calling out and alerting any demon nearby that there was danger. Instead, he pulled the sprite until they were face-to-face, peering deep into his eyes.

"Mine."

Instantly, the pale eyes glazed over as Xi used his ability to take command of the fey's mind. Most vampires could only use compulsion on humans, but Xi was strong enough to control lesser demons.

"Where is Lynx?"

The sprite nodded toward the larger tunnel behind him. "That way."

Xi lowered the sprite and shoved him in the general direction. "Take me."

The fey's face was slack, but he followed Xi's command without hesitation. Together, they moved through the darkness, heading toward the open space, which smelled of rich herbs and sharp fruit. The fey seemingly kept their area cleaner than the predatory demons. They weren't, however, any neater. The space was crowded with bedding that was spread across the cement floor and piles of clothing and personal items. As if the owners had tossed them aside in a hurry. Xi clenched his fangs, briefly afraid that the imp had already left. Then he caught the unmistakable scent of cloves.

Searching the shadows at the far end of the space, Xi shoved the sprite forward. As he hoped, a tall, slender male with long copper hair and a narrow face stepped out of a hidden passage. He was dressed in jeans and a sweatshirt with the Chicago Bears logo on the front, and as he stepped into the space, he was munching on an apple.

This had to be Lynx.

"What the hell, Colly?" the male snapped as he studied the sprite. "You're supposed to be headed to the airport."

"Lynx." Xi stepped next to the sprite.

The imp frowned, but he was more confused than alarmed. There were enough vampires in the rebellion not to set off immediate alarms.

"Who are you?"

Xi touched the sprite on the back. "Return to your duties," he commanded.

Silently, Colly turned to leave. The sprite would eventually wake from the compulsion with no memory of having seen Xi.

Dismissing the creature from his mind, Xi concentrated on the imp, who was picking his way through the checkboard of blankets and mattresses to stand in front of him.

"I asked a question," the male said.

Xi arched a brow. Most imps were ballsy. This one was straight-up suicidal. Probably because he had been singled out to create the curses for the rebellion. It made him mistakenly believe he was indispensable.

A shame Xi didn't have the time or interest to rid the fey of his misplaced arrogance.

Grabbing the front of the sweatshirt, he yanked the imp forward. "Mine."

Lynx blinked. Obviously stronger-willed than the sprite. "Let me go, leech."

Xi released a burst of power. "Mine."

"Not until—"

"Come with me," Xi interrupted the slurred words, turning to head out of the open space.

The imp obediently followed him, although Xi could sense him battling against the compulsion. His hold wouldn't last long.

Zigzagging back through the passages at a dizzying speed, Xi at last halted in front of the cell. Brigette stepped forward, but he lifted his hand in warning. He couldn't risk having the imp distracted. Not when his hold on the creature was so tenuous.

Grabbing Lynx by the arm, he pointed toward the small box. "Remove the curse."

The male licked his lips, a sheen of sweat forming on his forehead. "Maryam," Lynx rasped.

Xi's fingers dug into the male's arm. "Remove the curse."

"No."

There was the sound of a bone shattering as Xi tightened his grip. "Remove the curse."

Lynx whimpered, the sweat dripping down his face as he desperately tried to battle against the compulsion. Then, with slow, jerky movements, he reached out to touch a finger to the box. He spoke soft words in a language Xi didn't understand, and Brigette abruptly stepped back. As if she could sense something happening with the magic. Xi hoped the male was destroying the curse, not setting it off. His inability to detect what

Lynx was doing was unnerving as hell. Like playing Russian roulette. Only with a curse that could end his life—and Brigette's—without them having any hope of fighting against the unseen enemy.

At last, a tendril of smoke curled out of the box, and the scent of crushed cloves tainted the air.

"Is the curse gone?" Xi asked Brigette.

The female leaned forward, sniffing the box. "Yes."

Relief flooded through him. The first hurdle had been cleared. Now to deal with the next dozen.

Lifting his arm, Xi slammed his fist into Lynx's face. The creature's eyes rolled back, and he slid to a puddle of unconscious imp on the dirt floor. Xi's fangs throbbed in anticipation. His impulse was to kill Lynx. Not only because his magic had threatened Brigette; the imp needed to be destroyed before he could create more lethal bombs.

Unfortunately, Lynx was the only one who could deal with the other curses. Which meant he had to stay alive.

For now.

Motioning for Brigette to back away, he waited for her to crouch down and cover her head with her arms. The curse was gone, but the C-4 remained. Once she was braced, he kicked the door open. There was a loud explosion that launched Xi through the air and into the wall. A shower of dirt and rocks from the ceiling dusted him as he groaned from the impact. There'd been some damage, but he was already healing.

He was far more worried about Brigette.

Rushing forward, he met her just as she was squeezing past the mangled door. She was dusty, with a fleck of blood on her face, but there didn't appear to be any major damage.

Thank the goddess.

He reached out. Every instinct urged him to wrap her tightly in his arms. Not only to reassure himself that she was unharmed, but to absorb her fragrant heat. The fear that he might not be able to rescue her had left him chilled to the bone.

Ironic for a vampire.

But there was a warning voice in the back of his mind, reminding him that the danger wasn't over. Reluctantly, he contented himself by lightly brushing the dust from her cheek.

Once they were safe, he'd hold her tight against him. And never let her go.

Not ever.

Thankfully unaware of the primitive decision that had already been made deep in his soul, Brigette turned to glance at the unconscious imp.

"You can compel demons?"

He was caught off guard by her question. She'd been trapped in a cage with lethal silver bars, they'd just avoided being annihilated by a curse, and they had a limited time to get out of the tunnels before they exploded, and she was focused on his compulsion skills?

Then he realized why she was troubled. No doubt, she was searching her memories to determine if he'd ever manipulated her with his powers.

"I can only compel lesser demons and only for a short amount of time," he assured her. Then, reaching down, he grabbed Lynx by the ankle. "Let's get out of here."

She fell into step beside him, and together they moved toward the larger tunnels, dragging the imp behind them.

"We need to warn Styx that these tunnels will explode as soon as Maryam leaves," Brigette at last muttered.

"Does he need to warn the human authorities?"

"No, the C-4 is a way to spread the curse to a wider area, not to bring down any structures. We need to get every demon out of Chicago." She grimaced. "Plus all the other cities we saw on the map."

Xi tried to think of the logistics it was going to take to empty the city of every single demon. It boggled the mind. Even if they had a means to send out a generalized warning—which they didn't—there was no way to convince thousands of demons to flee. It would be like herding cats.

"Never going to happen."

She sent him a frustrated glare. "We have to try."

Xi didn't miss her obvious concern for the lives of the demons. Whatever she'd been in the past, she no longer was willing to put herself before others.

"I might be able to do something for Chicago," he told her, reaching into his pocket with his free hand to pull out his phone.

"What?"

"Call Viper," he said, punching in the number.

She arched a brow. "That's your plan?"

"That's it."

"Okay."

Chapter 14

Levet had his arm stretched out, the doulas stone glowing in his hands. The magic was pulling him down the narrow streets, as if he had a hunting dog on the leash. It yanked him through London and into Chelsea.

He'd expected the stone to pack a punch of magic. All good things came in small packages. But he wasn't pleased to be hauled through puddles or jerked off his feet when the stone was particularly enthusiastic.

Jogging beside him, Troy dodged a streetlamp. "Slow down."

Cursing the stupid stone, Levet tried to dig in his heels. "I cannot. The magic is pulling on me like a—" Levet screeched as he was whipped around a corner down a narrow alley. He was still screeching when he was rudely slammed into a wall. Bouncing off the hard bricks, he landed on his derrière. Rubbing his squashed snout, he climbed to his feet. "Ow."

Troy planted his hands on his hips and glanced around the cramped space. There was nothing to see beyond the brick buildings that framed the alley. No doors. No windows. No manhole that would lead to the sewers beneath the street.

Nowhere for the vampire to have disappeared.

"Your doohickey is broken," Troy growled in disgust.

Levet scowled, holding out his hand, where the stone continued to glow and pulse with magic.

"It is not broken."

"Are you telling me that we're following a vampire who can walk through a solid brick wall?"

Levet gave the stone a good shake. It instantly tried to slam him against the wall. Levet heaved a sigh, staring at the bricks.

"Perhaps he rested here before being picked up in a car," he hesitantly suggested. It wasn't a very good guess. The stone should have followed him even if he'd traveled in an automobile.

Troy stepped past him, laying his hand flat against the bricks. "Or before a portal opened."

Ah. That made much more sense, even though most vampires detested traveling with magic.

"*Oui*, or before a portal opened," Levet agreed. "Can you sense anything?"

Troy closed his eyes, no doubt absorbing any lingering magic on the wall. At last, he nodded his head.

"One was opened here."

"When?"

"Months ago. The residue is barely detectable."

"Can you follow it?"

"No." Troy opened his eyes, firmly shaking his head. "Even if it had just opened, I could only get within a general area with my own portal. This one is too degraded to tell more than the fact that it was created by a nymph."

Levet wrinkled his snout. What sort of nymph would be willing to work with a leech…

"Oh." With a blink, Levet took another look around. He'd been so distracted at being jerked and tugged by the stone that he hadn't realized precisely where he was. Now he had a very good suspicion who had opened the portal. "Male or female?"

"Female."

Levet smiled, bending down to sweep away the dust covering the cobblestones. "Step back."

Troy muttered something about a brain filled with chunks of stone, but Levet ignored him. The imp couldn't be talking about him. His mind was sharp as a…um…as sharp as something or other.

"What are you doing?" Troy demanded as Levet continued to clean off the cobblestones.

"This neighborhood is controlled by a nymph called Cleo."

Troy made a sound of surprise. "A nymph controls the neighborhood? Does Victor know?"

Victor was the vampire clan chief of London. And, like all leeches, he believed that he was in charge of everything and everyone in his area.

"He leaves her in peace," Levet told his companion. "Cleo was here before the Romans ever built the first fort and cunning enough to have bartered and blackmailed her way to gaining the support of the local demons. She was dug in so tightly that no one dared to try and challenge her. Not even Victor." Levet shrugged. "Although I suppose the leech could destroy her if she was foolish enough to try and threaten him, or his claim over London."

"Good for her," Troy murmured. "I admire a fey who can climb the ladder of success."

Levet snorted. "You're not going to be so happy when you discover her price for offering us information."

Troy shrugged. "It's not going to bother me one way or another. This is your quest, not mine."

"I thought we were partners," Levet complained. What was the point in having the flighty imp along if he wasn't going to share the potential cost? "You know, like Sonny and Cher."

"I'm just along for the ride."

Levet sent the male a frustrated glare. "I do not know what that means."

"It means that you're paying the price," Troy drawled. "Not me."

"You are a terrible KISA," Levet muttered.

"I'll take that as a compliment. I've never had any aspiration to be a knight in shining armor."

Levet clicked his tongue. The male's ego was nearly as bloated as a vampire. Maybe even a dragon.

"You take everything as a compliment."

"Of course. It's the only way to fully enjoy being in the company of others." Troy leaned against the wall, making no effort to help. "Otherwise, I might as well stay as secluded as your poor Inga."

Levet coughed as dust filled his snout, but he didn't stop. Dawn was beginning to creep over the horizon. He needed to find the mark that would open the entrance to Cleo's hidden lair.

"She is not poor Inga," he muttered. "She is the Queen of the Mer-folk."

"And yet so alone," Troy drawled.

Levet sat back on his heels, his wings drooping. He could still see Inga's face as he told her that he was about to leave. Her disappointment was like an anchor that weighed down his heart.

"That is true," he admitted. This imp might annoy him. Really, really, really annoy him. But there was no doubt that Troy actually cared about Inga and her future. He was the one creature who would understand Levet's struggle to support the ogress without endangering her position as queen. "And I am not entirely certain how to make things better. I can offer her my companionship."

Troy rolled his eyes. "I'm sure that's a source of great solace to her."

Levet stiffened. Yep. Really, really, really annoying. "I am. She adores me."

"She also adores psychedelic muumuus and raw liver on banana bread," Troy pointed out in wry tones. "That might suggest she doesn't always have the best taste."

"Hey."

"But she has the heart the size of a dragon," Troy smoothly continued.

Levet nodded sadly. The female had been wrenched from her mother's arms and sold into slavery when she was just a baby. She'd been told her family hated her. And she had been manipulated into betraying her people by the former king. "*Oui*. It is not only large, but tender. She has been hurt too many times."

"So why not stay at her side and protect her?"

Levet winced as the imp's words scraped across his raw nerves. "I would if she were simply an ogress. But she is the Queen of the Mer-folk. They will never allow her to sit on the throne unless she earns their respect." He heaved a sigh. "Something she will never earn if she depends on *moi* to offer her courage."

Troy shrugged. "They have no choice but to allow her to sit on the throne. Not as long as she holds that big-ass trident."

Levet wasn't nearly so nonchalant about the magic of the Tryshu protecting Inga. It did, after all, have some weird mystical power to determine who should lead and when it was time for a new ruler.

"How long will the Tryshu keep her as queen if she cannot lead her people?" he asked.

Troy blinked, as if he hadn't considered the possibility that the trident might decide to reject Inga.

"So you abandoned her for her own good?" he finally demanded.

"I did not abandon her," Levet snapped. "I am fulfilling my duty, just as she is fulfilling hers." He returned his attention to the cobblestones. The mark had to be somewhere. "At least I hope she is," he breathed in a soft voice.

Troy shoved himself away from the wall. "I smell...figs."

The words had barely left his lips when a rich, female voice floated through the alley.

"Levet. I didn't know you were going to visit. You should have called first."

Levet cautiously straightened at the unmistakable reprimand. Cleo had opened a portal, but she hadn't stepped through.

"I am just passing by," he assured the nymph.

"It is still rude to enter without permission." The scent of figs intensified, drenching the air with outrage. "And you brought along an uninvited guest." Troy was wise enough to hold up a hand in a gesture of peace. "I am—"

"I know who you are, Troy, Prince of Imps," the tart voice interrupted. A half dozen nymphs rushed from the shadows, at the same time, another dozen appeared on top of the nearby buildings, pointing crossbows that were loaded with iron arrows. They wouldn't kill Levet, but they would seriously injure Troy. All fey creatures were allergic to iron.

For several minutes, the warriors simply surrounded the alley, not speaking but silently making certain that Levet and Troy didn't try to escape.

Then, there was a stir of warm air, and a female stepped out of a portal. She was small and slender, like all nymphs, but instead of the usual golden hair, Cleo possessed raven curls that framed her pale, perfect face and tumbled down her back. Her eyes were also darker than other nymphs, closer to cognac than gold. But it was her vibrant sensuality that was causing Troy to struggle to catch his breath. The very air seemed to sizzle with sex.

She was wearing a long, black-and-gold gown that matched the warriors' uniforms, and an emerald the size of an egg hung around her neck.

"Why are you in my territory?"

Levet cleared his throat. He wasn't afraid of Cleo. He didn't fear any demon. Well, he might be the teensy, tiniest bit nervous around dragons. They were absurdly temperamental. But he was in a hurry. He didn't have time to sneak his way out of Cleo's dungeons.

"We are on the hunt for a vampire."

"Vampire?" She arched a brow, gliding forward. The air warmed, spiced with the scent of figs. "Dangerous business."

Levet shrugged. "It is what I do."

"I remember." Cleo reached up to touch the emerald that hung around her neck. Several centuries ago, it had been stolen by a jealous lover. Levet had overheard the male trying to barter the gem to an imp in Dublin and had taken steps to remove the rare emerald from the vengeful jerk. A few nights later, he returned it to Cleo. Not for a reward. He simply enjoyed thwarting the two males who'd tried to take advantage of a female. Of course, at the time, he hadn't realized that Cleo was one of the most powerful creatures in all of Great Britain. "It's because I owe you a debt that I haven't punished you for trespassing."

Levet shifted his weight from foot to foot. Cleo ruled her territory with an ironing board. No, that wasn't right. An iron fist, *oui*. If there was a portal opened, then she was the one who opened it.

"We...um...could use your assistance," he told the female.

The cognac eyes glowed with a warning taste of her power. "You invade my territory, and now you ask for my help?"

Levet blinked. "It was not much of an invasion."

The cognac gaze turned toward Troy. "You know how I feel about royalty."

Troy shrugged. "Probably the same way I feel."

Cleo took a step toward the imp, her gaze running over his poison-green spandex jumpsuit. It was impossible to know from her beautiful features if she was amazed or traumatized by the sight of the bizarre outfit. Levet was betting on traumatized.

"I've heard about you, Prince of Imps," she murmured.

A smile tugged at Troy's lips, a combination of captivation and odd wariness. As if he wasn't sure what to make of the lovely nymph.

"I'm afraid I can't return the compliment," he said.

There was a ripple among the guards. Like a breeze rustling through grass. Clearly, they thought the words were an insult to their leader.

Cleo tossed her glossy raven curls. "It wasn't a compliment."

Troy chuckled. "Touché."

The nymph turned back to Levet. "What do you want from me?"

"The vampire I am hunting disappeared through a portal." Levet waddled forward, touching the brick wall at the end of the alley. "Here."

Cleo shook her head. "You must be mistaken. Victor and I have a bargain. There have been no vampires in the neighborhood."

"He would have come through several months ago," Levet told her.

A speculative expression settled on the nymph's face. "You can follow a trail that is months old? Impressive."

Levet held out his hand, exposing the stone. "Only with assistance."

Cleo leaned forward, studying the small object that continued to glow with magic. "What is it?"

"A bauble that belongs to the Queen of the Mer-folk."

Cleo reached out her hand. "Can I have it?"

Levet quickly closed his fingers around the stone and lowered it. He wasn't done with his hunt. He was going to need the stone.

"Inga might be open to negotiations," he hedged, not about to bluntly refuse the female's request. Cleo hadn't earned her position by being a kindly, forgiving soul. She was as ruthless as a scorpion when she wanted something. He hid his arm behind his back. "Once my quest is complete."

She pursed her lips, as if debating whether or not to simply take the stone, then she sniffed. "What is your interest in the vampire?"

"The Anasso believes that he is the leader of a rebellion."

"Sounds like leech business."

Levet swallowed a sigh. "So I've been told."

"Why should I help?" Cleo demanded.

"The King of the Vampires would be in your debt."

"Tempting." She didn't appear particularly impressed with that reward. "What else?"

Levet tried to think of the best means to tempt her. "I suppose there might be a monetary reward."

Cleo shook her head. "I want a favor."

Ah. That didn't seem so bad. Levet owed lots of favors. Most of the creatures forgot the debt in a century or two.

"Very well. I will owe you a favor."

"Not from you." Cleo pointed toward Troy. "From him."

The imp widened his eyes, pressing his hand to his chest. "Me? No way."

Levet smiled. "Done."

Troy's breath hissed between his teeth. "Wait. You can't barter with me, you ugly lump of granite."

Both Levet and Cleo ignored the male's protest. The bargain had been made. It was ridiculous for the imp to continue bleating about it.

"The vampire approached me six, maybe seven, months ago," Cleo said. "He needed to leave London without being traced."

Levet felt a tingle of excitement. That had to be the vampire they were chasing. "Did he give you a name?"

"He didn't offer, and I didn't ask."

"What did he pay you?"

The cognac eyes narrowed. "That's confidential."

Levet shrugged. How much the leech was willing to pay might give some indication of how desperate he was to keep his identity hidden. Not that it mattered. Levet was hunting him down, one way or another.

"Can you open the portal again?" he asked.

Cleo paused, no doubt considering the odds of being punished by the vampires. Then, with a lingering glance toward Troy, she moved toward the wall. Laying her hand against the bricks, she murmured a word of power.

"There."

A shimmer of magic spread over the grimy stones, revealing an opening that was large enough for an ogre to walk through. It was a display of her massive power.

"Troy."

The imp scowled. "What?"

"Don't forget. You owe me."

Troy parted his lips, but Levet stomped his foot on the idiot's toes. He was going to get them tossed into the dungeon.

"*Merci, ma belle.*" Levet performed a deep bow. By the time he straightened, Cleo and her soldiers had disappeared. Levet grimaced. The fact that she left without saying goodbye meant the clock was ticking. They had a precious few minutes to get out of the area before she returned. And the next time it wouldn't be so civilized. Levet scurried forward. "Let us go."

Troy stomped next to him, obviously in a mood. "You are amazing, you know that?"

Levet never slowed. "Amazing in a good way?"

"Amazing that you stroll through the world creating one disaster after another. And yet you remain completely unscathed while everyone around you is shit on," the imp muttered.

Levet rolled his eyes. What a whiner. Lifting his hands, he shoved the imp forward. Troy released a roar as he tumbled into the portal, cursing Levet in several different languages.

Levet clicked his tongue and followed behind the imp. "And people claim I never shut up."

Chapter 15

Brigette leaned against a tree, trying to pretend a nonchalance that was betrayed by the shivers that shook through her body.

It'd been over three hours since they'd fled the depths of the tunnels and hidden near the main entrance to watch the demons creep out in small groups and scurry away. Each time a shadow appeared, Brigette's gut clenched with fear. Eventually, Maryam would crawl out, and the lethal curse would be triggered.

She remained on edge even after Viper arrived with the large coven of witches, who spread through the streets, marking out spells with soft chants as they circled wider and wider.

The theory was that the dampening spell would prevent the curse from leaving the tunnels. But theory and fact were not always the same thing.

It wasn't until Xi appeared around the corner and hurried to stand next to her on the narrow street that the shivers eased. She swallowed a sigh. Obviously, her fear wasn't just about Maryam. She'd been afraid that...

What?

She fiercely refused to examine what was rubbing her nerves raw. This wasn't over. Not yet. She couldn't allow herself to be distracted.

"Well?" she asked as he stepped next to her, the cool wash of his power a welcome relief as it defused the anxious heat that thundered inside her.

"The witches have finished casting the spell."

Brigette clenched her hands together. "Do you think this will work?"

Xi reached to grasp her hand, his head turning to watch the old, crumbling building across the street. It had once been an old pumping station, but it had long ago been abandoned. The station remained in derelict condition, but the demons had reopened the access point inside to avoid being seen by the humans as they entered and left their temporary lair.

"Only one way to find out," he murmured. "Unfortunately."

Just days ago, Brigette would have jerked her hand away. She didn't like that touchy-feely crap. Not even when she was facing potential death.

Now she squeezed Xi's fingers, allowing his presence to offer her comfort.

"Did Viper contact Chiron?"

"Yes."

Brigette studied his tense profile. "But?"

"But Ulric is visiting the in-laws."

Brigette was confused. As long as Ulric didn't enter Dreamscape, then the bomb wouldn't trigger. Or, at least, that was what Roban had claimed. That gave them time to locate the thing and get it out of harm's way.

"That's good, isn't it?"

"They are rare zephyr demons and live in some remote hole in the ground. Which means that Ulric is out of contact. There's no way to warn him not to return."

"I need to go to Vegas." Brigette pushed away from the tree, prepared to take off for Nevada. That second. It didn't matter if she had to run the entire way; she was going to do whatever necessary to protect Ulric.

"Viper is sending Lynx in Styx's jet," Xi hurriedly assured her, thankfully not pointing out that she'd plotted a painful death for Ulric not so long ago. "He'll defuse the curse before the bomb can be triggered."

Brigette chewed her bottom lip. "I don't trust the imp."

"He's a rat," Xi reminded her. "And, like all rats, he'll do whatever it takes to stay alive. He's already pledging loyalty to Styx and revealing the location of the curses he created. He knows the only way to keep his heart from being carved out of his chest is if he does everything in his power to stop Maryam and her rebellion."

She reluctantly nodded. Xi was right. The imp was like most of Maryam's collection of ruffians—out for themselves. Once the word got out that the rebellion was a bust, they'd be turning on each other like rabid curs. "What about the other rebels?"

"Styx has taken the Ravens with him to capture the demons headed toward the airport, while Viper has his clansmen surrounding the parking lot where Maryam left the vehicles. Most of the traitors should be rounded up before dawn."

"So it's over," she murmured, trying to make herself believe the words.

Xi glanced back toward the pumping station. "As soon as we have Maryam and Roban locked in the dungeons." His jaw clenched. "Or dead."

"What are they waiting on?"

Xi shrugged. "Maybe they decided to remain safely hidden while they send out their devoted followers to risk death. They wouldn't be the first leaders with more bravado than courage."

It was possible. After all, Brigette had only known them a few days. But Maryam hadn't struck her as the type of leader who would cower in the shadows. This was personal for her. She would want to witness the destruction of her enemies with her own eyes.

Plus, she was a vampire. Every leech was a control freak.

Brigette scoured her mind, trying to recall her limited conversations with the female. They'd discussed the rebellion in general terms, but Maryam hadn't trusted Brigette enough to give step-by-step details. Only Roban had...oh.

"One way or another," Brigette breathed.

"What?"

"That's what Roban said when he locked me in the cell," she told Xi. "He made it sound as if there was more than one plan."

"It doesn't matter." A cold smile of anticipation curled Xi's lips. "Once they come out of the tunnel, we'll have them."

He was right. As soon as they'd contacted Viper, Brigette had clearly pinpointed the exits from the tunnels. They were all being watched by the vampire's clansmen. It was now just a waiting game.

A shame she wasn't in the mood to wait.

"Maybe I should go down and get them," she suggested.

Xi was shaking his head before she finished speaking. "We can't be certain that there aren't other nasty surprises waiting inside. She'll come out."

Brigette clenched her hands. She wanted to be doing something. *Anything.* "I'm not the most patient creature."

Xi arched a brow. "Shocking."

She sent him a frustrated glance. "Not all of us can be cold-blooded."

A tingle of electric power crawled over her skin, making her shiver as Xi stepped toward her. "Is that what you think? That I'm cold-blooded?"

Tilting back her head, she studied the pale, chiseled features. In the silvery moonlight, he was just so damned...perfect. A fantasy that might disappear in a wisp of smoke.

She shivered again, longing to reach out and touch that flawless face. "Just stating a fact."

His lips parted, revealing the tips of his razor-sharp fangs. "My temperature might not run as hot as a Were, but there's nothing cold about my blood." Unlike her, Xi didn't hesitate to reach out and run his fingers over her cheek. His cool touch set off ripples of excitement that made her toes curl. "Not when I'm next to you."

Heat stained her cheeks as her musky scent of arousal perfumed the air. Now wasn't the time to get all hot and bothered.

Pretending she wasn't embarrassed, she turned her head away. His dark, mesmerizing gaze made it difficult to think clearly.

"Is that a line?"

"Line?" he asked in confusion.

"A pickup line."

Xi allowed his fingers to brush down the curve of her throat. "If you have to ask, then it's not a very good one."

Brigette kept her gaze locked on the pumping station. Her instinct was to make some snarky comment. Or shove him away. It was terrifying to acknowledge how deeply he was etching himself onto her heart. Onto her very soul.

"I haven't flirted in over five hundred years," she admitted with a rueful sigh. "I'm a little rusty."

"Me too."

Her gaze snapped back to his face. Was he joking? He looked serious, but it was hard to tell with Xi. He had a wry, unexpected sense of humor. But there was nothing but a fierce desire smoldering in the dark eyes.

"You weren't trapped with an evil beast," she finally said. It was impossible to believe that females wouldn't have been doing everything in their power to try to attract the attention of this male. "Why would you be rusty?"

"Being a Raven to Styx is a full-time position. I've devoted my time and attention to securing his position as the Anasso."

"No females?"

"None that tempted me to forget my duty to my king." He lowered his head, scraping a sharp fang along the line of her jaw. "Not until now."

She swayed forward, as if drawn to him by a primitive spell. "Not so rusty."

"When this is over—"

His soft pledge was brought to an abrupt end as a violent tremor shook the ground. Knocked off balance, Brigette was pitched forward, landing heavily against Xi's hard body. His arms immediately wrapped around her, pulling her close.

"I got you."

There was another tremor, and another. Xi and Brigette remained tightly clenched together, neither of them speaking. There was no need to discuss what was causing the small earthquakes. They both knew that Maryam had left the tunnels and set off the explosions.

Braced for a painful death, Brigette felt each second tick past at a sluggish pace, as if the very world had slowed to a mere crawl. Then, when no hideous death appeared to snatch her into the jaws of the netherworld, she tilted back her head to exchange a relieved glance with Xi.

But even as his head lowered, as if he was going to kiss her in celebration, Brigette was pulling out of his arms and sprinting toward the pumping station.

Xi raced to jog next to her. "What are you doing? Brigette..."

She ignored his exasperation. Lowering her head, she sucked in deep breaths as she circled the building. Maryam hadn't left the tunnels from this exit. Which meant she had used one of the others.

"Call Styx and warn him that Maryam isn't here," she muttered, her head bent low as she ran through the dark streets.

Sucking in deep breaths, Brigette absorbed the scents that filled the air. She could easily shuffle through the mundane smells of the city, along with the humans, but it took a concerted effort to pick through the numerous vampire scents that flooded the area.

Pain slammed into her as she instinctively attempted to call on her wolf, only to have it refuse to answer. It didn't matter how much time passed, she would never be used to the loss of her animal. Or the knowledge that it was her own damned fault that the best part of her was buried forever.

Grimly shoving aside her aching regret, Brigette followed the tunnel that was beneath the streets. Maybe if she backtracked, she could find where Maryam escaped.

Focused on the hunt, Brigette was distantly aware of Xi running beside her, his dagger clutched in his hands. He was protecting her so she could concentrate on tracking her prey. As if they were true partners, not just strangers temporarily thrust together.

Strange sensations swirled through her, a mixture of pleasure and longing and fear. Pleasure at the realization that she wasn't alone as she flowed through the darkness. Longing for a future where Xi was always at her side. And fear that she would, all too soon, be back in her desolate village. Isolated and forgotten.

A familiar scent jerked Brigette out of her dark thoughts. Thank the goddess.

Coming to an abrupt halt in the center of the street, she knelt next to the heavy manhole.

"Maryam came out here," she said.

Xi knelt beside her. "Alone?"

"No, Roban's with her." Brigette leaned down to touch the manhole. The scents were distinct, but already fading. "They escaped at least half an hour ago. The triggers must have been set to give Maryam and Roban plenty of time to get out of the area before going off."

"Dammit, I should have thought of that," Xi growled, his face tight with self-disgust. "I need to warn Styx."

Brigette straightened. "You tell him. I'll follow the trail."

"We'll follow the trail." Xi pulled out his phone, hitting speed dial. "We're in this together, right?"

In this together...

Brigette tried to squash her fierce stab of satisfaction. She wasn't entirely successful, but at least she didn't blush. She was going to take that as a win.

"What about the other rebels?" she asked as soon as Xi finished his call and returned his phone to his pocket.

"Styx and Viper have it under control. The important thing now is to capture Maryam."

Brigette nodded, following the trail at a swift jog. They'd traveled straight south for several blocks, heading toward the sprawling suburbs.

"They aren't going to the airport," Xi muttered.

"Or the parking lot," Brigette added.

"So where the hell are they going?"

Brigette picked up speed. "Only one way to find out."

* * * *

Levet stumbled over Troy as he hurried forward. The stupid male had stopped just inches outside the exit of the portal. Worse, he had his arms folded over his chest and a dangerous expression on his face.

"Someday..." Troy growled as Levet regained his balance and flapped his wings to get rid of the dust.

"*Oui.* I know." Levet waved an airy hand. "You will rip off my wings or chop off my head or some other nasty punishment. I have heard them all."

Troy's eyes flashed with a predictable fury. "I'm sure I could come up with a few new ones."

Levet ignored the male's yakking. He had more important things to worry about than a pissy imp. Like figuring out where they were.

Turning in a slow circle, he discovered they were on a high bluff overlooking a wide, muddy river. Oh. Continuing his circle, he caught sight of exactly what he'd been expecting.

A farmhouse.

There was nothing to make it special. It looked like every other farmhouse in the Midwest. It had two stories, with a wraparound porch and a sharply angled roof. It was painted white, although it was peeling in more than one place and the gutters were drooping.

A rolling yard surrounded the house, dotted with a handful of outbuildings along with a fringe of trees. The pungent scent of ancient ash and oak and flowering dogwoods spiced the air. It looked charming and rustic and wholesome.

The sort of place that would welcome you with a warm meal and a kindly smile.

Thankfully, the locals had long ago learned to avoid the place as if it was infested with the plague. Only the call of an owl disturbed the heavy silence.

The house was, of course, a mere diversion. It was the series of caves that stretched for miles beneath the rolling hills that interested the vampires who inhabited it.

Levet clicked his tongue. "We are back where we started."

Troy sent him a baffled glance. "Not exactly. Chicago is at least a couple hours north of us."

"*Oui*, but I have been here before."

"So?" Troy shrugged. "You're thousands of years old. I imagine you've been everywhere before."

Levet sniffed. The male made him sound as if he was ancient. Granted, he was no spring turkey, but he was still in his prime. Indeed, if he was any more prime he would be…Well, he wasn't sure what he would be, but it was very, very prime.

"I have been here recently," he clarified.

Troy wrinkled his nose, his gaze skimming over the bluff to the river far below. "I can't imagine why. There's nothing here but mud and bugs. Two things I detest."

Levet shrugged. He wasn't fond of mud either, but he wasn't complaining. At least not out loud. Squaring his shoulders, he took charge of the situation.

"Follow me."

Troy hesitated before reluctantly falling into step next to Levet. "What are you leading me into this time? Quicksand? A dragon's snare? The pits of hell?"

Levet nodded toward the nearby house. "There."

Troy sniffed the air. "It smells like vampires."

"Below us is the Anasso's old lair," Levet said, picking up his pace. "It is now used by the Ravens."

Troy's eyes darted side to side, as if expecting a leech to leap out of shadows. The imp wasn't afraid. He was too arrogant for that. But no demon would willingly trespass in the King of the Vampire's private territory.

"Shouldn't we call and let them know we're coming?" Troy demanded. "I already owe a strange nymph some mysterious debt. I'm not adding vampires to the list."

"Styx will not mind," Levet blithely assured his companion. "Besides, it will soon be dawn. I need to get out of the sun."

Troy heaved a resigned sigh. "I don't suppose they have a Starbucks in there, do they? I'd kill for a blueberry muffin and a cappuccino."

Levet pressed a hand against his rumbling stomach. How long had it been since he'd last eaten? Too long.

"Mmm. Blueberry muffins."

Chapter 16

Styx was leaning against the mantle of the marble fireplace, sipping a well-earned glass of aged whiskey. The long, elegant room had dozens of chairs and sofas and puffy things that Darcy called chaise lounges, but he never sat in them. They were froufrou furniture from the palaces of France and built for beauty, not to bear the weight of a six-foot-five vampire.

But while he never felt completely comfortable in the room, he did love the aged, leather-bound books that lined two of the walls and the large window that offered a view of the rose garden.

Standing next to the side table, Viper poured himself a glass of the whiskey. The younger male had arrived moments ago, his face more pale than usual and his immaculate velvet jacket coated in dust. Styx might have poked fun at his friend if he hadn't been equally unkempt. It had been a long, tense night that he hadn't been entirely sure they were going to survive.

It had taken its toll on all of them.

"How many?" he asked as Viper strolled to stand next to the window.

Viper knew exactly what he was asking. There was only one thing on their minds right now. Capturing every rebel who skulked out of the tunnels before they could carry out their traitorous plans.

"We collected sixty-three as they were leaving the tunnels and another fifty who made it to the parking lot."

Styx nodded. "There were nearly two hundred scattered throughout the airport."

"I have several squads sweeping the city for any rebels who might be trying to sneak away."

"Good." Styx drained his glass and set it on a bookshelf. They had no idea exactly how many demons had been working with Maryam, but he was confident that they'd already scooped up the majority of them. "I've put out a reward for any rebel found hiding. It's large enough to encourage every demon in the city to join the hunt. Eventually, they'll all be rooted out."

Viper ran a weary hand through his hair. "You got ahold of all the clan chiefs?"

"They're going to contact the local covens to create the same dampening spell we used here. That should prevent any accidents until the imp can disable the devices."

Styx shuddered. He'd seriously underestimated Maryam. He accepted that she was trying to topple him as king, but it hadn't occurred to him that she would be willing to destroy thousands and thousands of demons to accomplish the task.

She was no longer a nuisance. She was a crazed maniac bent on genocide.

As soon as she was in his hands, she was a dead vampire.

Unfortunately, he had no idea when that would be.

As if able to read his dark thoughts, Viper glanced around the library. "Where is Xi?"

"On the hunt for Maryam and Roban."

Viper stiffened, his fangs lengthening at the realization that the leaders of the rebellion were still on the loose.

"They weren't headed for the airport?"

Styx's jaw tightened. He'd expected to find the female vampire waiting for a flight to Vegas after Xi had revealed her bitterness toward Chiron for supposedly betraying his people. Instead, he'd just received a call telling him that they'd managed to sneak past the circle of warriors they had guarding the streets.

"Nope, they escaped through a secret tunnel. Right now, they're moving south."

Viper muttered a string of curses. "Does Xi have the Were with him?"

"Yes." Styx's brows pulled together as Viper polished off his whiskey in one gulp. "Is that a problem?"

"It's possible the female is leading him into a trap."

Styx shrugged. That had been his first thought as well. Brigette had proven she was willing to sacrifice anyone, including her own family, to gain what she wanted. There would be no reason she wouldn't destroy Xi. But his Raven was confident the Were had changed. He had to trust in Xi's ability to judge the female's character.

Viper, however, wouldn't be so easy to convince. The male was even more cynical than he was.

"He's been with her for the past few days. Why wait until now to hurt him?" Styx demanded.

"I still don't like it."

"Neither do I, but someone has to capture Maryam, and I can't take the risk she is trying to lure me from the city." The heavy chandelier hanging from the center of the ceiling swayed back and forth, the lights flickering, as Styx struggled to contain his burst of frustration. He wasn't the sort of demon who liked sitting on his ass while his people put themselves in danger. He was the sort that liked to be in front, swinging his massive sword and stomping creatures beneath his heavy boots. Being king, however, meant he occasionally had to grit his fangs and do what was best for everyone. "We need to be prepared."

"True." Viper's dark eyes flashed with a glittering hatred. "Maryam has proven to be a cunning opponent. She might have expected you to disrupt her initial plans."

"If I was leading this rebellion, I'd assume that shit would go south," Styx agreed. "And I would also make sure that plan B was a knockout punch."

Viper grabbed the bottle of whiskey and headed toward one of the chaise lounges. Flopping onto the brocade cushions, he opened the bottle and made himself comfortable.

"I'll stay here until the bitch is captured."

"What about Shay?"

"She's staying with Dante and Abby."

Styx nodded. Dante's mate might have started her life as a human, but she'd been infused with the essence of a goddess. She could kill with a single touch.

"Formidable protection," he murmured.

Viper took a swig of whiskey, straight from the bottle. "Don't tell her that. She thinks she's there to protect them."

There was a sharp tug on Styx's heart at the fond resignation in his friend's expression.

"Yeah, the only way I could convince Darcy to remain in Kansas City was to tell her the pups need her," he said, the aching need to hold his mate in his arms almost overwhelming.

The two males exchanged a glance filled with a shared pain at the necessity of putting duty to their people above their own needs.

"Any luck on tracking down who might be the mystery manipulator?" Viper turned the conversation. There was no point in wallowing in pity. Being a leader meant sacrifices.

"I suspect it might be Ian."

"Ian?" Viper stared at him, almost as if he was wondering if Styx was joking. "I thought he was dead."

"We all did. Presumably, the word of his demise by his servants was greatly exaggerated."

"Why would they claim he was dead?"

"That's an intriguing question with no answer."

Viper paused, as if trying to imagine why anyone would pretend to be dead. It was a dangerous game, considering that any demons nearby would pillage the lair as soon as word got out that the vampire was dead.

"Who told you that he was still alive?" he finally asked.

"Locke."

Viper arched a brow. "You went to see Locke?"

"He might live in isolation, but he isn't a hermit. I thought he might have information."

"Oh, I don't doubt his ability to collect the latest news. I'm just shocked that he would be willing to speak with you."

Styx grimaced. His friend's surprise was predictable, but it still hurt to think of how many relationships had been shattered when he'd been forced to destroy the former king. Locke was his brother, but now they might as well be strangers.

Or enemies.

"I'm not sure I would say that he was willing," Styx admitted. "He did, however, tell me that Ian showed up at his lair in Iceland a few months ago."

Viper studied him with a dark, searching gaze. "You believe him?"

Styx considered the question. Once he'd returned to Chicago, he'd been instantly confronted with the news that the rebels were on the move and that Maryam was plotting to destroy thousands of demons. He hadn't had much time to reflect on his conversation with Locke.

"For now," he finally said. Unless the former Raven had changed drastically over the past few years, he had no talent for lying.

"If Ian was pretending to be dead, why would he seek out Locke?"

"Locke wasn't sure." Styx's lips twisted. "He offered Ian the same lack of welcome that he offered me."

"Locke always was stubborn."

Styx sent his friend a sly smile. "Isn't there a saying about a pot and black kettle?"

Viper blinked, his expression one of faux innocence. "I don't know what you're talking about. I'm not stubborn. I'm firm in my resolve."

"Shay says you're as firm in your resolve as a Missouri mule."

Viper held up the whiskey in a mocking toast. "True." Taking a deep drink, he set the bottle on the Persian carpet. "Did Locke tell you anything about Ian that might help? Like where we can find him?"

"No. The only thing he said was that Ian mentioned something about a resurrection."

Viper looked as confused as Styx felt. "What does that mean?"

"I have no idea." Styx started to shake his head in frustration, only to hesitate. Resurrection. It could mean a lot of things. A return to old days. Or a birth of new days. Even bringing the dead back to life, although vampires considered creating zombies an abomination. Besides, Ian hated everyone. He wouldn't try to bring them back from the dead. Styx abruptly froze. Ian hated everyone...except the former Anasso. "Shit." Styx turned his head toward the window. It was dark, but he could sense the coming dawn.

Viper rose to his feet, obviously sensing the tension that tightened Styx's muscles into knots.

"What is it?"

"I know where Ian is."

* * * *

Xi didn't know how far they'd traveled. They'd been running for over two hours, cutting through empty fields and down gravel roads as Brigette followed Maryam's trail. He knew that they had angled west, and that they had avoided any cities, probably because they suspected that Styx had "kill on sight" orders sent to every vampire in the world.

As dawn neared, Xi expected the desperate traitors to find some abandoned farmhouse or hidden cave where they could spend the daylight hours. Instead, the trail led them to a highway that cut through the rolling fields and, at last, to an aging motel that was miles from the nearest civilization.

Halting in the shadows of a hedgerow, Xi watched as two forms entered the room at one end of the U-shaped building. Maryam and Roban. Satisfaction blasted through him. It wasn't that he didn't trust Brigette's nose. Even without her wolf, she possessed a far greater sense of smell than he did. Still, he wanted visual confirmation that the female vampire hadn't been able to trick them into chasing a false trail.

"Gotcha," Brigette muttered, her face flushed and her eyes sparkling from the long chase. Even her curls were more fiery than usual, cascading down her back in wild abandon. She looked exactly as she was meant to look. A powerful predator who loved being on the hunt.

He reached to lightly touch her arm. He didn't want her rushing in and giving away their presence. Not until they knew what the two traitors were doing here. And, more importantly, if they were alone.

"Stay here," he murmured, pulling out his dagger before he straightened.

"Xi," Brigette growled.

"They can't sense my presence," he reminded her.

Her eyes glowed with frustration, but before she could argue, he was heading toward the highway, his movements so fast he was nothing more than a blur. Once he neared the motel, however, he made a wide half circle to cautiously approach from behind.

Testing the air, he easily picked up the scent of the vampire and Were, but there was nothing else. No demons, no humans. Not even a stray raccoon. The place might be abandoned, but there was some sort of magic that kept it free of vermin.

It had to be a haven. A sort of demon safehouse that was created to serve as a temporary resting place. The layers of magic prevented humans and stray animals from entering. It also rejected any demon who stayed for more than a night or two. This place was for transient shelter. It wouldn't allow any creature to nest.

Cautiously, Xi studied the two-storied brick structure. It was originally built by humans, fifty or sixty years ago. The rows of windows had been boarded over, and the doors were built out of a thick steel that had long ago rusted. The roof, however, had recently been replaced, and the parking lot was cleared of any trash. There was nowhere to hide. And no way to sneak up on the place.

Dropping low to the ground, Xi used his powers to disguise his presence as he crept toward the window at the end. Unfortunately, he couldn't physically hide from view. He had to hope Maryam hadn't been worried enough about being followed to keep watch.

At last reaching the back wall, Xi straightened and pressed his back against the weathered bricks. Then, inching toward the boarded window, he slowly smiled in satisfaction. He could hear the sound of low voices from inside the room.

From the beginning, Maryam had managed to stay one step ahead of them. Maybe her luck had just run out.

"Dammit." That was Roban's voice, followed by the sound of heavy footsteps, as if the male Were was pacing the floor.

"Well?" Maryam demanded.

"Nothing. No one is answering their phone."

Even through the thick brick wall, Xi could feel Maryam's icy reaction to the lack of response from her people.

"There's something wrong," she snapped. "I told you that I should stay and make sure the others escaped."

"If you had stayed, then you would have been captured," Roban protested. "Or worse."

"Or I could have prevented disaster."

"How?" The chill pulse that seeped through the bricks was joined by a blast of heat from the Were. Obviously, tempers were frayed. Which only made them more dangerous, Xi silently acknowledged. Nothing was more lethal than a cornered demon. "Obviously, we were betrayed," Roban continued, his voice vibrating with tension. "I told you that you couldn't trust that Were."

Xi narrowed his eyes. Did Roban actually believe that Brigette had betrayed them? He'd trapped Brigette in the cell to die when the tunnels exploded. But if he had proof, why didn't he just share it with Maryam?

The female vampire clearly shared his confusion. "We have no evidence she was involved."

Roban snorted loudly. "Did you see her during the evacuation?"

"No. I didn't see a lot of my people, but that doesn't mean they betrayed me," Maryam pointed out in dry tones.

"It no longer matters," Roban muttered, as if aggravated that he couldn't convince the female to accept that Brigette had been the cause of their current troubles.

Probably because he was smart enough to realize that someone was going to have to take the blame for the failure of their rebellion. And he didn't want the shit falling on his head.

On cue, tiny fractures began to form in the bricks as Maryam lost control of her temper. "Months of plotting wasted and my army captured or dead, and it doesn't matter?"

Roban seemed to sense that he was losing control of the situation. Xi didn't know what would happen when Maryam reached her breaking point, but he suspected it involved bloodshed.

"We must concentrate on the future," Roban hastily urged. "We can still strike a killing blow."

There was a tense silence, the bricks continuing to crack and pop behind Xi. Then, perhaps realizing she was in danger of collapsing the building, she finally leashed her burst of anger.

"If we've been compromised, what makes you think this new plan will work?"

"Because I didn't share the details with anyone but you and my brother."

Xi felt a pang of surprise. He assumed any backup plan would have been made by the vampire, not the Were.

"And you trust your brother?" Maryam demanded, her voice edged with frustration. She was smart enough to realize that putting her fate in the hands of Weres wasn't the best choice.

"He's family."

"Is that supposed to impress me?"

"No." Roban's voice was wry. "To be honest, my sister tried to eat me a few weeks after I was born, but Stewart will do anything for money."

"Nice recommendation."

"Rebellions aren't built on loyalty or honor or any other noble crap," Roban informed his companion. "They're a mess of greed, grievances, and ugly power grabs."

Xi surprisingly found himself agreeing with the male. Too many times, even the most noble causes became tainted by dark hungers.

"What was your motivation if it wasn't to protect the Weres?" Maryam's words were sharp with accusation.

"You know why." Roban paused. "To please you."

"Get some rest," the vampire snapped. "We finish this when your brother arrives tonight."

Chapter 17

Brigette was across the highway, standing just out of range of the motel. She had no intention of hiding in a hedgerow while Xi confronted the traitors. Still, she was careful to ensure she remained distant enough not to give away her presence. As much as it aggravated her to admit it, Xi's skills were much more valuable than her own. At least when it came to collecting information.

Pacing back and forth through the empty field, she kept her gaze locked on the dingy motel. It felt like an eternity passed, although she logically knew that it had only been a few minutes before a dark form abruptly appeared in front of her.

She sucked in a deep breath, her tension easing as he released his powers and the feel of his presence washed over her in an icy wave. It was almost as if her inner wolf was desperate to catch his rich, male scent. That it needed to know he was near.

Which was not only a ridiculous delusion, but a dangerous one. Her wolf was buried too deep. Hoping it would return was only asking for heartache.

Shaking off her dark thoughts, she met his chiding gaze with a lift of her brows. She wasn't a dog. She didn't stay put just because someone told her to stay.

"Were they alone?" she asked.

He nodded. "The motel is empty except for them."

That seemed odd, but she didn't bother to question the lack of customers. Instead, she studied his lean, perfect face, trying to determine what he'd discovered.

"And?" she prompted.

"And we need to get a room."

She blinked, her heart slamming against her ribs. He wanted to get a room? Together?

"Excuse me?"

His lips twitched. "Sun and vampire don't mix. I need to find shelter."

"Oh." She clenched her teeth. She wasn't going to blush. "What about Maryam and Roban?"

He grimaced. "I could overhear most of their conversation. They're waiting for Roban's brother, who is arriving later tonight."

"So this is an escape attempt?"

"No. As you suspected, they have something else planned."

Brigette glanced toward the motel. "Did you hear any details?"

"No, but Maryam knows that the Chicago rebellion has gone to hell. She'll be desperate to strike some blow against Styx."

She sent him a puzzled glance. If Maryam and Roban were alone, it seemed like the perfect opportunity to bring an end to their treachery.

"Shouldn't we capture them before that can happen?"

A hint of fang was visible, as Xi no doubt considered the pleasure of dragging the two back to Chicago in silver shackles. Or maybe he intended dispose of them in the motel room.

Brigette was voting for the second choice. She had a personal score to settle with Roban. One that was going to end with one of them dead.

Xi shook his head. "We can't do anything until Roban's brother arrives. He might finish the job, even if Roban is dead. Whatever the job might be." He turned to scan the motel, at last pointing to the far side of the U-shape. "The room on the end should offer us a clear view of the parking lot and Maryam's door." He reached to grab her hand. "Stay close, and my powers should help cloak your scent."

He didn't wait for her agreement as he tugged her against his body and cautiously headed toward the motel. Not that Brigette was going to argue. As much as she wanted this ended, they couldn't ignore the risk of not having a backup plan already in motion.

With a speed that left her breathless, they were crossing the field and then entering the motel room. The door slammed behind them, and Brigette tugged her hand from Xi's grasp. It wasn't that she resented his touch. Just the opposite. The cool pressure was addictive. It would be all too easy to cling to his slender fingers and pretend that she would never have to let go.

Unnerved by the thought, Brigette turned in a slow circle, taking in her surroundings. The room was plain, but it was surprisingly clean. There was a bed shoved against the far wall and three chairs beneath the boarded window. Each were a different size, from teeny tiny to one that was large enough to easily withstand the weight of a full-grown troll. Like Goldilocks, she inanely thought. *One was too small, one was too large, and one was just right.*

Obviously, this place was designed to offer shelter to whatever demon happened to be passing by.

With a shrug, she turned her attention to the opening, which revealed an attached bathroom. Thank the goddess. Nothing would feel better than a hot shower right now.

Well, maybe one thing…

A white-hot hunger blasted through her as she noticed Xi studying her with a brooding expression. As if he was lost in his own thoughts of what it would mean to spend the day trapped in this small room.

Her mouth dried to the texture of the Sahara Desert, even as her palms were coated in a damp sweat. Weird. But then, this male managed to cause all sort of strange and wonderful sensations.

But even as he took a jerky step toward her, he abruptly stiffened, his head tilting back as if he was sniffing the air.

"It's almost dawn," he murmured. "We need food and clean clothes."

Disappointment punched her with enough force to make her grunt, but, grimly, she held his gaze. He was right. This was the perfect time to get supplies.

"I'll go with you," she said.

He shook his head. "I need you to stay and keep an eye on Maryam."

"You just pointed out that it's almost dawn. She's not going anywhere."

He arched a brow. "Do you really want to take a chance of having them sneak away?"

Her lips parted to insist there was no way they were going to leave at this hour, only to snap them shut. Maryam had proven to be a survivor. If she suspected, for a second, that they'd been trailed to this motel, she would be plotting a way to escape.

She folded her arms over her chest. "Fine."

His lips twitched as he leaned down to brush his lips down the stubborn length of her jaw.

"I won't be long."

That was true enough, Brigette acknowledged, as he silently slipped from the room. She could catch the scent of dawn swiftly approaching. He would have less than half an hour to get supplies and make it back to the room.

Refusing to worry, Brigette took the opportunity to enjoy a hot shower, savoring the clean water as it washed away the filth from the tunnels. She might be evil, but that didn't mean she had to smell bad.

Then, using one of the fluffy towels to dry off, she pulled back on her old clothes. Xi might have many talents, but he was a male. The likelihood of him being able to find clothes that not only were suitable, but also the right size, was zero percent. Maybe less.

She'd just finished using the disposable toothbrush when the door was pushed open and Xi appeared carrying two bags. He opened one of them to place what smelled like a turkey sandwich and a bag of chips in a cellophane container on the big chair. Her mouth watered, and she told herself that it was a response to the turkey, and not to the tall, dark, gloriously sexy male.

The second bag he tossed in her direction. "I had to guess at your size," he said.

She snatched the bag out of the air and pulled out the pair of jeans and sweater that were folded inside.

Her brows arched as she realized that they were not only what she would have chosen, but they were a perfect fit.

"You guess remarkably well," she murmured.

He moved to stand directly in front of her, his cool power flowing around her with his intoxicating scent. She would never again smell cedarwood without the memory of this male haunting her.

Of course, it was very likely that he would haunt her even without the scent.

He was etched so deeply on her soul, there was no way to get rid of him. No matter how many centuries passed.

"I've paid attention," he assured her.

"Paid attention to what?" Her voice was ridiculously husky.

Xi stepped even closer. Close enough for her to appreciate the velvet darkness of his eyes and the flawless perfection of his pale skin.

"Everything."

Brigette sucked in a deep breath, savoring the shiver of awareness. During the long hours they'd raced in pursuit of Maryam and Roban, she'd been exhausted, frustrated, and terrified she might fail to prevent whatever horrifying plan they had devised. And she was still all those things, but for the moment, the sensations that sparked through her body overwhelmed everything else.

She hovered between sanity and the urgent desire that pulsed through her with a raw, primitive beat.

It'd been so long.

And she'd never, ever needed a male like she needed Xi.

Plus, the sun was shining. They were trapped in the private motel room. It offered the perfect opportunity to forget her worries and concentrate on something less stressful.

Not that being near Xi didn't involve stress. But it was stressful in that delicious, heart-pounding, tingly-all-over sort of way she craved.

The endless reasons she should give into temptation raced through her mind as she glanced down, stroking her fingers over the cashmere softness of the sweater he'd brought her. A distant memory of taking pleasure in her rich gowns and satin slippers echoed like a picture that was faded and fuzzy.

"I spent centuries wearing whatever was available. I lost all interest in material things," she admitted in low tones, lifting her head to meet his mesmerizing gaze. Another shiver raced through her. "I lost interest in a lot of things."

"Including your own happiness?"

Brigette tossed the clothes onto the smallest chair, the familiar guilt pressing against her with an unbearable weight.

"Power was more important."

"And now?"

"Now, I don't deserve happiness."

He brushed his fingers over her cheek. "Do any of us truly deserve happiness?" The tips of his fangs gleamed in the dim light. "We simply grab it when it's offered."

Brigette's gaze locked on the fangs. Weres didn't drink blood, but claws and razor-sharp teeth were always a part of sex. At least, if it was good sex.

The awareness that had been ignited from the moment she'd caught sight of Xi blazed through her. More than that, there was an awakening of...something in the center of her being. A sense of emerging from a darkness that had enveloped her for hundreds of years.

Please don't be hope, she silently begged.

She pressed her hands against his chest, dismissing her pang of fear. Beneath the thin material of his black sweater, she could feel the steely hardness of his muscles.

"How do you grab happiness?"

Xi's eyes darkened, and an icy breeze tugged at Brigette's hair. As if he was losing his fierce control over his emotions. Excitement blasted through Brigette. She wanted him to lose control. She wanted him raw and abandoned.

"Do you want me to demonstrate?"

Her hands trembled as they stroked over his chest. Xi wasn't the only one losing control.

"I…" The words threatened to lodge in her throat. "I want you."

Xi gathered her in his arms. "How much?"

Brigette struggled to focus on his words. It wasn't her fault. Being pressed against Xi's hard body was turning her brain to mush.

"What?"

He smiled, revealing his huge fangs. "How much do you want me?"

Oh. Her mouth went back to the Sahara Desert. Hot and dry. "A lot."

Xi chuckled as her words came out as a croak. Lowering his head, he used the tip of one fang to trace the line of her jaw.

"Amateur."

Brigette felt as if there was a vice around her chest, making it difficult to breathe. It'd been so long, and the need swelling inside her was more intense than she'd ever expected.

"What are you talking about?"

"I need to hear more than just a lot," he complained, nipping her lower lip. "I want you to tell me that you want me so much that you ache."

It took a moment for Brigette to realize that Xi had sensed she was being overwhelmed. His teasing was an effort to ease her tension.

The knowledge melted her heart in a way that was far more dangerous than the desire pulsing through her.

Brigette scored her nails down his chest. "I want you more than that turkey sandwich and potato chips that are calling my name."

"Better." Xi lifted his head, his eyes smoldering with a dark fire. "I want to taste you from the top of your silken curls to the tips of your tiny toes."

She pressed her nails deeper and was rewarded by his low grunt of desire. "How do you know my toes are tiny?"

Xi smiled at the unmistakable challenge.

"Let's find out." Holding her gaze, Xi gracefully lowered himself to his knees. Then, wrapping one hand around her calf, he lifted her foot off the ground and pulled off her boot and sock. "Just as I suspected." He kissed the tip of each toe. "Teeny tiny perfection."

Brigette's heart quivered, something more than mere lust cascading through her as he tugged off her other boot and sock to nibble her toes. She reached down to touch his dark hair. It was as soft as satin beneath her fingertips. Her hand drifted to the amazing tattoos, tracing the sinuous snakes that coiled along the sides of his skull.

At the same time, Xi's hands skimmed upward to efficiently deal with the holster that held her dagger before unfastening her jeans and shimmying them down her legs.

A frost coated the paneled walls as Xi took in the sight of her lacy panties. Brigette shivered, but it wasn't from the cold. Inside, she was a raging inferno.

"This is unexpected," Xi growled.

A stupid blush touched Brigette's cheeks. "They were in the clothing that Maryam gave me when I first arrived in Chicago."

"She might be evil, but she has fine taste in lingerie," Xi murmured.

"I thought they were stupid," Brigette said, her blush deepening. "But I didn't have anything else, so I wore them. Then...I decided that I like the feel of lace and satin."

"Me too," Xi whispered. "But I prefer the satin of your skin."

Grasping her hips, Xi held her steady as he nuzzled a path of kisses over her lower stomach. Pleasure poured through her, air squeezing from her lungs as he used the tip of his fang to slice through the side bow of her panties.

The bit of lace floated to the worn carpet like a broken butterfly. Or a flag of surrender, she wryly acknowledged. She'd known this moment was inevitable, even when she was battling against her fate.

The scent of cedarwood drenched the air, along with her musky passion. It was enticingly erotic.

Xi obviously agreed as he tightened his grip on her hips and skimmed his lips down her inner thigh. Brigette hissed as her fingers gripped his hair. His lips were cool, contrasting with the heat of her skin. And the sharp points of his fangs sent jolts of bliss zapping through her like tingles of electricity.

Instinctively, she tipped back her head as he tugged her legs wider. She'd been hoping for a little stress relief. And this was a legendary stress reliever.

Legendary.

She swallowed a scream as his tongue found the tender skin of her cleft. The cool strokes sent flames of need surging through her body. Vampires weren't supposed to have any magic, but his tongue was bewitching her in a spell of pure bliss.

The world melted away until there was nothing but the torturous pleasure of his tongue and her soft pants that filled the cramped room. At last, Brigette's toes curled, and her back arched as an explosive orgasm threatened to rip her apart.

No. Not like this.

"Xi..." Her voice was harsh with the effort of leashing her hunger.

He tilted back his head as her words faltered. "Yes?"

Brigette became lost in the dark temptation of his eyes. "I can't remember," she breathed.

A wicked smile curved his lips. "Good."

With an effort, Brigette gathered her shattered thoughts. She might not deserve happiness, but she was going to do what Xi had suggested. Grab it. With both hands.

"I want to see you naked." She spoke her fantasy out loud.

Slowly, Xi straightened, the air sizzling as his frosty power slammed against her molten heat.

Ice and fire.

An explosive combination.

"You're getting better at this," he assured her, toeing off his boots.

"Maybe you can teach an old dog new tricks," she teased, relishing the sight of the vampire strip show.

First, the thin sweater was pulled over his head and tossed aside. Next, the black jeans were yanked down so Xi could step out of them, leaving him gloriously naked.

Silence filled the room as Brigette slid a slow, appreciate gaze from head to toe and all the delicious places in between. The broad width of his chest, the slender waist, and the impressive thrust of his erection.

She reached out to touch the thick arousal, but Xi was already stepping forward to pull off her sweater, along with the bra that matched her panties.

"We'll learn together," he growled, his fingers trailing over her shoulders and down to cup her breasts in his palms.

Brigette shivered. Partially in pleasure and partially in unease. She was a lone wolf, right? But his words were conjuring the image of being something beyond alone.

"Together," she whispered.

He studied her with a searching gaze. "Does that scare you?"

"It terrifies me," she admitted with a stark honesty.

A vast emotion stirred in the depths of his eyes. "Me too."

They stared at one another, an emotion she wasn't ready to name swelling between them. Then, as if realizing Brigette was on the verge of panic, Xi used his thumbs to tease the tips of her nipples.

"How much do you want me?" he asked in a low voice.

Brigette growled, relieved to focus on the hunger gnawing inside her. Passion was uncomplicated. Exactly what she needed in this moment.

Pressing her hands against his bare chest, she shoved him backward. Xi made a sound of surprise as he was knocked off balance. Brigette shoved again, and he ended up sprawled across the bed.

"I'm not very good with words," she told him with a smug smile. She liked having him spread-eagled beneath her.

He flashed his snow-white fangs as an invitation. "Then show me."

* * * *

Xi watched Brigette with a painful tension. He didn't doubt that she wanted him. Her hunger sizzled in the air. And the musky scent of her arousal teased at his nose like the sweetest aphrodisiac.

But she was terrified of allowing herself to be vulnerable. Her past had taught her that intimacy meant pain. And, worse, she was convinced she deserved to be hurt. He sensed she was caught between fear and the passion that smoldered in her eyes.

Xi held himself still, even as he smiled in challenge. He wasn't going to press her into anything that she might regret. They both had had enough of that in their lives. But he wasn't going to let her use the mistakes she'd made in her life to destroy her future.

Braced for rejection, Xi's dead heart clenched as she released a soft sigh and moved to crawl onto the mattress.

"I can show you," she murmured.

She crouched between his legs, like a wolf about to pounce. Xi shivered. It was sexy as hell. Then, lowering her head, she took his straining erection between her lips.

Xi cursed, his back bowing off the bed. He'd known making love with this female would be different from any of his previous lovers. There was an intensity to their attraction that threatened to consume both of them. But the ecstasy that crashed through him as her mouth slid up and down his cock made his body tremble and his fangs throb.

He reached to grab her arms, pulling her up his body so he could claim her lips in a kiss of stark need. She parted her lips, returning his kiss with a fierce urgency that made him shiver.

Wrapping his arms around her, Xi rolled until she was pinned beneath him. Were females were notoriously violent lovers. A thought that would normally intensify his anticipation. What was more erotic than a female who demanded satisfaction?

But they couldn't risk alerting Maryam or Roban that there was someone else staying at the haven. They might come looking to see who was there.

Gently tugging her arms over her head, Xi urged her to grasp the slates of the headboard. Her lips curved with a slow smile of anticipation.

If Xi had had a beating heart, it would have halted at the sight of her spread beneath him.

Nothing had ever been so beautiful.

"I want you, Brigette," he murmured in a soft voice.

She wrapped her legs around his waist. "How much?"

Xi positioned his cock at her entrance, sliding the tip into it. He wanted to savor each thrust. Each caress. Each cry of pleasure.

"A lot," he growled, slowly plunging deep inside her.

Chapter 18

Brigette brushed kisses over Xi's broad chest, savoring the cool, satin perfection of his skin. She didn't know how much time had passed. It felt as if it'd been mere minutes, but she knew that it had to have been several hours.

Time really did fly when you were having fun, she drowsily acknowledged. And there was nothing more fun than explosive, toe-curling sex with a gorgeous vampire.

She smiled as his arms tightened around her and a low growl rumbled in his throat. Xi's heart might not race, and his skin remained cool to the touch, but she didn't have to guess whether or not he was thoroughly sated. Not only did the scent of cedarwood drench the air, but she could feel the small vibrations that raced through his body from his most recent orgasms.

Xi pressed his lips against the top of her tangled hair, his fingers trailing down the curve of her spine.

"Well?" he murmured.

She tilted her head back in surprise. Surely, he couldn't need reassurance. She'd nearly bitten her tongue off to keep her screams from giving away their presence.

Then, meeting the dark mystery of his gaze, she realized that his question went beyond sex. It veered into dangerous territory. Territory she wasn't prepared to enter.

She forced a teasing smile to her lips, determined to keep him focused on their physical connection. That she could handle.

"Not bad," she assured him.

His brow arched. "Not bad?"

"For an old man."

"I'm not old," he protested. "I'm experienced."

She allowed her fingers to roam over his pale, stunningly beautiful face before moving them to trace the elegant tattoos on the sides of his head.

"Anciently experienced," she helpfully pointed out.

His lips parted to show a hint of fang. "You're welcome."

She shivered. He'd scraped the fangs over her skin and used them to nibble at her most tender parts, but he'd been careful not to draw blood. She understood the care he'd taken, but there was a part of her that deeply resented the fact that she would never feel those long, sharp teeth sliding deep into her flesh.

She arched against him. "Hmm."

He bent his head, his lips touching the tip of her nose. "There's a smile on your face." He nibbled kisses down to the valley between her breasts. "But I sense a conflict in here."

On cue, her heart jerked and skidded, hitting against her ribs. She felt a nearly overpowering urge to cup the back of his head and urge him to sink those fangs into the curve of her throat. Or maybe the plush softness of her breast.

Dangerous territory...

She shivered, lowering her hands to lightly press them against his chest. "I was debating whether to satisfy my hunger for that turkey sandwich or my hunger for an arrogant leech."

His dark eyes flared with an emotion. Disappointment? Then, with a speed that no other creature could match, he was out of the bed to grab the sandwich and chips.

Returning to the bed, he stretched onto the mattress beside her and laid the food between them.

"Eat," he commanded. "I need you to keep up your energy."

With a snort, she picked up the sandwich and ate half in one bite. The meat was processed and the bread stale, but it tasted like ambrosia. It'd been too long since her last meal, and she'd burned through a massive amount of energy.

"I'm a Were," she told Xi, munching through a handful of chips.

"And?"

"And my energy is ten times greater than any leech." She sent him a mocking smile. "With or without a turkey sandwich."

The rich scent of Xi's desire flooded the air. Brigette was instantly on fire for his touch.

"Finish your meal, and we'll see who has the superior vigor," he told her.

Two more bites and the sandwich was gone, along with the last chip. She even licked the salt from her fingers. Yum. At the same time, she glanced at Xi from beneath lowered lashes.

"Are you one of those males who always has to win?"

The scent of cedarwood pulsed through the air, as Xi's snowy white fangs fully extended. "That depends."

"On what?"

"If I am in battle, I have to win."

"I'll give you that one."

"And I would suggest you never play hide-and-seek against me."

She rolled her eyes. "Considering your unique talents, I can guarantee that I'll avoid playing any childhood games against you," she said in dry tones. "Anything else?"

Without warning, he turned his body, rolling on top of her to press her flat against the mattress. He gazed down at her startled face, his expression suddenly somber.

"I have to win you." His voice was low, but she didn't miss the urgency in each word. "Forever."

She hissed, her hands pressing against his chest as she turned her head to the side. "Xi."

"No. Don't look away," he commanded, waiting for her to reluctantly turn back and meet his fierce gaze. "We've been dancing around this since we caught sight of each other."

"I don't dance," she ridiculously muttered.

A rueful smile touched his lips. "No, you're more a bob-and-weave fighter, but it's time to stand still and accept what's happening between us."

She dug her nails into his skin. She'd been so determined to avoid this conversation. And if Xi had any sense, he would want to avoid it as well.

The mere thought of this magnificent creature being trapped with a jaded, evil-tainted Were with a bad attitude was enough to make any demon cringe in horror.

"Please don't make this complicated," she pleaded in a husky voice.

"It's been complicated from the beginning."

He was right. There'd been a primitive tug between them from the moment they'd crossed paths. As if some mystical fate had decided their futures long before they were created.

But she'd ruined any opportunity that might have been hers if she'd chosen another path. And Xi was just another victim of her selfish choices.

Thankfully, she could prevent him from paying the ultimate sacrifice. And that's exactly what she was going to do.

"Xi." She brushed her hands down his bare chest. "I just want to spend today with you."

"And then?"

"Then we capture Maryam and Roban," she said. "Along with whoever is working with them."

"And then?"

She glared into his beautiful face. Why couldn't he let this go? She was trying to protect him.

"I return to my home."

"You have no home."

Brigette flinched at his words. Not just because they were harsh, but because they were painfully true.

"I don't think a vampire who lives in a cave can have an opinion about anyone else's house," she told him in tart tones.

The dark gaze swept over her face. "I'm not talking about a place to live. I'm talking about a family."

A muffled sound of pain was ripped from her throat. Biting her lip, she battled back the tears she refused to shed.

"I can't do this," she rasped.

"Brigette." He lowered his head, burying his face in her hair as if absorbing the musky scent. "What are you afraid of?"

That was easy enough.

"I had a family. And I destroyed them."

He frowned at her blunt response. "And you're not done punishing yourself?"

She shrugged. It was true enough, although it wasn't the entire reason she felt compelled to push him away.

"I don't deserve a family."

His fingers feathered down her cheek, his cool touch sending sparks of hunger shooting through her body.

"Neither do I, but I'm willing to grasp whatever happiness that's offered," he told her.

She pressed him away, her teeth clenched. "I can't dishonor their memories. I can't."

There was a tense silence, then Xi pressed his lips to the hollow beneath her ear.

"Brigette," he whispered.

She held herself stiff. It was that or melt into a puddle of goo. "What?"

"If I stop talking, will you hold me?"

Regret sliced through her. She hated the note of pleading in his voice. Xi was a proud, honorable male who deserved a female who could not only stir his passions but bring him respect as his mate.

Instead, all she could offer was shame.

She should push him away. This had already gone too far. Instead, she wrapped her arms around his neck.

"Yes," she breathed, her voice thick with longing. "Yes, please."

Xi muttered low words of approval, settling next to her as he pulled her tightly against his hard body. Brigette nestled her head onto his chest and savored the feel of his cool power that washed over her.

A few more hours and she would walk away, she silently promised.

Forever.

* * * *

Despite Brigette's emotional outburst, she drifted into a deep sleep. No doubt because she was exhausted. Or perhaps it was because she was enveloped in the strength of Xi's arms. There was nothing like the comfort of knowing she was protected by one of the most powerful creatures in the world.

Still, she wasn't so complacent that she didn't wake the second she caught a whiff of a male Were. Her eyes snapped open, and she sucked in a deep breath. Yep. Definitely Were. And definitely not Roban.

Slipping out of bed, Brigette silently pulled on her clothes, including strapping on her dagger. She had a feeling she was going to need it.

"What's going on?"

Brigette turned her head to discover that Xi was not only awake, but fully dressed. She shook her head. The male was like a ghost, moving through the world with barely a ripple.

"There's a Were in the parking lot. I need to take a look." She nodded across the room. "Go into the bathroom and shut the door."

Annoyance twisted his lean features, but with a jerky nod of his head, Xi headed into the attached room. Once certain that the vampire wasn't going to turn into a pile of ash from a stray shaft of lingering sunlight, Brigette tugged open the door and peered through the narrow crack.

Her stomach dropped at the sight of the dark-haired male leaning against the silver Hummer parked across the lot. The male was thinner than Roban and attired in an expensive cashmere sweater and black slacks, but there was no doubt that the two were related. The stranger had the same harshly carved features and a shaved head. He also had the same arrogant expression.

There was the sound of metal scraping against metal, and Brigette crouched low. Maryam's motel door was opening to allow Roban to slip out before he hastily closed it again. The sun was beginning to set, but it was still bright enough to cause a vampire serious harm.

Barely daring to breathe in case she gave away her presence, Brigette strained to hear the conversation floating from below.

"You're early," Roban snapped, shoving his hands into the heavy leather jacket he'd pulled over his predictable flannel shirt and jeans. "I told you to wait until after sunset."

"Tough. You know how I feel about vampires," the newly arrived Were drawled. "The only good leech is a dead one."

The smell of musk blasted through the air. The two might be brothers, but this wasn't a joyous family reunion. In fact, there was an unmistakable prickle of violence that Brigette could feel even from a distance.

"Careful, Stewart," Roban warned.

"You might be willing to hump a vampire, but I'm only here for the money." Stewart held out his hand. "Cash only."

"It will be yours once you've gotten me inside the house."

Brigette clenched her hands, willing them to be more specific. A "house" told her jack shit about where they were going.

Stewart dropped his hand, a sneer twisting his lips. "Why, bro, I'm beginning to think that you don't trust me."

Roban shook his head in disgust. "Not as far as I can throw you."

Stewart shrugged, opening the driver's door of the Hummer. "Let's get this over with."

"Getting me into the house isn't the only thing you're getting paid for," Roban snapped. "Do you have it?"

Stewart paused, as if having second thoughts. Then, with a growl loud enough to resonate through the parking lot, he reached into the pocket of his jeans and pulled out something that looked like a necklace. He handed it to Roban, who immediately turned back toward the motel.

"I need to give this to Maryam before I leave."

"That leech has your balls in a vice grip." Stewart climbed into the vehicle. "It's pathetic."

"Just wait here. I'll be back in a few minutes."

Shit. Brigette closed the door and straightened. At the same time, Xi was stepping out of the bathroom.

"They're leaving," she told him in a clipped voice. She didn't have time to argue. "I have to follow."

His brows snapped together, his features hard with a combination of fear and frustration.

"Brigette."

"I know." She sent him a rueful smile. "You keep an eye on Maryam." He held out his hand. "Wait."

"I can't. They're in a car. I'll have to find one to keep up with them," she told him, not bothering to mention she'd only driven on a handful of occasions.

"Don't..." His words faltered, as if he couldn't force them past his lips. "I have no plans to die," she assured him. "Not yet."

His dark eyes smoldered with a thunderous emotion as he forced himself to take a step back, shrouded in the shadows.

"I hate this."

"I'll be fine."

"Come back to me," he whispered as she opened the door and cautiously slid out of the room.

Chapter 19

Styx knew he was a control freak. His mate, Darcy, told him that he was obsessively anal and borderline OCD. Viper called him an overbearing dickhead with trust issues. He didn't mind. Being the Anasso meant that he had to be prepared to take command of any situation.

Tonight, however, he willingly allowed Viper to drive as they headed south at a speed that would have them thrown in jail if a human cop happened to catch sight of them. An unlikely event, considering they were on roads that hadn't seen anything faster than a tractor in decades.

He wanted to concentrate on his upcoming encounter with Ian. If he was right and his former brother was in his old lair, then he needed to be prepared.

They were driving along a high bluff overlooking the Mississippi River when Viper asked the question that had, no doubt, been on his lips since they'd retreated to their separate rooms to rest for the day.

"What makes you think that Ian is headed to the caves?"

"When we first encountered Ian, he was a feral beast who'd been rampaging his way across Siberia," Styx said, grimacing at the memory. The male had been as large as a bear, with shaggy gray hair and pale eyes that had glowed with a frenzied insanity. "I wanted to have him destroyed. It was obvious that he possessed a vicious temper and an addiction to causing pain."

Viper kept his hands lightly on the wheel. Despite the fast speed and rough roads, the Jaguar skimmed along as if it was gliding on air. The benefit of state-of-the-art suspension.

"I assume the old Anasso didn't agree?"

Styx absently stroked his fingers over the hilt of his sword, which was angled between his spread legs. The Jag was smooth, but it wasn't the roomiest vehicle. And since he was double the size of most men, it meant a tight squeeze.

"He claimed that every vampire could be salvaged, no matter how violent they might be. At the time, I admired his loyalty to his people. Now..." Styx shook his head.

"What?"

Over the past few years, Styx had learned more and more about his former master. Most of it awful. It made him wonder how he could have been so blind for so long.

"Now I wonder if he kept him because he knew that Ian was utterly devoted to him and would do anything he commanded. No matter how heinous."

Viper nodded. "Like having a rabid dog chained in the front yard?"

"Exactly."

They slowed as the road narrowed to a dirt path. They were getting close. "Even if he is feral, he should know you can't resurrect a vampire," Viper pointed out. "Unless he thinks you can glue a bunch of ashes back together."

Styx shuddered. He devoted a lot of energy to suppressing the memory of his master's death.

"Yeah, I've never heard of a vampire resurrection, but then again, I never heard of a spirit who could drain the power from Weres or an evil beast who could corrupt magic," Styx said in dry tones. The past few years had been filled with one shock after another. Resurrection didn't seem so crazy on the scale of utter insanity he'd been battling.

"Magic doesn't work on vampires," Viper insisted.

Styx shrugged. "As I said, Ian was never stable."

Viper turned onto the short drive that led to the top of the bluff. "What does a delusional resurrection have to do with the rebellion?"

Styx tensed as the white farmhouse came into view. He'd been back here a hundred times. It's where most of his Ravens lived. Hell, he'd lived here himself before mating Darcy. But he'd never allowed himself to think about his former master. Or the fact that the caves were more or less his mausoleum.

"I don't know. It's possible that he wanted me dead before our master returned," he said in absent tones. "I am, after all, sitting on his throne."

Viper sent him a mocking glance. "Yeah, there's nothing more annoying than returning from the dead, only to find someone sitting on your throne."

"Or, worse, trapped in the caves with my Ravens." Styx snapped his fangs together, his fingers tightening on the hilt of his sword. "Of course," he growled. "I've been so blind."

Viper stopped the car next to the house. He turned to eye Styx in confusion.

"I'm still blind. What are you talking about?"

"You destroyed the Anasso in his private cavern," he said, as if the younger vampire might have forgotten.

Not many creatures realized that it had been Viper, not Styx, who'd lopped off the previous Anasso's head. At the time, they'd decided that it would be easier for the vampires to accept Styx as the next king if they believed he'd killed his successor. It wasn't unusual in the demon-world for the role of leader to be decided in a battle to the death. Plus, Viper had been newly mated. The last thing the male had wanted was to be hounded by those vampires who wanted revenge for the death of the previous king. Or, worse, a challenge to take the throne.

Styx had reluctantly taken responsibility. For both the death of the Anasso and accepting the duty of king.

"Yeah, I remember." Viper's jaw tightened. "He was about to kill Shay."

"So if you were going to resurrect him, where would you go?"

Viper switched off the powerful engine. Instantly, a deep silence settled around them. It was more than just the quiet of an isolated spot far from a human town. This was the stillness of a place where powerful demons gathered. Woodland creatures were wise enough to avoid the area.

"I suppose I'd go to where he died," Viper said, following Styx's train of thought. "Although I can't imagine there's anything left but a charred spot on the ground."

Styx nodded toward the house, which was the main entrance to the extensive caves that tunneled beneath the bluff.

"And how would you get to where he died if the place was surrounded by a dozen of the toughest, most skilled warriors in the world?"

Viper muttered a low curse as he finally realized what Styx was implying. "He had to get rid of the Ravens."

"Yes. And what better way than to stir up a revolution against me?"

Viper frowned, as if considering the events of the past weeks. "I can understand the annoying harassment that started all of this, but to try and destroy the clan chiefs along with thousands of demons? That seems a little extreme."

Styx shrugged. "Ian's an extreme kind of maniac."

Viper tapped his slender fingers on the steering wheel, obviously wondering what the hell he'd gotten himself into. Styx didn't blame him. This wasn't the first time Styx had dragged the younger male into a potential deadly encounter.

"If we're going to be facing him, maybe you should tell me more about this Ian," Viper at last said.

Styx shuffled through his memories, dredging up the first time he'd encountered Ian. It should have been a difficult task, considering the number of creatures he'd known during the endless years he'd been roaming the earth. Who could remember them all? But the night they'd stumbled across Ian would be forever seared into his mind.

"I'm not entirely sure what happened in his past," Styx said. "But when we found him in the wilds of Siberia, he'd just slaughtered an entire tribe of tundra fairies."

"Back in the dark ages, most vampires were savages." Viper flashed a mocking smile. "Including you."

"He not only slaughtered them; he'd also skinned them to make his clothing and filed their bones to make spears."

Viper blinked. Most vampires were jaded. It was tough to live for thousands of years and not see the very worst of both demons and humans. Wars. Plagues. Pollution. But there was something particularly noxious about a creature willing to abuse a dead body.

"Gruesome," Viper muttered.

"It gets worse," Styx warned. "There were also hints that the fairies had been alive while they'd been flayed and their bones removed."

Viper shook his head. "Enough."

"You asked."

They exchanged a glance of pure disgust, then Viper visibly turned his thoughts away from the mutilated fairies.

"I assume you managed to tame him?"

"He developed a veneer of civilization," Styx said. "Honestly, he rarely spoke or went out into public. He spent most of his time in the deepest bowels of the lair, protecting the vaults that held the master's most prized possessions."

"Alone?"

Styx nodded. He'd been in charge of the Ravens, and he'd deliberately chosen duties for Ian that would keep him far away from the others.

"Yeah. Always alone."

Viper narrowed his eyes, as if he'd been struck with a sudden inspiration. "What was in the vaults?"

Styx wasn't entirely sure what his friend was asking. "The usual. Treasures, private correspondence..." He struggled to think of anything else. "Oh, and a few rare artifacts."

"What kind of artifacts?" Viper pressed.

Ah. Styx belatedly realized where his friend was headed.

The artifacts.

"The former Anasso was a brutal warrior with a talent for inspiring his people, but he was also wise enough to realize his enemies possessed powers he couldn't fight against," Styx mused.

"Magic?"

Styx nodded. "That was his greatest fear. A fear that only became worse as the tainted blood drove him insane. He was constantly seeking new ways to protect himself. Illusions, artifacts—"

"The blood of a Shallot demon," Viper interrupted in a harsh voice, a nearby tree tilting to a weird angle as the ground beneath it collapsed.

Viper had the ability to loosen the dirt and bury anything, no matter how large.

"Yes." Styx still felt guilty that Viper's mate had nearly been sacrificed to keep their former master clinging to life.

Viper regained control of his temper. "Could some of the artifacts have included death magic?"

"Possibly."

Viper continued to tap his fingers on the steering wheel. "So let's assume Ian possessed some magical item he believed was capable of bringing his master back from the dead. Then he needs to get into the caves where you killed the Anasso to perform his ritual."

"Yes."

"But the caves he wants to enter just happen to be littered with Ravens."

Styx arched a brow. His warriors were the most elite fighters in the world. "I'm not sure littered is the correct term."

"Polluted?" Viper offered. "Infested?"

"Forget it."

"Anyway, Ian decides he has to clear out the warriors," Viper continued. "A task that was easier said than done."

"No shit," Styx said dryly. It would take an entire army to overwhelm his Ravens.

"The most obvious choice would be to kill you."

"A task that is much easier said than done," Styx echoed Viper's earlier words.

"No shit." Viper echoed—or was it re-echoed?—Styx's words. "And there's no guarantee it would lure the Ravens from the caves. He needed them to face an enemy that would be dangerous enough to draw them out and elusive enough to keep them distracted."

"A rebellion," Styx murmured.

"It makes sense."

"It does," Styx agreed. "If it had been one direct attack on me, the Ravens would have come to my defense, but they would have returned as soon as the danger passed. This way, the guards have spent the past weeks focused on the constant barrage of annoying incidents, along with trying to discover who was behind the trouble. And since Brigette revealed the presence of Maryam, they haven't returned here at all. Ian has had free access to search the caves for the precise spot our master was killed."

Styx's gaze returned to the house. He was aggravated that he hadn't suspected that there was more to the rebellion than a random attempt to steal his throne. There had been something strange about it from the beginning. Then, again, Ian had taken great care to avoid being detected, including the rumors of his recent death.

"What are his powers?" Viper asked.

Styx took a second to conjure up the memory. Ian had been violent, brutally strong, and unpredictable. But he was trying to pinpoint the male's unique skills.

"I remember he could create ice," he at last said.

Viper made a sound of surprise. "That's it?"

"Not just frost. But a thick layer that can trap a demon," Styx warned. "I once saw him halt a charging troll with the stuff."

"Anything else?"

Styx shoved open the door and wrestled his way out of the cramped car, careful not to stab himself. Having a massive sword was handy when he needed to cut off heads, but it had its own challenges.

"Probably," he muttered.

There was a brush of cool air, and Viper was standing beside him. "Great."

Styx strapped the sword across his back, sending his companion a humorless smile. "Are you ready?"

Viper moved forward. "Bring it on."

* * * *

For one of the rare occasions in his life, Levet decided to allow discretion to be the better part of velour. Or was it valor? Whatever.

Instead of entering the caves through the front door, he led Troy through the woods until they came to the hidden entrance that he'd used years ago to rescue Shay.

It was just as unpleasant now as it had been back then.

Dark and dank, with a sour stench that made Levet's snout curl in distaste. It was as if the smell of fear and madness had combined into a toxic brew and penetrated deep into the bowels of the earth.

Walking beside him, Troy shuddered. "Why would anyone choose to live in these nasty caves?"

Levet understood the male's disbelief that any creature, even a leech, could linger a second longer than absolutely necessary in such inhospitable surroundings. But he'd spent more than a few decades in precisely this sort of place. When a demon needed to disappear, there was no better place than a hole in the ground.

"They're private," he said with a shrug.

"And damp. And moldy. And cramped," Troy complained, muttering a curse as he was forced to bend over to enter a narrow passageway. "I've banged my head a dozen times."

Levet sniffed. He had no sympathy for the imp. Not after spending the entire day listening to the annoying creature complaining. Really, the male was ridiculously sensitive at the thought of being indebted to Cleo. Why worry about something that might not happen for years? Maybe centuries.

Levet preferred to ignore the bad stuff that was waiting to happen. Why ruin today with worries about tomorrow?

"You should not be so large," he told his companion.

Troy clicked his tongue. "Not all of us can be mini versions."

"True," Levet agreed, glancing down at his short legs. Long ago, he'd resented his height-challenged stature; now he took great pride in stuffing so much awesomeness in such a small package. "Only a lucky few are chosen."

"Some say chosen. Some say cursed," Troy taunted.

Levet stuck out his tongue. "You are just jealous."

"Right now, I'm just sore, and in dire need of a shower." Troy groaned as they reached a larger cave and he was able to straighten. He placed a hand on his lower back, as if it was aching. "Plus this place is giving me the creeps."

"*Oui.* It is creepy." Levet glanced toward the shallow basin in the center of the stone floor. A small pool of stagnant water remained, although any hint of personal belongings had been hauled away and burned. "This is where Damocles lived."

"Who?"

"Damocles." Levet shuddered. The creature might have looked like an angel, but he had a heart filled with evil. "He was an imp who acquired the drug-addicted humans that provided the tainted blood for the previous Anasso."

"An imp pimp?"

"*Oui.* He kept the poor creatures pinned down here like cattle."

Troy's gaze skimmed over the barren cave with something that might be regret.

"Unfortunately, there are a few of my fellow imps who will do anything for a price."

"I am acquainted with one or two of them," Levet said, smirking at his companion.

"Hmm."

"Wait." Troy reached out to grab the top of Levet's wing.

Levet scowled. Rude. "What is it?"

"Magic."

Tugging his wing out of the male's grasp, Levet concentrated on the strange vibrations that pulsed against him.

"What sort of magic is that?" he demanded in confusion.

"Death magic," Troy breathed.

Well, that couldn't be good. Scampering across the cave, he headed into a nearby tunnel.

"Come on."

Chapter 20

Brigette managed to acquire a car less than a mile from the motel. The acquiring took the form of stepping in front of an automobile that was speeding down the highway. Once it squealed to a halt, she pulled the screaming woman out and tossed her aside. Then, squashing her six-foot frame into the compact car, she hit the gas and managed to catch up to the Hummer.

Brigette had expected to arrive at their destination within a few minutes. Why stay at that motel unless it was close to where you were going? It couldn't be for the upscale accommodations. Instead, they traveled for over an hour. Long enough for dusk to paint the sky in shades of peach and soft rose. And long enough to make her muscles tense and a headache form behind one eye.

She'd driven a few times, but never on a highway. And never in pursuit of a Hummer that was traveling well over the speed limit. Staying far enough away not to attract attention, she'd clenched the steering wheel in a death grip and clenched her teeth until they threatened to shatter.

They were approaching a large city that the signs indicated was St. Louis when the Hummer finally slowed and veered onto a narrow road that headed into an elegant suburb.

Winding through tree-lined streets, Brigette glanced toward the houses, which went from big to bigger to enormous. The space between them also became wider and wider. As if they wanted to be close enough to be seen and envied by their neighbor, but far enough to avoid having to acknowledge one another's presence.

At last, they reached the end of a cul-de-sac, and Brigette parked the car, while the Hummer continued down the driveway that headed toward the massive mansion. She hurriedly abandoned the stolen vehicle and jogged down a slope to hide in the shadows of a tall hedge.

Crouching low, she allowed her gaze to take in the house, which was built to curve along the ridge of the hill. It was large enough to fit an entire horde of orcs in comfort, with floor-to-ceiling windows that offered a view of the nearby lake. There was also the thick scent of curs threaded through the evening breeze.

Curs?

What the hell was this place?

She was sorting through the various possibilities when she was distracted by the sound of footsteps. Pressing deeper into the hedge, she watched as Roban and his brother hurried toward the lake. Her brows arched in confusion. She assumed they were going inside.

Her confusion only deepened as they halted next to a large dumpster that was partially disguised behind a wooden grotto.

What were they doing? Planting a bomb? Or was the bomb already there and he was intending to trigger it?

The possibility had her inching her way forward. She wasn't sure how she was going to stop Roban, and not for the first time, she regretted the fact that she'd avoided most human technology. If she had a phone, she could call Styx. Despite the scent of curs, the vampire might know why Roban would choose this particular spot and could warn whoever lived in the mansion.

Careful to stay downwind, she circled the grotto to watch the two men shoving aside the dumpster. They were exchanging a low conversation, then without warning, the brother stiffened. As if Roban had just said something that shocked him.

The air heated as the two males exchanged a muttered argument, and then without warning, Stewart was turning to stomp his way back up the hill, and Roban was suddenly disappearing from view.

Brigette hesitated. She wasn't sure what to do. There was no point in returning to the motel. Night was creeping in, which meant that Maryam would soon be leaving with Xi on her trail. Or more likely, Xi would lose patience and kill her before she could cause any more chaos.

And there was no use trying to warn whoever was in the house. They would either assume she was completely nuts or, worse, believe she was the danger. She did, after all, have a reputation of being utterly evil.

Her only hope was to kill Roban before he could trigger the bomb.

Squaring her shoulders, she darted toward the grotto. A damned shame she didn't have Xi's ability to disguise her presence. Then again, the sudden stench of trash was potent enough to mute her scent. Her lips twisted. She never thought she would be happy to be near a pile of rotting garbage.

She dropped to her stomach as she reached the edge of the cement pad beneath the grotto. Peering through the wooden slats, she could see that the dumpster had been shoved aside to reveal a hidden tunnel.

That's where Roban had disappeared.

And where she had to go to stop him.

Refusing to give herself the opportunity to second-guess her impulsive decision, she crawled on her belly across the cement pad. Once she reached the square opening, she sucked in a deep breath. Rich soil, musty air, and Weres.

Outside the house, there might be curs, but inside were a number of very powerful pureblooded Weres.

Brigette's jaws clenched. A part of her had known that Roban would seek to hurt his own people. He had the same restless dissatisfaction etched on his face that used to plague her. The sort of restlessness that led to outrageously awful decisions.

Pulling her dagger from its holster, she clenched it tight as she inched her way through the tunnel carved into the earth. It was not only pitch-black, but the heavy scent of Were also meant that she would be almost on top of Roban before she sensed his presence. Of course, she couldn't risk allowing him to reach his destination before she could carve out his heart, she sternly reminded herself.

She picked up her pace, brushing her shoulder against the side of the wall to detect any openings. She was too close now to lose track of Roban in a side tunnel.

Thankfully, he continued straight to the end of the tunnel, where an iron door had been carved into the foundation of the house above them.

Brigette halted, watching as the door was pushed open from the inside. Stewart? Probably. The male must have access to the house and a familiarity with the security system. Which was why Roban needed him.

She waited until Roban had disappeared from view before cautiously following behind. Trying to take on two male Weres was going to be... suicidal, but she didn't have a choice.

Not now.

Entering the house, she took a second to glance around the vast, open space of an unfinished basement. There was nothing to see but bare concrete, with steel posts to hold up the massive weight of the mansion. Well, nothing unless you counted the dead Were that was sprawled on the floor with a small silver arrow shot directly through his heart.

Stewart.

Brigette grimaced. Not at the sight of the dead demon. The male had obviously betrayed the Weres in this house by helping Roban to sneak through the hidden passage, and in turn, he'd been betrayed by his brother. Karma was a bitch. As she knew all too well. But she hadn't suspected that Roban had a weapon hidden beneath his jacket.

A silver arrow, no matter how small, was a death warrant for a Were if it penetrated the heart.

Sliding along the edge of cement wall, she searched the darkness for any hint of Roban's location. It was disorienting to go from the cramped space of the tunnel to the open emptiness of the basement. At last, she caught sight of a bulky form headed toward a set of stairs in a far corner.

Once again, Brigette gave herself no time to think of the consequences. Heading straight toward Roban with a short burst of speed, she lifted her hand that held the dagger. As if sensing her approach, Roban halted, but before he could turn and fire his crossbow, she tossed her dagger, hitting him in the center of his back.

It was a risky move.

The blade missed his heart. And now she was without a weapon.

On the plus side, the dagger was imbedded deep in his flesh in a spot that he couldn't reach to pull it out. The silver in the blade would not only swiftly drain his strength; it would also prevent him from shifting into his wolf.

Roban grunted, stumbling to his knees as if thrown off balance by the pain of the wound. He was also kind enough to drop the small crossbow from his nerveless fingers. With a powerful jump, she was flying through the air to snatch the weapon off the cement.

Swearing at the unexpected attack, the Were lifted his head to stare at her in blatant disbelief. "You."

Brigette smiled, pointing the crossbow at the center of her heart. "Did you miss me?"

His jaw clenched, his eyes glowing as his wolf struggled to burst through his skin and rip out her throat.

"You're just full of surprises, aren't you, bitch?" he spit out.

"Better than what you're full of," she taunted.

He snapped his teeth together, the air heating from the force of his fury. "How did you escape?"

She shrugged, not about to reveal anything about Xi or the fact that he was currently keeping an eye on Maryam.

"I have skills you can only dream of possessing."

He curled his lips in disgust, no doubt assuming she was referring to her defunct powers from the Beast.

"You call them skills. I call them evil."

"So says the male who just killed his own brother," she countered.

He jerked in surprise. "How did you know Stewart was my brother?"

"He looks just like you," Brigette smoothly lied. "Oversized head with no neck. Lots of muscle without much power."

Roban hesitated, his breathing labored. The silver was sapping him of his strength.

"I couldn't trust him," the male grudgingly confessed. "I could see in his eyes that he was going to betray me." His lips curled. "Just as I could see it in your eyes."

She narrowed her gaze, not entirely believing his claim. He'd been arguing with Stewart before he entered the hidden tunnel. It'd been more than a fear of betrayal that had caused him to end his brother's life.

Now, however, wasn't the time to worry about the fratricide.

"Some people might call that paranoia," she drawled. "Seeing betrayal in everyone's eyes."

He scowled. "Are you claiming you didn't run to the vampires and rat us out?"

"Of course I did."

"I knew it," he hissed. "I told Maryam you couldn't be trusted."

"Don't give yourself any props. It didn't take a lot of brains to guess that I would turn on you. I am evil, after all."

He turned his head to spit on the cement floor. "Bitch."

"Original." Brigette rolled her eyes before glancing toward the nearby stairs. "What is this place?"

"You don't know?" he mocked.

Brigette slowly turned her head to meet the male's taunting sneer. Just as slowly, she tightened her finger on the trigger of the crossbow.

"Maryam might let you be a smart-ass around her, but I'll carve out your tongue and chop it up for my dinner. Talk."

The sneer remained, but Roban couldn't hide the genuine fear in his musky scent or the sweat that coated his bald head.

"It's the royal household of Salvatore," he reluctantly admitted.

"The King of Weres," Brigette breathed.

Hatred smoldered in Roban's eyes. "The one and only."

That explained the obscene size of the house, as well as the curs. Salvatore was rumored to have a vast army of the creatures as his personal guard. It didn't, however, explain why they were there.

Surely, Styx would have warned Salvatore about the cursed explosives and the need to have the local witch coven provide a dampening spell, wouldn't he? Of course, Roban couldn't know what exactly had happened in Chicago. He might believe that the bombs had gone off as he and Maryam had intended.

"Did you plant an explosive here?" she demanded.

"Naturally."

The word came too easily not to be a lie. If there was a bomb, he would do whatever necessary to keep her from finding it.

She shook her head. "You wouldn't be within a hundred miles of this place if it was ready to explode," she murmured. "You must have brought it yourself."

Eying him up and down, she tried to determine if was carrying some sort of explosive device. He was obviously hiding all sorts of nasty surprises under that jacket.

Then again, maybe the device was already planted somewhere in the house.

Which meant she couldn't kill him until she discovered exactly what was going on.

"Enjoying what you see, bitch?" Roban jeered.

Brigette made a loud gagging sound. This male was cruel and sweaty with a sour scent that made her shudder in revulsion. Just the opposite of Xi's cool, sleek perfection. The vampire was a male that a female could enjoy ogling.

For an eternity.

"You disgust me, but this won't be the first time I've had to hold my nose and do what was necessary to get what I want," she muttered.

He tried to snarl, but it ended up more as a whimper. The silver was not only causing him pain, it was draining his skin to a weird shade of ash.

"What do you want, traitor?" he demanded.

She shrugged. "I wanted to be left alone in my deserted homeland, but you just couldn't let me be."

"If you wanted to be left alone, you would never have come to Chicago." He ground his teeth. "What do you want?"

Xi...

Brigette hurriedly squashed the dangerous thought. The delectable vampire was the one thing she could never have.

"To forget." The words were out before she could halt them. "To sleep without nightmares."

"I can help." He leaned forward, as if willing her to believe his sincerity. "We all have demons to battle."

"We do." She met his fierce gaze with a humorless smile. "I battled mine and destroyed everyone I loved. What you offer is a temporary sense of victory, followed by endless regret."

His brows snapped together. "I'm not destroying my family."

Brigette deliberately glanced toward the motionless form across the basement. "Again. You just murdered your brother."

"I told you. He was going to betray me."

"And the king?" She tried to urge him to reveal his plans for Salvatore. "Why would you want him dead?"

"We have no need for leaders. The Weres were meant to roam free."

Brigette snorted. For a male who'd managed to manipulate hundreds, maybe thousands of demons, he was terrible at lying.

"That's just stupid," she snapped. "Weres are animals at heart. We possess an instinctive need for a pack and an alpha."

A low growl rumbled in his throat, but he was too smart to try to convince her that wolves could suddenly become loners.

"Salvatore is too concerned with the politics of vampires and fey and every other demon," he said in snarled. "Not to mention his pack of squalling whelps. He hasn't bothered to care about his people for a very long time."

Brigette ignored the male's petty complaints. Instead, she sniffed the air. Roban's true reason for trying to kill Salvatore was laced in his scent.

"You're jealous."

He jerked, trying to pretend confusion at her accusation. "What?"

"You want to be Salvatore."

"Bullshit."

"There are very few things I can claim to be an expert on," Brigette said, in dry tones. "Jealousy is one of them. I smell it on you."

Roban leaned back, the frustrated animal inside him glowing in his eyes. "You can't smell shit. Your wolf is dead."

She ignored his attempt to rattle her. There was nothing he could say that would make the loss of her wolf any worse than she had already endured.

"Does Maryam believe that you're doing this to free your poor oppressed people?" she asked. He glanced away, and Brigette's lips twisted. "No, she's not that gullible. You tried to convince her that you're doing it for her, didn't you?"

"I am."

Brigette shook her head, a queasiness rolling through the pit of her stomach. This male was self-absorbed, greedy, and willing to sacrifice anyone to get what he wanted. Just like she used to be.

"You're doing it for yourself," she insisted. "You think if you kill Salvatore, then you can take his place as king."

His lips parted. Was he going to deny her accusation? Then he shrugged, obviously realizing he couldn't fool her.

Not when she'd been the ultimate queen of treachery.

"Why not me?" He tilted his chin, his expression arrogant. "I'd be better than that selfish bastard who forgot who helped put him in power."

"What are you talking about?"

"I was in Italy when he first claimed the crown. I could have sided with the numerous Weres who wanted to challenge him, but I stood with Salvatore." His features tightened with a blatant craving for power. "A mistake."

"This isn't about Salvatore's ability to govern. Or what you did in the past."

His hands clenched, as if willing his claws to emerge so he could slice open her throat.

"You know nothing about it."

"I know that if you truly thought Salvatore was a bad king, you'd face him in a one-on-one battle. That's the way a true leader is chosen." She glanced around the empty basement. "Instead, you're sneaking through hidden tunnels like a coward to stick a knife in his back."

"I don't have a knife." He reached beneath his jacket, and Brigette snarled in warning. "Easy," he murmured, pulling out a small object that was shaped like an oval. "I have this."

Brigette leaned forward, studying the object. It looked like a miniature pineapple and smelled...nasty. She wrinkled her nose. There was a harsh chemical stench that caused the hair on the nape of her neck to rise. Thankfully, she couldn't detect any magic. Which meant it wasn't cursed.

"What is it?" she asked.

"An experimental human invention."

She sniffed again. There was a tang of metal power, but no C-4. "A bomb?"

"An incendiary explosive," he corrected.

"What does it do?"

"It combusts to spread sheets of flames that are impossible to put out." An unmistakable anticipation tightened his features. "It doesn't have the capacity to kill large numbers, like our cursed bombs, but it is lethal in small spaces, and there is no way to defuse it. Not even with magic."

Brigette slowly smiled. She had the information she needed. Now it was time to put an end to this male.

"Clever, but, thankfully, useless once you're dead."

Roban lifted his hand, as if preparing to toss the device in her direction.

"Put down the crossbow, or we'll both be sorry."

"I'm not afraid to die." Her finger tightened on the trigger. "Are you?"

His eyes glowed. "No. I lied."

"Lied about what?"

With a speed that shocked her, Roban was surging to his feet, knocking the crossbow from her hand. Shit. She'd allowed herself to be lulled by the assumption that the silver was draining his powers. Obviously, he'd been exaggerating the extent of his injuries.

Damn drama queen.

Leaping forward, he lifted his hand over his head before slashing it downward. "I do have a knife."

Brigette saw a glint of silver, and she jerked to the side. It wasn't enough to prevent the blade from stabbing deep into her chest, but it prevented the killing blow.

Not that she was going to let Roban realize he hadn't succeeded in his effort to destroy her.

Collapsing on the ground, Brigette rolled to the side. She didn't have to pretend she was mortally wounded. She could feel the warm blood pouring out of the wound to pool on the cement and the shocking pain as the silver began to spread its poison through her body. If she didn't remove the blade, it would soon kill her.

But angling her arm to hide the hilt of the knife, she kept Roban from seeing that he'd missed her heart.

"Die, bitch." He spit on her face and grabbed the crossbow before heading toward the nearby stairs.

Brigette kept her eyes closed as he left the basement, but she didn't miss the sound of his occasional stumble and the loud rasp of his breath. He was injured badly enough to slow him down.

Which meant she still had a chance to stop him.

Clinging to that hope, she reached up to yank the knife from her chest.

* * * *

Maryam didn't bother with a car as she left the motel and headed south. She had the speed and the stamina of a vampire, plus it was faster to cut straight through the empty fields than to use the highway.

Avoiding the farmhouses that were always home to yapping dogs, she flowed through the darkness with powerful ease. It felt good to be out of the tunnels and to run beneath the moonlight. And if she was honest, it felt good to be away from Roban.

The Were had started as a loyal partner. A male who would do whatever she asked without complaint. It was only in the past few weeks that she suspected he had ulterior motives for joining her rebellion.

Not that she was any better. Roban was right when he claimed that the revolution wasn't about honor or duty or anything else she'd tried to make herself believe. She wanted to pretend she was doing this to protect the vampires from being enslaved by the Anasso, but deep in her heart, she knew that she wasn't that noble.

The scrolls that she'd been given had offered her an excuse to strike out. To purge the bitter hatred that had been stewing inside her for centuries. It was only when she'd realized her efforts to overthrow the Anasso had failed that she understood it had never been her true objective.

Her real goal didn't need hundreds of demons. Or Roban.

Just herself.

Reaching the banks of the Mississippi River, she continued south, heading toward the orangish glow of light that was reflected in the night sky. Once, she halted, her skin tingling as if she'd just brushed by a hidden vampire. Glancing around, she could see nothing but the usual woodland animals and a dancing swirl of lightning bugs.

She frowned, then shaking off the sensation of being watched, she continued forward.

Nothing was going to distract her from her target. Not this time.

Resuming her swift pace, she reached the suburbs and circled the large lake that was framed by sprawling mansions. She'd never been to this part of St. Louis, but she easily caught the pungent stench of curs.

A dead giveaway to the location of the King of Weres.

Cautiously approaching the house, she searched for any hint of Roban. His brother was supposed to open a hidden tunnel that would allow them to enter the lair without being detected.

It wasn't until she passed by the grotto that she found his trail. It was nearly disguised by nasty garbage. With a shudder, she forced herself to approach the grotto and drop through the opening in the cement slab.

This had better be the passage into the house. Otherwise, she was going to skin Roban and hang his pelt on her wall.

Traveling down the dark tunnel and through the open door into the basement, Maryam halted long enough to study the dead Were on the floor. This had to be Stewart, Roban's brother. She dispassionately took in the sight of the silver arrow sticking out of the male's chest before shrugging and heading across the cement floor. The male had been an idiot to trust Roban. And he'd paid the price.

She halted again as she neared the stairs. This time, she bent down to study the blood that was smeared across the cement. Were. But not the same Were.

Dipping her fingers in the dark liquid, she licked the sticky substance clinging to her skin. Roban. He'd been badly wounded, judging by the amount of blood. But he wasn't the only one. She touched another puddle of blood before tasting it.

Shock jolted through her.

Brigette.

What was the female doing here? Roban had tried to convince her that the female was determined to betray her. Was he right? Had she somehow discovered their plans and come here to warn Salvatore?

Or...

Were the two working together? Had Roban pretended to hate the female so Maryam would suspect that they'd formed a secret partnership?

Maryam straightened, shaking away the sudden fear that she was walking into a trap. The blood indicated that the two had been in a vicious battle that had left both of them wounded. Whatever was happening between them had nothing to do with her plans.

Dismissing them from her mind, she pulled out the necklace that Roban had convinced his brother to bring to the motel. It was a medallion in the shape of a wolf's head. An ugly piece of metal tied to a leather strap. Hardly her preferred style of jewelry, but it was created by Salvatore to invite a vampire to enter his home.

It was the only way she could pass over the threshold.

She walked up the stairs, entering the pantry. The small room was lined with cupboards and shelves, with an opening into the brightly lit kitchen. Maryam turned away from the main area of the house, choosing the servant's staircase on the opposite side instead.

There was a hum of energy that filled the air and the smothering heat of having so many powerful Weres in one house. It made it almost impossible to locate the female she wanted. Thankfully, there was currently only one

Were in the mansion who was mated to a vampire. Latching onto the cool scent, she followed it up to the third story and turned to the right.

The furnishings were elegant, with polished wood paneling on the walls and soft peach carpets on the floors. Overhead, an open-beamed ceiling gave an illusion of cozy warmth. There was, however, an echo of emptiness, assuring her that she was in the guest wing of the house.

Reaching the end of long hallway, Maryam paused to press her hand against the closed door. Inside, she could sense a Were, but nothing else. Perfect.

Grabbing the handle, she shoved the door open, not surprised to discover that it wasn't locked. This was the lair of the King of Weres. Who would be stupid enough to invade it?

Stepping over the threshold, Maryam swept her gaze over the large suite that was decorated in soft shades of peach and cream. There was a sitting area with a small sofa and two matching chairs, and across the room was a small, delicate female just finishing the task of smoothing the comforter over a wide bed. Although Weres could tolerate sunlight, they were nocturnal creatures who preferred to hunt beneath the moonlight. Obviously, Darcy had just gotten up and was preparing for the night.

Turning at the sound of Maryam's entrance, the female revealed her short, spiky blond hair and large green eyes. Her heart-shaped face and fragile features made her look like a human teenager rather than a vicious, predatory werewolf.

Maryam wasn't fooled. This female could shift into her animal and rip off her head if she wasn't careful. Which was why she'd come prepared.

Reaching into the black Dior handbag she'd matched with her cashmere sweater and black slacks, she pulled out a small handgun that was loaded with silver bullets. One shot through the heart and the bitch would be dead.

But first, she wanted to make sure that this female knew exactly why she was there.

"Darcy?"

"Yes?" The female studied her with more curiosity than fear. "Who are you?"

"Maryam."

The air was filled with a sudden blast of heat as the female belatedly realized precisely who had intruded into her private rooms.

"The traitor," she muttered, stepping away from the bed. Was she hoping to make a dash toward the door?

Maryam shook her head. No, it was more likely she was hoping to reach her phone, which was on the nearby nightstand.

"Good guess, Darcy," she mocked, lifting her hand to reveal the handgun.

Darcy stiffened, clearly aware of the danger she was in. Still, her expression remained one of disdain.

"That's Queen Darcy to you, leech," she chided Maryam.

The agonizing pain that she'd kept suppressed for centuries erupted in one glorious explosion of fury.

The heat in the air was replaced by a coat of ice, the walls cracking beneath the force of her power.

"You will never be my queen, dog," she snapped, instantly regretting the loss of her usual cool composure.

She wanted to be in command of this encounter. To face this female with a dignity and grace that honored the memory of her dead mate. But just seeing the Were standing there, alive and glowing with happiness, when her own heart was shattered...

It was too much.

"You're right. I won't be your queen, because you'll soon be tried and convicted for your attempt at mass murder," the female said, her tone filled with a smug assurance that only inflamed Maryam's fury.

Did the bitch think she had the right to judge her?

She was surrounded by luxury, adored by her family, and treated with a respect she'd done nothing to earn. Most of all, she had the unwavering love and loyalty of her mate.

Maryam resisted the urge to step forward. She was in command of the situation, but she wasn't going to forget that there were several Weres and curs roaming through the house. She needed to be prepared for a quick exit.

"It was a revolution," she corrected in sharp tones.

Darcy folded her arms over her chest, as if she didn't have a care in the world. "It was a psychotic hissy fit that failed."

Maryam narrowed her eyes, struggling to leash her temper. "It's true that I failed to destroy the Anasso. But I can have the next best thing."

"What's that?"

"Destroying his mate." She smiled. Just saying the words felt good. As if they purged as small amount of the bitterness gnawing inside her like a corrosive acid. "As the Anasso destroyed my mate."

Darcy blinked, her expression confused. "Styx killed your mate?"

"The previous Anasso."

"Oh." Her confusion remained. "What does that have to do with Styx?"

She didn't bother to lie. Not now. This was, at last, the time for her to be honest. With herself. And with this female who was about to be sacrificed.

"He snatched away my opportunity for revenge," she replied, revealing the hatred that burned in her unbeating heart. "I should have been the one to strike the killing blow. It was my right."

Darcy's lips parted, genuine horror in her green eyes. "You've started a revolution that threated to destroy thousands of demons because you were peeved you didn't get to kill the Anasso?"

Maryam hissed. "You have no idea what it means to lose a mate."

"No, I don't, thank the goddess." Darcy shook her head. "But I can't imagine that killing innocent creatures would make me feel better."

Maryam shrugged. "We each grieve in our own way. I only wish that Styx could be here to see the female he loves scream in pain."

Aiming the gun at Darcy, she was placing her finger on the trigger when the shrill shriek of an alarm blasted through the house.

Shit. It had to be Roban.

Momentarily distracted, Maryam cast a quick glance over her shoulder. Any second, the guards would be filling the hallways. She needed to finish this and...

The sound of running footsteps warned her that she'd allowed herself to be dangerously sidetracked. Quickly spinning back, she saw Darcy sprinting across the room. Instinctively, she pressed the trigger, assuming that the Were was intending to tackle her to the ground. It wasn't until the bullet flew wide of the mark that she realized she'd miscalculated.

The female was clever enough to feint an attack before she veered to the side and, with one smooth motion, leaped headfirst through the window.

Maryam cursed at the sound of shattering glass. The Were was trying to escape. Without bothering to consider the consequences, Maryam surged forward, leaping through the opening of the broken window and landing on the soft ground below.

The house was now ablaze with lights, the alarms shrilly piercing the air and the thunder of footsteps warning that the guards were searching for any intruders. Maryam ignored the commotion, furiously focused on the scent of the fleeing dog.

She raced along the narrow path that led toward a nearby conservatory. Did the female think she could hide among the daffodils and petunias? Or was there some hidden trap she was intending to spring?

It didn't matter.

Nothing mattered but striking the killing blow.

The blow intended for the previous Anasso.

The image of Styx howling in pain when he discovered that his mate was dead had just managed to form in her mind when there was a blur of movement from a nearby hedge. She came to a halt, baffled when she couldn't catch any scent or sense any presence.

What had caused the shadow?

Waving the gun from one side to the other, Maryam was prepared to shoot anything that moved.

Unfortunately, her grim determination couldn't protect her from the mystery attacker who had already managed to circle around her. She felt the necklace yanked away from her throat at the precise moment the silver blade was shoved through her back and directly into her heart.

"Nooooo!" her scream of fury echoed through the air as she fell to her knees.

How could fate be so cruel as to snatch away her chance of revenge?

It wasn't fair.

It wasn't...

* * * *

Xi held the necklace in his fingers as he watched the female tumble face-first onto the ground. Seconds later, the slender form shuddered, the flesh cracking like an empty shell. Then, with an unnerving speed, Maryam was gone, and nothing remained but a layer of ash on the dew-kissed grass.

Lingering long enough to make sure the traitor was well and truly dead, Xi turned away.

He no longer had any interest in the female. Any threat she posed was over, and with the necklace he'd taken from around her throat, he could now enter the house.

His only thought was reaching Brigette.

Chapter 21

Styx grimaced as they entered the long open space with a low ceiling and a thick smell of mold. He had avoided this particular cavern, and none of his Ravens had a reason to be in this part of the vast maze of tunnels and caves.

It was here that Styx and Viper had battled against his old master, and the darkness that had been a part of the previous Anasso's soul seemed to linger. Cautiously glancing around the empty space, Styx frowned. He could feel Ian's presence. It pulsed through the room with a raw, savage force. But he couldn't see him.

"Styx, be careful," the younger male warned. "There's someone—"

The words were still on his lips when a blast of ice shot down from the ceiling, aimed directly at Styx.

Shit.

Styx braced himself for the impact, but before the sheet of ice could slam into him, Viper was leaping in front of him. Styx cursed, watching helplessly as the ice slammed Viper against the wall and crawled over him like a living force. Within seconds, the male was completely encased in a layer of frost. Like a frozen cocoon.

An unwelcome sense of déjà vu clenched Styx's stomach, forcing him back to that horrifying night when he'd been forced to destroy his old master.

He'd been in this cavern with Viper, finally forced to witness the spiraling madness that consumed the once proud King of the Vampires. And when his master had tried to strike a killing blow against Viper, it'd been Styx who'd stepped in front of his friend to take the blow, while Viper had used Styx's massive sword to end the Anasso's life.

Now the battle had been reversed. Viper had sacrificed himself so Styx could end the threat to the vampires.

Shaking off his fury at allowing Ian to catch them by surprise, Styx lifted his sword and glared at the male who dropped from the ceiling.

"Release him," he snarled, warily studying the male, who stood in the center of the cavern.

Ian had changed. A shocking realization, considering that vampires didn't age. His large frame had thinned to the point of emaciation. And his once-lustrous gray hair was now a lank curtain that framed his gaunt face. He was wearing a heavy leather coat that looked worn and frayed, along with slacks that were coated in dirt. As if he couldn't be bothered with his appearance.

His eyes, however, still burned with the same frenetic fire.

"Did you hear me?" Styx snapped. "Release him."

Ian smirked. "Poor idiot," he taunted, glancing toward Viper, who was barely visible beneath the ice. "Yet another victim of your bloated ego."

Styx cautiously moved forward. He couldn't sense anyone else in the cavern, but he'd been caught off guard once; he wasn't going to let it happen again.

"Ian—"

"Take another step, and I'll destroy your companion," Ian interrupted, lifting his hand toward Viper.

"Don't," Styx rasped, coming to an abrupt halt. He had no idea if Ian could actually kill Viper with his ice, but he wasn't going to risk his friend's life.

"That's better." Ian smiled with smug satisfaction. "I'll admit that I didn't expect to see you here."

Styx lowered his sword. He was going to have to somehow distract Ian long enough to strike a killing blow. His lips twisted. Yeah. No problem.

"I didn't expect to see you anywhere," he said, stepping to the side so he was standing between Ian and the helpless Viper. "You were supposed to be dead."

Ian shrugged. "I needed to disappear."

"Why?"

The vampire reached beneath his coat to pull out a rolled sheet of parchment that was tied with a leather strap. He waved it toward Styx.

"I was searching for this."

"What is it?"

"A scroll my master collected centuries ago."

Styx frowned. He couldn't detect magic, but he could smell the aged blood that clung to the parchment. In the olden days, witches often used sacrifices to create their spell.

"Magic," he muttered.

"A very ancient magic."

Styx glanced from Ian to the blackened stain on the stone floor, where his master had died.

"Do you really believe you can resurrect the Anasso?"

"Resurrect?" Ian looked momentarily baffled. As if Styx was speaking in a foreign language. Then his lips curled in disdain. "Ah. You've been talking to Locke."

There was no point in denying his conversation with their fellow Raven. "He said you were planning a resurrection."

Ian shook his head. "You can't bring a vampire back from the dead."

Styx blinked in confusion. Obviously, this male wasn't the complete nutbar that he'd suspected, but that didn't mean he wasn't plotting something nefarious.

"Then what are you resurrecting?" he asked.

"The future."

"Is that supposed to make sense?"

Ian gave another wave of the scroll. "This spell will take me to my master."

Okay. He was right the first time. This male was a total nutbar. "He's dead."

Ian's eyes smoldered with a pale fire, as if he was being consumed by some intense emotion burning deep inside him.

"I am well aware of that," he growled.

"Then how can the magic take you to him?"

"It will return me to the last moments of his life."

Styx tried to sort through the words. Was Ian saying he could use the magic to see what had happened just before the Anasso was killed? He'd heard that a few rare imps could try to peek into the past. But he sensed the male was hoping for more than a glimpse of his former master.

"Time travel?" he finally demanded.

"A brief visit." Ian shrugged. "The witches created this as a way to say goodbye to a loved one. Or pass along important information."

Styx resisted the urge to roll his eyes, covertly inching closer to the male. Any witch willing to use blood magic had no loved ones, dearly departed or not. It was, however, quite likely that witches used the magic to retrieve spells or incantations that might be lost by an unexpected death of a coven sister.

"You want to say goodbye?"

"No." Ian snapped his fangs, like a rabid dog desperate to bite their enemy. "I want to be there so I can destroy you before you can strike the killing blow."

Styx arched his brows. He thought trying to resurrect a vampire was crazy. But Ian's belief that he could travel back to the moment when the old Anasso had died and somehow keep Viper from lopping off the male's head was even more insane. There were strict limits on magic that prevented meddling in timelines.

"You can't alter the past," he said, as he took another step. And then another. He was still too far to risk an attack, but he was gaining ground. Right now that was enough.

"Watch me." Ian removed the leather strap, tossing it away.

"Why?" Styx loudly demanded. He had no idea what the spell would actually do, but he didn't want to find out.

Ian sent him an impatient scowl. "What?"

"Why now?" Styx asked. He just wanted to keep the male talking until he could get close enough to strike. "Why didn't you use the scroll as soon as you discovered the Anasso was dead?"

A shadow passed over the male's face, as if he was haunted by a dark memory.

"I wasn't in my right mind after I leaned what had happened."

"You mean you went insane?"

Ian's features hardened at the question. "My servants were forced to chain me in my lair to keep me from walking into the sunlight to end my grief. Eventually, I regained command of my emotions. I no longer wanted to die. I wanted *you* to die." A layer of ice flowed across the floor, threatening to freeze Styx's boots to the stone. "But, more importantly, I wanted my king returned."

Styx shrugged. He had no sympathy for this male. He was a savage beast who should have been put down centuries ago.

"Where did you get the scroll?"

"It was left behind in the hidden vaults of our London lair." Ian confirmed Styx's theory.

"Is that also where you found the scrolls that convinced Maryam that I was intending to enslave the vampires, not to mention confining the Weres to their homeland?"

Ian jerked, as if he was shocked that Styx had managed to figure out that he was responsible for manipulating Maryam into betraying him. His jaws clenched with annoyance, but he forced a smile to his lips.

"Very good."

Styx stepped forward. "Why her?"

Ian waved a dismissive hand. "I traveled with the master to deal with the clan chief of St. Petersburg after her refusal to bend the knee. After the chief was dead, I watched her mate battle through a dozen warriors trying reach the Anasso to annihilate him. That much pain and fury would never go away. It festers until it must be purged." Another layer of ice formed on the floor. "I know."

"You used her to distract me so you could enter these caves," Styx said.

Ian unrolled the parchment, preparing to read the incantation written on it in blood. "I needed the ashes to bind the spell to my master."

Styx lifted his sword. It was soon going to reach the point where he had no choice. He either launched his attack or the bastard completed the spell.

"But you didn't dare confront my Ravens," he taunted, no longer trying to disguise his approach.

Ian squared his shoulders, clearly welcoming the impending battle. "There was also the hope that the rebels might get rid of you." A savage snarl curled his lips, revealing the fully extended fangs. "Now I'm glad they didn't. I want to kill you now and then again in the past. Double the pleasure."

"Better vampires than you have tried." Styx stepped to the side, slowly circling closer. "And failed."

* * * *

Brigette easily followed Roban through the vast mansion, despite her weakened condition. She didn't need her wolf to track the trail of blood that stained the peach carpets. Obviously, the male hadn't been able to dislodge the dagger stuck in the center of his back.

Thank the goddess. Although she had pulled the knife from her chest, she no longer had the ability to heal like a regular Were. The wound in her chest not only hurt like a bitch, but it was draining her strength at an alarming rate.

Heading up the stairs, Brigette followed the blood spatter to the end of a long, paneled hallway. Then, without hesitation, she pushed open the door and stepped into a large room with a peach velvet sofa and two rocking chairs beneath a bay window.

She frowned. This wasn't the master suite. This was...

Horror clenched her heart as she glanced toward the opening, where she could see into the connecting room. Inside, she could see the bunk beds and piles of toys.

A nursery.

No. No, no, no.

Struggling to think clearly, Brigette was forced to shove aside her revulsion as Roban stepped out of the inner room. The male came to an abrupt halt at the sight of her, a flush of anger staining his face.

"You."

Brigette spread her feet and prepared for battle. "Like a bad penny."

"Christ." The male stepped forward, lifting his arm to reveal the crossbow he held in his hand. "Why won't you die?"

Brigette shrugged. "A question I've asked myself."

"It doesn't matter." Roban glanced over his shoulder. "It's too late to stop me."

It felt as if her stomach dropped to the tips of her toes. "You've planted the bomb in the nursery?" She returned her gaze to his face, studying the blunt features that were tight with pain and something else...not regret. But resignation. As if he understood he'd crossed a line, but was unable to stop his evil compulsion. "What's wrong with you?"

Roban licked his lips; then, with an effort, he was squaring his shoulders. "You were right."

"Right about what?"

"The only way to become the king is to defeat Salvatore."

She frowned. When Roban had been describing the device, it had sounded as if it had a limited range. So why not put it in Salvatore's bedroom?

The answer hit her as Roban glanced away in embarrassment. "But you can't. Not in a fair fight," she said.

"No." Roban shrugged. "But after he's weakened by the death of his pups, I'll have the chance I've always dreamed of."

"That's why Stewart was arguing with you," she spat out, each word thick with loathing. "He realized that you weren't trying to kill Salvatore, but were cowardly intent on murdering those innocent babies."

"He was willing to do anything for cash. Until I asked the location of the nursery," Roban muttered. "I could see he was getting cold feet."

"So you killed him."

A sour scent of desperation tainted the air. The male was on the edge of madness.

"He shouldn't have developed a conscience." Roban turned his back to stab her with an accusing glare. "Just as you shouldn't have."

"You're probably right."

Brigette gripped the knife in her hand. Then, without warning, she leaped forward. Roban had been expecting her attack, and the second she moved, he was pressing the trigger on the crossbow.

A silver arrow flew through the air, heading straight for her heart. Brigette whipped around so the projectile hit her in the side. It plunged easily through her flesh, scraping a rib before penetrating her lung.

Brigette was barely aware of the pain that tore through her; instead, she focused on the male, who was desperately trying to back away. Ramming him into the wall, Brigette plunged the knife into the center of his heart.

"It's too late. You can't stop the device," he choked out. "It's already set to go off."

Brigette twisted the blade until the life seeped out of the male's eyes. "I'm not going to fail. Not this time."

"Too late," he rasped, sliding down the wall to collapse at her feet. "Too...late..."

"No," Brigette muttered, heading into the connecting room.

She didn't have to stay. She could already smell Roban's death, and soon his body would be consumed with the flames that would return his soul to the wolf-spirit. He was no longer her worry. But saving the pups...

Dropping to her hands and knees, she searched underneath the beds, in the closets, and through the pile of toys. At last, she found the device hidden behind a laundry basket, and scooping the pineapple-shaped object off the floor, she returned to the outer room.

She wasn't going to be too late, she told herself over and over. For the first time in her life, she had the opportunity to truly make amends for what she'd done in her past, and failure wasn't an option.

Pausing long enough to grab one of the rocking chairs and toss it through the window to set off the alarms, she raced out of the nursery and toward the servants' staircase.

At one point, she thought she heard a male calling her name, but it was hard to be sure. Her heart was thundering, and the shrill alarms were piercing her poor ears. Besides, it didn't matter. She had one job. And nothing was going to distract her.

She crossed the pantry and headed toward the opening to the basement. Once she was there, she could toss in the device and close the door.

A fantastic plan. Unfortunately, she was just inches away when there was a faint hiss and the pungent stench of chemicals assaulted her nose. As she launched the device toward the doorway, the flames abruptly exploded.

Most of them raced toward the basement, but enough of the chemicals had spilled on Brigette to ensure her destruction. With a resigned acceptance that her end had finally arrived, Brigette watched the flames crawl up her arms.

"I love you, Xi," she murmured, conjuring the image of the male who had become the center of her existence.

An odd peace surrounded her, as Brigette dropped to her knees and bowed her head in defeat. Just the thought of Xi was enough to protect her from any pain as the fire consumed her.

Chapter 22

Levet's pace slowed the closer he came to the large cavern. It wasn't just the memory of their battle against the demented Anasso that caused his feet to drag, although the heavy atmosphere pressed against him like a shroud of doom. *Non*, it was the layer of frost that was making the stone beneath his feet perilously slippery.

A shiver shook through him as the neared the arched opening. "It's cold," he muttered.

"Really, really cold," Troy agreed, walking next to him with a grim expression. The imp clearly hated the dark, soggy maze of caves. Not surprising. Fey creatures adored sunshine and open meadows.

Or, in Troy's case, tawdry strip joints and loud music.

"Someone should tell the vampires that it is rude to go about covering everything in frost," Levet complained as he slid forward, barely preventing himself from skidding straight into the cavern ahead of them.

Troy snorted. "That sounds like a job for a gargoyle."

Levet shrugged in resignation. "I suppose it will be my duty. Everything else is."

A loud roar echoed through tunnels, shaking the earth and threatening to tumble thousands of tons of rocks on their head.

"Styx," Troy hissed.

No other demon had the sort of power to cause destruction on such an epic scale. Well, perhaps dragons. And Jinns. Oh, and his beloved Inga, now that she held the Tryshu in her mighty hands.

Levet shook away the distracting thought, forcing himself to peer through the opening.

As he expected, he discovered Styx in hyper-battle mode, the massive sword cutting huge swaths through the air and his fangs fully extended. Levet shivered. The male was a pain in the derrière, but there was no arguing that he was an impressive warrior.

His attention turned to the vampire Styx was attempting to sever in half with his oversized sword.

"Who is that?" he asked, running his gaze over the male vampire with his stringy gray hair and skeleton body.

Troy shook his head. "I don't recognize him."

Levet wrinkled his snout. "He smells weird."

"Weird? What does that mean?"

"Odd. Peculiar. Abby normal."

Troy made a sound of annoyance. "I know the definition. What's weird about his smell?"

Levet studied the too-thin vampire as he stood in front of Styx. He didn't possess the talent to see auras around creatures, but he could smell them.

"It's tainted," he said.

Troy sucked in a sharp breath. "Evil?"

"Madness."

Together, they watched as the strange male lifted his hand to shoot out sheets of ice that threatened to slice off Styx's head. The Anasso leaped to the side, smashing the frozen projectile with his sword. The ice shattered to fall harmlessly to the ground, but even a quick glance was enough to reveal that Styx was being subtly herded into a shallow alcove. Once he was cornered, he wouldn't be able to avoid the lethal shards.

"Shit," Troy abruptly muttered. "Look over there."

Levet glanced in the direction Troy was pointing. At first, all he could see was a lump of ice that covered the far wall. Then he caught sight of silver hair and a furious male face.

"Viper," he breathed in amazement. "He has been turned into a lollipop."

"A popsicle."

"Same thing." Levet waved his hand in an airy motion, fascinated by the sight of the powerful demon frozen solid. Could he see what was happening? Could he hear the battle? Would he mind if Levet took a selfie with him and posted it on Instagram? So many questions...

"We need to get him out of there," Troy abruptly announced. "As much as I might dislike the smug bastard, I have a feeling that whoever would replace him as the clan chief of Chicago would be much worse."

Levet wasn't nearly so certain. Who could be worse than Viper? Then again, Shay would be devastated to lose her mate.

"*Oui.* You assist Viper," he murmured, spreading his wings and stiffening his spine. "I will offer my considerable skills to aid Styx in his battle."

"Wait." Troy reached out to lay a restraining hand on his shoulder. "What are you going to do?"

Levet clicked his tongue. What a stupid question. "Use my magnificent magic."

"Absolutely not."

Levet's tail snapped angrily around his feet. "You're not the boss of *moi.*"

"Do you see that scroll in the vampire's hand?"

Levet turned to glance toward the stranger, belatedly noticing the curled parchment the creature was clutching. "Of course I see it. I am not deaf," he muttered.

"It's an ancient spell. And, even from here, I can sense it's unstable. One of your whacky fireballs and you'll blow us all to the netherworld." Troy glared down at him. "Got it?"

"*Oui.* I got it." Levet waved a dismissive hand toward the imp. "Go, do something with the Viper-frosty-pop."

Troy muttered beneath his breath, entering the cavern and inching his way along the wall toward Viper. Levet headed in the opposite direction. He didn't know what he was going to do without his magic. He needed to distract the creepy vampire long enough for Styx to do something with his big sword. Like chop off the male's head.

He managed to sneak close enough to feel the full effect of the vampire's icy power. Any closer and his poor tail would be frostbitten. So now what?

Glancing around, he looked for some sort of weapon. There was nothing. Not unless he counted the big stone with a jagged edge that was inches from his feet.

Just in front of Levet, Styx was forced to leap again as the ice flew toward his throat. He landed lightly despite his massive size, but the ice beneath his feet caused him to slip. There was a shout of victory from the strange vampire as he lifted his hand to hit Styx with yet another blast of ice.

Sacre bleu. It was now or never.

Reaching down, Levet grabbed the stone and tossed it with all his might at the attacking vampire.

The rock flew through the air, heading straight for its target, but just as it reached the stranger, the male moved to the side. It wasn't that the vampire realized the rock was coming; he was simply trying to find a better angle to strike at Styx. But the small step was enough to allow the rock to fly harmlessly by, instead thumping the King of the Vampires right between the eyes.

Levet stomped his foot in frustration, his hand rising. He didn't care what Troy had said. He was going to use his fireballs. He might cause a ginormous explosion, but at least he would have halted the battle.

But even as he called on his magic, the unknown vampire was spinning to glare at him in dazed confusion. Obviously, he hadn't realized that Levet had managed to sneak up on him.

The momentary distraction was all that Styx needed. Holding his sword in both hands, he held it high and then swooped it down to slice off the vampire's head in one clean sweep.

Levet widened his eyes as the head bounced at his feet and then exploded in a puff of ash.

"I did it," he breathed, glancing up at Styx, who was still holding his sword, a bloody wound in the center of his forehead from where the rock had smashed into him. "I saved the world. Again!"

Epilogue

It had been a busy three weeks since the night that Styx had confronted Ian in the caverns. He'd personally taken the imp to each location where the cursed explosives had been planted, making sure that each and every one of them had been destroyed. Then he'd searched through the tunnels to gather clues to those who'd been involved in the revolution. Many of them had left behind personal items that would allow his Ravens to make sure they'd already been captured or to track down those who were still trying to hide from his judgment.

And, of course, he'd been consumed with the need to spend quality time with his mate. Just the thought that he might have lost her was enough to give him nightmares.

Tonight, however, he'd refused to consider his endless duties. This evening, he was going to enjoy the pleasure of Viper's company and a very expensive bottle of brandy.

Sitting in his private office, Styx was settled in his heavy leather chair, while Viper was leaning against a bookshelf, a crystal snifter held in his slender fingers. The younger male had fully recovered from being coated in ice and, as usual, was dressed in an elegant velvet coat and satin pants.

"Have you heard from Xi?" Viper asked.

Styx grimaced. "No. The last I knew, he was headed to Ireland."

"Is that healthy?"

"I've asked Cyn to check on him." Styx felt a familiar frustration. He'd been too late to track down Xi. By the time he'd learned that Brigette had sacrificed herself to save Salvatore's children, the male had already disappeared. "It's all I can do. At least for now."

Viper lifted his glass in a somber tribute to the courageous Were. "I was so worried that the female was going to betray us, it never occurred to me that she might prove to be a hero."

"We all owe her a debt of gratitude." Styx lifted his own glass. "A damned shame she isn't here for us to tell her."

They both took a drink of the wicked-smooth brandy. Then Viper glanced toward the painting of a beautiful female with bright green eyes and spiky blond hair that hung above Styx's desk.

"How is Darcy?"

Salvatore's lips twitched. He was still infuriated that his mate had been targeted by Maryam. And that he hadn't been there to protect her. On the other hand, his fierce spitfire of a mate was more than capable of taking care of herself.

"More than a little pissed that Xi managed to kill Maryam," he said dryly. "She'd been waiting around the corner with a wooden stake she was hoping to stick into her heart."

"Sweet, gentle Darcy?"

"She's pure demon when it comes to protecting her family."

"Understandable." Viper moved to take a seat opposite Styx, his expression suddenly weary. "Is it over? Ian is dead. Along with Maryam and Roban."

"I'm still investigating the rebels. Most of them were there for a free meal and a warm place to sleep, but there are a few who are eager to continue the revolt." Styx's lips curved with a smile of anticipation. There were some parts of his job that he truly enjoyed. "I would like to have a personal conversation with them."

"I hope the conversations are short and brutal."

"Those are the best kind."

They exchanged an amused glance. "Indeed they are."

About to polish off the last of his brandy, Styx caught the unmistakable scent of granite. That could only mean one thing.

His peaceful evening was about to be destroyed.

Surging to his feet, he watched in annoyance as the tiny gargoyle waddled into his office.

"Who the hell let you in?" he growled.

Levet stuck out his tongue. "Darcy, of course. She adores me."

She did. That was the only reason this aggravating creature wasn't stuffed and mounted over his fireplace.

"Get out," Styx snapped.

Levet puffed out his chest, his ugly little features set in a stubborn expression. "Not until I receive my reward."

"Reward?" Styx frowned in confusion. "Reward for what?"

"For saving you."

The chandelier overhead trembled at the force of Styx's blast of temper. "You hit me with a rock."

"*Oui.* I was trying to distract the bad vampire."

"Then why didn't you throw a rock at him?"

"I missed." Levet smile was pure innocence. "But it worked out for the best. The vampire was distracted, and you cut off his head. Winner winner turkey dinner."

Styx narrowed his eyes. He wasn't fooled. Not for a minute. The little bastard had deliberately hit him with that rock.

"Someday," he snarled.

* * * *

Xi finished polishing the brass knob he'd just installed in the wooden door and stepped back. It'd taken almost two weeks and his super vampire speed, but he'd finally finished building the cottage in the center of the devastated village.

The white stones and thatched roof looked out of place against the landscape, which was a sickly gray from the evil that had cloaked this place for so long. But the toxic fog was gone, and eventually the heather and sage would return. When that happened, he would plant a garden at the back of the cottage.

Satisfied he'd created something that would make Brigette proud, he pulled the two daggers from beneath his coat.

He held the matching pair flat in his palms, the memory of finding Brigette's weapon in the basement seared in his mind.

He'd been so close.

After using Maryam's necklace to enter Salvatore's lair, he'd easily caught the scent of his female. He'd raced through the house, determined to protect her, but even as he'd charged into the pantry, the flames had engulfed her. When the fire had at last faded, there'd been nothing left but the dagger.

Numb with disbelief, Xi had grabbed the weapon and headed to Ireland. At first, he didn't know why he was compelled to travel to the remote, devastated village.

Was it his grief? Was it driving him to be closer to the one place Brigette called home? That would be the reasonable place to mourn her loss. But even as he'd huddled in the barren landscape, the ocean wind whistling a soulful song over the shattered foundations, he'd realized it wasn't enough.

He was still numb, waiting for the crippling pain to hit.

He needed to build a shrine to his mate, he'd realized. A place where he could feel her presence. Or perhaps he just needed to stay busy to maintain his sanity.

Whatever the reason, his task was completed. Now he was going to…

His thoughts were fractured as the daggers slowly lifted off his palms.

Xi hissed in horror as they floated midair. Magic. It had to be. But how?

He stumbled back, watching as the daggers began to spin, twirling faster and faster as a bright glow surrounded them.

"No!" Xi roared in fury.

The dagger was his last tangible connection to Brigette. He damned well wasn't going to let it be destroyed.

Impervious to the potential danger of touching the glowing magic, Xi reached out to snatch the daggers. His fingers passed through the unnatural light, wrapping around a thick hilt. There was a sizzle of energy that crackled like electricity. Or a lightning bolt.

Expecting to be scalded by the weird magic, Xi instead found himself pulled forward by the weight of the dagger. With an effort, he regained his balance, frowning in confusion. It wasn't until he lifted his arm that he saw that he wasn't holding a dagger, but a sword.

Somehow the magic had fused the two daggers to create a new weapon.

In amazement, he studied the slender silver blade, with its exquisitely thin edge, before turning his attention to the hilt, which was designed with intricate symbols.

What was happening?

Did the village still possess the magic of the Weres who lived and died here? That would explain the sudden musk that teased at his nose and the distant howl…

Wait. A howl?

Spinning toward the nearby cliff, he watched in amazement as a large, white wolf padded toward the village.

If his heart was beating, it would have halted at the sight of the creature.

He'd never seen anything so magnificent.

There was a proud elegance in the creature as it moved toward him, then there was a shimmer of magic, and the wolf transformed into a beautiful, naked woman.

She was tall and slender, with brilliant red hair that now had a streak of pure white above one temple. Her eyes were golden with the power of her beast, but Xi knew that they would melt to a rich brown when he held her in his arms.

Brigette.

Falling to his knees, he allowed the sword to drop.

Suddenly, he understood.

He understood why he hadn't been able to grieve. Why he'd been compelled to travel to this place. Why he'd built the cottage.

His soul had known his mate wasn't dead. He'd been preparing to be reunited with her.

But understanding in his heart didn't explain it to his brain.

Waiting until she was standing directly in front of him, Xi straightened, his hand tentatively reaching out to touch her cheek. A lingering fear was banished as he felt the warmth of her velvet-soft skin and caught her sweet scent.

She was different. He could sense her wolf prowling just below the surface. And there was that amazing streak of white in her hair. But this was Brigette.

His woman. His mate.

"How?" he rasped, his fingers trailing down the curve of her neck.

She leaned against him, the heat of her naked flesh driving away the ice that had formed in the center of his being.

"I'm not sure," she told him. "One moment, I was being consumed by the flames, and the next, I was transformed into my animal form, lying in a misty darkness. I assumed my wolf had called me to the spirit-world."

Xi continued to stroke his fingers downward, tracing the strong width of her shoulder. His bold warrior.

"Maybe you were protected because your wolf was in hibernation."

She circled her arms around his neck, her fingers tangling in the short strands of his hair.

"Or perhaps I still have some of the Beast's magic running through my veins." She shrugged, her expression distracted. As if she was already forgetting her time in the darkness. "All I know is that I suddenly woke at the bottom of the cliff. That's when I caught your scent." She paused, glancing around as if noticing for the first time where they were. "What are you doing here?"

"Waiting for you."

She blinked at his simple words. "For me?"

"Yes."

"How did you know I'd be here?"

Xi glanced down at the sword that he'd dropped at the sight of Brigette. The silver blade shimmered in the moonlight, and the ground around the weapon had turned from ash gray to a soft, tender green. As if the magic in the sword was healing the land.

Giving a shake of his head, Xi returned his attention to Brigette. Later, he would sort through the strange events of the evening. For now, he intended to savor the miracle he'd been given.

"You're my mate." He bent down to sweep her off her feet, cradling her against his chest.

"My wolf agrees," she growled, using her elongated fangs to scrape the skin of his chest.

Xi shuddered with pleasure. Soon he would have his fangs buried deep inside her as he claimed her as his mate. And he very much hoped she would do the same. Sex with this Were was going to be wild, and fierce and potentially dangerous.

Was there anything better?

"A very smart animal," he whispered.

Brigette parted her lips to answer, only to snap them shut when she realized where he was carrying her.

"Did you do this?" she breathed, her eyes wide as she took in the small cottage.

"It's just a beginning," he assured her, pushing open the door with his shoulder and carrying her over the threshold.

She reached up, framing his face in her hands as she regarded him with a fierce intensity.

"A new beginning."

"Together."

Bending his head, he allowed his fangs to lengthen. "Forever."

Printed in the United States
by Baker & Taylor Publisher Services